Across the room, Sunny drew a finger across her throat, frantically gesturing for Rory to cut it short. Esther, he noted, hadn't moved, her expression as bewildered as he felt.

"Powell's back," he said to Esther.

She pushed off from the wall. "Thank you." They stood toe to toe, Esther's chin level with his eyes. "I think Sunny wants you."

Rory looked in the dispatcher's direction, his gaze passing over the security monitors on the way. On the center screen, Chief Mansfield's face stretched from edge to edge. Clutching the phone to his ear with a beefy hand, he glared into the camera.

The chief wanted him. Rory's mouth went dry. He swallowed hard as the first hit of adrenaline kicked in. Hot damn—it was about time!

Praise for Gone Astray

"Gone Astray is a delight with a police detective who has health conditions, self-doubts, and a love interest who is believable. Rory Naysmith is an older cop, who arrives to a new job in a new town where he knows no one and gets saddled with a cold case and a rookie cop, young, inexperienced, and eager as a puppy to please. I strongly urge you not to start reading at bedtime—you'll get no sleep as you read until you finish what I hope is the first of many in a series."

~*Lenora Rain-Lee Good,*
author, Jibutu: Daughter of the Desert

"The beautifully detailed world Terry Korth Fischer creates in a cold Nebraska winter along with a finely tuned mystery makes Gone Astray a winner. Excellent first novel!"

~*Teresa Trent, author: Pecan Bayou and Piney*
Woods Cozy Mystery series.

Gone Astray

by

Terry Korth Fischer

Gone Astray

Cover Art by *Kim Mendoza*

The Wild Rose Press, Inc.
PO Box 708
Adams Basin, NY 14410-0708
Visit us at www.thewildrosepress.com

Publishing History
First Edition, 2021
Trade Paperback ISBN 978-1-5092-3525-4
Digital ISBN 978-1-5092-3526-1

Published in the United States of America

Dedication

To Holly

Acknowledgements

I want to thank my brother-in-law, Sergeant James Simmons, Retired, who selflessly answered my questions and allowed me a glimpse into the workings at an eleven-person police department. Any mistake in police procedure is because I didn't ask the right questions.

To my sister, Holly, who named my protagonist, Rory Naysmith—best flawed detective name ever.

Thanks to the dedicated team at The Wild Rose Press for the opportunity to make this book happen. Special kudos to my editor, Kaycee John, whose patience and time are truly appreciated.

To my many writer friends who gave encouragement, critique, and guidance: Pat, Lenora, Dixie, Liz, Teresa, Mary, and Kristen.

And, last but not least, to my readers. I am so lucky to have you all on my team.

Chapter One

The station felt as placid as a church sanctuary on Monday afternoon. Rory Naysmith couldn't describe why the silence bothered him. The small Nebraska town couldn't solve all his problems, but he'd anticipated the move to the Winterset Police Department would put him back in the center of the action. A heart attack didn't end a man's career, not one as distinguished as his. He'd labored to build his strength and stamina levels back to pre-incident condition. He was confident he could take on all comers, and in Winterset, he would prove it to the doubters—those threatening to put him behind a desk. Or worse—retirement.

No way, not this detective.

The wall clock confirmed he'd been on page five for fifteen minutes, reading and then rereading the department's mission statement. He got the part about "vigilant service and unimpeachable integrity." His mind stuck on the words "respect of all citizens." He couldn't earn their respect by covering the duty desk for the day sergeant. No sir—no special privileges for the department's new, and only, detective.

His focus returned to the page and the Winterset Police motto, "Do the right thing just because it is the right thing." Who wrote stuff like that?

He looked suspiciously at Sunny Gomez, the station's civilian dispatcher. She sat at an L-shaped workspace with three oversized monitors. In a blue shirt with the required WPD patch, her dark hair bubbled in a riot of curls. Large hoop earrings touched her shoulders. She sat quietly, her attention riveted on the center screen.

When the phone rang, Sunny shook an arm in his direction, gold hoops swinging, gesturing for him to pick it up.

Rory rubbed a hand over his balding head and frowned before lifting the receiver. "Police Department, Detective Naysmith."

"Ryan. One-o-eight, Fifth Street. It's against the law to disturb the peace." Rory opened the desk drawer and pulled out a pad. "Yes, sir, there is an ordinance against excessive noise."

"You better get out here. My neighbor is hauling speakers out to his driveway, and I know he's plannin' on blastin' the neighborhood with his bee-whop." Mr. Ryan's voice sounded hoarse as if he'd been screaming. "This time, I want him arrested!"

"I'm sorry, sir, I don't think we can arrest your neighbor for having outdoor speakers."

Sunny twisted the top half of her body to face him, her slender fingers poised over the computer keyboard. She raised one perfectly arched brow.

"However, we can schedule an officer to do a drive-by to see he remains within the ordinance limit," Rory said in his civil-service voice, the one he reserved for children.

"What if he starts to play that puke-punk?" Ryan demanded. "Polluting the neighborhood with that filth.

2

What'll it take? I'll write a check. I'm desperate. He won't listen to reason. Says he's just gonna wash his car!"

Rory suppressed a smile.

Sunny shook her head in warning. Rory shrugged. "I'm sure the policeman's fund could use another donation, but we'll be vigilant and keep an eye on your situation. Thanks for calling." He returned the receiver to the cradle, tore the top sheet from the pad, and stood.

Crossing to her desk, he placed the sheet in her outstretched hand. A blue iced cake sporting a caped crusader filled one computer screen. Displayed with unbridled pride, tacked, taped, and pasted around the black monitor, the photos of Sunny's four children hammed it up in a colorful collage. He wondered which one would celebrate the super-hero themed birthday.

"Sunny, how do you manage?"

She eyed the slip of paper. "You handled that just right. Sergeant Powell's never that nice. Of course, he's young. Don't have the experience of an ol' geezer like you."

Rory winced. "Guess Mr. Ryan was lucky. When do we expect the sergeant back?"

"Should be any time now. Unless he extends his dentist appointment to make time to eat lunch with his wife. He don't appreciate the detecting you got to do."

Rory wondered what that meant but let it go. The cake disappeared, and in its place, a spreadsheet materialized.

"Let's run a car past his place."

"We will. Unless something more urgent comes along, 'cause placating citizens is part of the job. Plus, it gives the boys something to do besides hang around the station and bother the dispatcher." Sunny raised her mouse-maneuvering finger and waved a scarlet nail in the air for emphasis. "After you've been here a while, you'll get the hang of it."

Rory wasn't sure he'd ever get the hang of it. Drastically different from the Omaha precinct, Winterset Police shared office space with the town's civic leaders, and citizens paid their parking fines and purchased garage-sale permits at a walk-up window. The bulletproof glass, complete with money pass-through, made the station look more like a bank than a law-enforcement facility. The chief of police served as the city planner, and the town's only detective covered the sergeant's desk while the sergeant ran errands. What a waste.

He returned to the duty desk and picked up the police manual, but he found he couldn't concentrate. Through a floor-to-ceiling window, he looked out at the street. Autumn colors dominated the view, trees were beginning to drop their leaves, and everything seemed peaceful. Too peaceful. A car pulled into a parking slot in front of the station, and three women exited, two older and one much younger. Possibly a daughter. The daughter was tall, or perhaps the older ladies had reached the age where they had begun to shrink. The older women moved to the parking meter and stopped, holding an animated conversation while the younger one threw glances at the station. He'd never get used to being on display.

"They're on their way in," Sunny warned.

"You're clairvoyant?"

"They're having the same argument most citizens have. Why should they pay to park when they've

4

already paid taxes? You'll see. They pay but come in to complain. Or they don't pay and come in to complain. Either way, it sets the mood."

Rory followed the women's progress on the double rows of security camera monitors mounted on the wall dividing the office from the lobby. First, they appeared on the CCTV unit displaying the street in front of the station, then on the one focused on the building's front door, and finally, in the fish-eyed view of the cavernous vestibule as they approached the payment window. There, they stopped, clustered together in a tight knot, their backs hunched toward the camera.

He looked down from the monitors to the pay window and found their solemn faces peering into the office.

Sunny jerked her head toward the trio. "Told ya."

"Me?" Rory mouthed, stiffening.

The lacquered nail rose again. "I ain't the police. You take care of them; I'll man the phone."

Rory checked his watch, heaved a sigh, and stood. The three lower monitors displayed city vehicles in the back lot, the chief's office, and a vacant office with his unpacked boxes and barren desk. He longed to slip off and start his real job.

A voice brought his attention back to the women. "Hello? Hello?"

"Good morning, Mrs. Beauregard," Sunny answered, impatiently shooing Rory in the direction of their visitors.

"Yes, ma'am," Rory said, crossing to greet them. "Can I help you?" He noticed the tall woman taking a step back to allow Mrs. Beauregard to speak.

"Well, it's not to give the city another quarter. Where is Sergeant Powell? We have a crime to report."

"I can help you with that."

"All the same, I don't know you, and this is a delicate situation. You're not even in uniform."

"I'm a detective," he said. "Detective Rory Naysmith. I don't wear a uniform. What seems to be the problem?"

Mrs. Beauregard crouched, bringing her mouth even with the pass-through opening. "Sunny? Can you vouch for this man?"

"Yes, Marilyn. I think he's Catholic, but short of that, he claims to be trustworthy. Sergeant Powell is at the dentist again, having more work done on that root canal. You can come back in half an hour. He ought to be here then. Course his mouth will be frozen."

"We're here now. I guess this fellow will have to do."

Sunny lowered her voice. "You better let them in. Marilyn Beauregard isn't above going straight to Chief Mansfield if she thinks the situation warrants it."

Rory looked around the dispatch room. There were no visitor chairs, and once inside, there was a clear view of the overnight lockup room. They'd had a drunk in residence the night before. Luckily, he'd been sent to county jail that morning, but not before he'd deposited the evidence of his debauchery all over the concrete floor. The odor still permeated the office. An old gray metal desk with two chairs sat in the alcove, and somehow it didn't seem appropriate for the women.

"Where do I take them?"

"Use the interrogation desk. Lydia and her daughter won't be a problem, but Marilyn...Trust me, you don't want them to be too comfortable, or they'll stay all day." Rory led the women to the gray metal desk, snagging the sergeant's chair on the way and rolling it to a spot alongside the two already there. He arranged them so the women would be comfortable.

"I'll stand," the daughter said as the others settled onto chairs. She leaned against the wall where the rule used to take vital statistics was painted. Even slouched, her head hit the six-foot mark easily.

"As you like," Rory said. "So, ladies, what's this about?" He gave them his full attention. It didn't appear Powell would be back anytime soon; he'd have to deal with the women himself.

"I'm Marilyn Beauregard," she said. He placed her in his mother's generation, mid-seventies. And like his mother, he assumed she had a penchant for gossip and drama. "I've lived in Winterset for over forty years, way before the foreigners began to invade. Winterset is my home, and it isn't right that a person can't be safe in their own home."

"You say there's been a crime?"

"I hope you're qualified."

Rory patted his breast, checking his gun's position in the shoulder holster. He knew he'd brought with him the weapons a real detective needed—experience, attitude, and a ball-point pen. He held his tongue, recognizing his first opportunity to work on the "respect of all citizens."

"Yes. It is criminal. Criminal behavior." Marilyn Beauregard laid her hand on the arm of her friend. "Lydia is… Oh my, I'll need to start at the beginning." She looked over her shoulder at Sunny and then straightened. "It's convenient that when we need the police, the only time we've ever needed the police, Sergeant Powell is out."

The daughter shifted her body weight and began to study the toes of her shoes as if she'd just discovered she was wearing a pair.

"Lydia Mullins is my dear friend," Marilyn said, squeezing her partner's arm. "My dear friend and her daughter, Esther, have lived in Winterset all their lives as well."

Bingo. The young woman's relationship with the others was confirmed. And he had a name to put with her—Esther Mullins.

"All their lives," Marilyn repeated, "and now they are being terrorized."

Rory raised both brows. "Terrorized?"

Both women clutched the handbags in their laps and leaned forward. "Yes, Detective, *terrorized*."

The cell phone on Rory's hip vibrated. He unclipped it and looked quickly at the display. The chief, he noted, and put it back.

The phone rang at Sunny's desk. "Police department," she said. A moment later, she swung around to face Rory, her eyes wide, her mouth a straight line.

The door connecting the police department to the city offices opened, and Sergeant Powell stepped in. He cleared his throat, ran a finger around his starched collar, eyed the civilian trio, and gave Rory an accusing scowl. Leaving the scent known only to dental offices in his wake, he crossed to the duty desk in three long strides. He turned abruptly and faced the interrogation desk. "Stay on your own side of the road, Naysmith."

Marilyn Beauregard jumped to her feet. "Thank goodness." There was relief in her voice. "Dicky, that fellow is after Lydia again." Taking Lydia by the elbow, she wrestled her friend to her feet.

Rory stood and only then noticed Sunny frantically waving the phone receiver.

Marilyn addressed Powell. "When are you going to do something? This isn't the first time, and I guarantee you it won't be the last."

Powell didn't answer. Instead, he grabbed the chair belonging to the duty desk and began to roll it back toward his desk. The older women followed, Marilyn's voice rising as they went. "You promised to take care of it, Dicky. It's not right that we have to live in fear while foreigners run around free to threaten and terrorize…"

Across the room, Sunny drew a finger across her throat, frantically gesturing for Rory to cut it short. Esther, he noted, hadn't moved, her expression looking as bewildered as he felt.

"Powell's back," he said to Esther.

She pushed off from the wall. "Thank you." They stood toe to toe, Esther's chin level with his eyes. "I think Sunny wants you."

Rory looked in the dispatcher's direction, his gaze passing over the security monitors on the way. On the center screen, Chief Mansfield's face stretched from edge to edge. Clutching the phone to his ear with a beefy hand, he glared into the camera. The chief wanted him.

Rory swallowed hard as the first hit of adrenaline kicked in. Hot damn—it was about time!

Chapter Two

Feeling confident, Rory rapped on the chief's door and entered.

Bryce Mansfield, in his early fifties, had an abundance of gray hair, deep, hooded eyes, and a chiseled face. He stood at a large mahogany desk, scowling. Behind him, a credenza sat under a mound of papers. Sunlight streamed through the window and cast a checkerboard pattern on the opposite wall, the lines as ridged as Mansfield's expression.

"When I call," he roared, "it's front and center."

Rory frowned. They shared a history, police academy, Omaha's west side, and more than a few beers. Along the way, Mansfield had lost his sense of humor, but he was police chief, and his concerns would become Rory's concerns—another adjustment to endure.

The chief crossed the office and fiddled with the thermostat. A blast of hot air stirred the scents of Pledge and Lysol. "I need to call the mayor," he said, briskly crossing back and taking a seat behind his desk. "There's not much going on—not like we've had a bank hold-up or a kidnapping. Or a murder, or any of a dozen other things that could be worse. We're lucky we haven't had any of those here in Winterset, at least not yet." He rapped his knuckles on the desktop and cleared his throat. "The mayor, however, is worried. He's taken a personal interest in the department's handling of all new cases."

Mansfield picked up a report and read silently, leaving Rory standing in the middle of the room. Lowering the papers, he leered at him. "Personal, meaning he inquired on your progress."

"Progress on what? I just started," Rory said. "You have something? I'm ready."

"Sure, sure, I managed to put him off," continued Mansfield. "For now, that is. He thinks we'll damage his image with it going into the New Year. The beginning of an election year at that. What have you accomplished so far?"

With a heavy sigh, Rory took a seat. His chief wasn't offering an opportunity. This was an inquisition. "I'm getting familiar with the department and the policies. I've read some old case files. It's all in the report you requested." He nodded at the papers Mansfield held.

"Humor me," the chief said. "Which old cases?"

"An open case from last May, the truck stop hijacking. But there's nothing there to work with."

Chief Mansfield motioned for Rory to fill in the details.

"To refresh your memory, tire tracks from a heavy pickup, probably a dually, were found in the trees out at the interstate truck stop. According to the casebook, the driver didn't see anyone, not anyone he could describe or pick out in a line-up. The truck was clean. No prints. No damage. The load was hauled away, lock, stock, and light bulb." Rory grinned. When the chief didn't respond, he added, "Like a prior incident in March, they hijacked construction supplies passing through

11

Winterset, headed for destinations farther north. Both loads carried by independent drivers. The filed reports show the outfits had nothing in common. There are no new witnesses. And no activity since May. It's a dead end."

The chief harrumphed, skimmed the report, and flipped to the second page. "Got to have something more in common."

"Don't seem to." Where was this going? It was November. Surely, the chief didn't want to zero in on a cold case from last spring.

As if he heard his thoughts, Mansfield said, "The mayor thinks the truck stop is too close to Winterset. He thinks the citizens feel threatened." He looked up. "Solving this one will do the trick. Make you look good, and it won't hurt the department's image, either."

Rory wasn't convinced. "Wouldn't solving an active case be better?"

"Sure, if there was one."

"Powell's got someone named Beauregard with two other women, filing a terrorist complaint. Mullins, I think, is the other name."

The chief wet his lips and hunched forward. "Not Marilyn Beauregard?"

"Yes, I believe so."

The chief looked earnestly at Rory. "Mullins, an older woman with her daughter? Probably Esther." He paused, then added, "There's another daughter, Jesse, she's a local doctor and would be at the hospital this time of day. Good girls—both of them, Esther and Jesse. But Marilyn Beauregard." He shook his head. "It won't be anything we can sink our teeth into. Let's concentrate on the hijackings."

Bryce Mansfield had always been more politician than policeman. Rory crossed his arms over his chest. Mansfield knew his record, had witnessed his talent for unearthing criminal elements. Damn it. He needed something meatier, sexier—like an old-fashioned murder. "I don't think there's anything here. I'll spin my wheels."

Mansfield tossed the report in the filing basket. "I want you to solve it. I went out on a limb, bringing you in instead of a younger man. You have to prove your worth, Naysmith. Sure, twenty-five years on the job trumped all other comers, but the mayor reminded me just this morning that there were younger men qualified. Lots of them. And it isn't too late for me to bring one on board." Surprised at the man's willingness to throw him under the bus, Rory flinched. Why Mansfield thought men of their age needed to be behind a desk was baffling. He wasn't too old. All he needed was a case to prove his skills were still top-notch.

"Work this case first. And don't screw up. I want results. If you mess this up, it will reflect on the mayor. The mayor will see that it reflects on me. And I'll, well, you get my drift. Put this on the top of your priorities. And that's not a request. It's a command."

"Yes, sir." Should he salute? Would Mansfield dictate his every move? Where could he take this case? Especially without new evidence. "I've got—"

"Everybody's got stuff. Not everybody has the experience to juggle them. I've seen you in action. I want this case buttoned up. The sooner I can report something positive to the mayor, the better."

Rory swallowed. Sure, he could do it if he were in Omaha, where he had resources and knew the lay of the land. Leaving the city, he'd bypassed the need to start on patrol by landing the detective slot through his old academy friend. Unfortunately, coming in from the outside hadn't made him a favorite with the others. He'd already run into opposition, resentful glances, and outright hostility. Yet he knew he couldn't do this on his own. He'd waste valuable time familiarizing himself with the area. He might be able to pull it off, but right now, Winterset loomed like a rocky shore, and he'd be a man alone, floundering in the wake and struggling against the receding tide. It would be impossible without some form of help.

"I prefer to work alone," Rory said. "But in this case, I could use a hand."

"Can't do it, Naysmith. It's a small department, the holidays are coming on, the end of the year, take your pick." Mansfield went back to inspecting the reports, picking up a fresh one from the in-basket, dismissing Rory.

"I've only been in Winterset three days. I don't know the town or the people. The second set of feet will save time."

The chief paused. "Whining? The numbered streets run north to south, and the avenues run east to west." His lips twisted into a wry smile. "Okay, I'll let you have one officer. He's new. It will help me out more than it will help you. He can run errands. He's a native, and you can bring him along by showing him how a real man handles police work."

A rookie? Rory pulled on an earlobe. Not exactly what he'd had in mind.

"Make you look good." Mansfield winked. "Keep in mind that detecting isn't a two-person job. There's no budget for it. His time will be off the clock."

Rory was sure Mansfield had his own reputation in mind, but before he could lodge a protest or divert him, Sunny's voice burst through the intercom, rife with excitement. "Holy schmoley, Chief. We got a live dead one!" Her voice filled the chief's office. "You got Naysmith in there? He needs—"

Rory's heart jumped. Dead body?

Chief Mansfield grabbed the phone, cutting Sunny's voice off. "What ya got?"

While Mansfield listened, Rory checked the department cell at his hip. One call, Sunny. Crap. His first chance, and he'd almost missed it. His mind started to whirl.

The chief's hooded eyes turned to Rory. "I'll send him right out. Get Thacker on the horn. We'll need him to run Naysmith to the scene." He slammed the receiver down.

"It's the senior care home. The boys found a body in the vacant lot. They say you better take a look." His face lit with excitement. "This could be just what we need."

Rory felt his pulse ratchet up. "Who's Thacker? He the rookie you were talking about?"

Mansfield rose and began to pace behind the desk. "The boys responded to a call. Thought something looked funny and turned up a body in a pile of leaves. Sunny has the details. I want you out there."

"Thacker?" Rory asked, rising as well.

"Yeah, Thacker. No time to clear you for a city car. He can run you out and then stick around to assist."

"I'm on it, Chief."

Rory stopped at his office for his hat and the newspaper. He secured the door and entered the dispatch office to find Powell handling the duty desk and Sunny seated at her computer. On the bank of security monitors, he noticed a police unit pull into the back lot. "What ya got, Sunny?"

"I got Thacker waiting. I got the boys out at the care home with a dead body. And I got a headache."

"Right. I'll get the details from the lead officer."

He couldn't move fast enough.

****

Clarence Thacker carried a spit and polish affect and a broad face that would give him the perpetual look of youth. As Rory climbed into the cruiser, Thacker said, "Welcome to Winterset, sir. It is an honor to escort you." He spoke in a broad, melodious bass, a sincere and commanding voice that would create confidence in those he served far greater than his appearance ever would.

Before Rory was situated, Thacker threw the transmission into drive and squealed out of the lot. The momentum threw Rory against the door. Righting himself, he reached for the seat belt, surprised the rookie hadn't turned on the siren in his enthusiasm. There was no hurry—the guy was dead. "Your first body?"

Thacker's ears pinked.

Rory pulled the newspaper out and found the page with the sudokus. The puzzles were a nuisance, but according to his cardiologist, he should wrap his intellect around them, exercise his right brain, and keep his left brain in check. He'd see. It might keep his blood pressure under control. "It's best not to think about the body until you're there." He folded the sheet, making it easy to work the puzzle within the confines of the car.

Thacker quickly maneuvered the cruiser through town. Static crackled from the radio. The phone lying on the console had been turned to walkie-talkie mode, and through it they listened to the exchange between men at the scene. The car's interior was spotless, though with the lingering impression that desperate men had ridden in back. It felt familiar, manly, and somehow comforting.

He was trying to place a three when Thacker said, "The perpetrator or perpetrators will have fled. No chance of apprehension at the scene."

Rory pushed the fedora back on his head and rubbed the crown of his forehead. "We'll see." He found the place for the three and scribbled it in with indelible ink. "Might not be a crime at all. Maybe some homeless guy lay down in an open field and quietly went to his final reward."

Thacker gripped the stirring wheel, tightening his knuckles. "I hope not."

From the corner of his eye, Rory saw the rookie wanted to pull the words back—astonished he'd said them out loud. He thought Thacker was too eager, something experience would smooth out, but he held the comment. After all, he hoped for the same.

They took the drive onto the care home property, pulling in behind a flashing cruiser. The Winterset Police were in full force, six marked cars with racks blazing. A dozen men combed the area, while a cluster of officers stood by the flapping door to a white trailer.

"What's the story?" Rory asked, shoving his hands deep in his pockets as they approached. If asked, he'd have said he did so in an attempt to appear non-aggressive, but in truth, it hid his excitement jitters.

Lloyd, a thin, angular man, said, "Happened this morning right at dawn. Jim and I were making a drive-by. Checking for vagrants or anything suspicious."

"You saw something odd?"

"There was a citizen complaint about a prowler. It was pretty quiet last night. We took the call around four. You wouldn't know, being a nine-to-fiver, but it breaks up the time and beats riding around in the car all shift trying to stay vigilant. Right off, we found this here construction trailer wide open. It took us a little longer to find the body."

"You found him?"

"Yeah. We're waiting for the coroner now. I called it in. They said we better have a detective take a look." He gave Rory a suspicious glare and headed to the rear of the property.

Rory and Thacker followed. At the edge of the property, the wind had swept a pile of leaves against the wooden fence. The body lay partially buried. "You've photographed the scene?" asked Rory.

"Yeah, we know how to do it. Don't worry, we done everything by the book."

Rory knelt beside the body. The top half of the dead man's torso was exposed where the wind had cleared away the fallen leaves. The man's weathered face was unshaven and severely beaten. He recognized Vietnam War campaign patches on the worn army jacket and noted thin threads poking through the fabric where his name patch should have been. Using a pen, he lifted the front of the tattered jacket and revealed a gaping wound.

"Not a lot of blood here," he said. "Did you move him?"

Lloyd's expression conveyed irritation. "We know better."

Rory shook his head. "There's the basic problem with mankind. You tend to your business, work hard, but there's always some fool right there ready to take it away. What do you think, mugging?"

Lloyd nodded, but Rory could see he didn't buy it. This wasn't a case of trespassing. From the look of things, it wasn't an accident, a foiled robbery, or a mugging gone wrong. It was murder, and this wasn't the place where it happened.

"Any witnesses? You talk to the complainant?"

Before Lloyd could respond, they were interrupted. "Yo, Lloyd, what ya find?" The newcomer was as wide as he was tall, his face alive with good humor. He carried a medical bag. Ducking under the police tape, he said, "You must be the new detective." He stuck a hand out. "Petey Moss. County coroner." Petey's rotund belly moved up and down as he pumped Rory's hand, and the action pushed the scent of Aqua Velva into the atmosphere around them.

"I suppose you want to know if he's dead?" Petey squatted beside the body, and Rory watched him conduct the exam. It didn't take long to confirm the death. "Yup, as a cinder block. Not a good spot for a nap."

Thacker wandered off. Rory stuck with the coroner while the body was removed and loaded for the journey to the morgue. He hated the time between discovery and the moment a case got turned over. He was itching to get started, but more, he hated the thought inexperienced law enforcement might contaminate the crime scene. He didn't know Winterset, and he didn't know this coroner. He wasn't about to let someone mess up his opportunity, so he would keep a watchful eye.

After the ambulance pulled away, Rory found the rookie kicking the cruiser's rear tire. "Find something?"

"Tire tracks. There must be a thousand vehicles through here in a week, each one with a driver, each driver with an agenda."

"Any look fresh?" Rory picked up a few loose pieces of gravel and rolled them around in his fingers. He let them fall to the ground. A stray dog wandered up to sit at his heels.

"Nah, as I said, perpetrators are long gone." Thacker hunkered down eye level with the dog and affectionately scratched behind its ears. "What ya think? He wasn't here for a nap."

Rory heard an ache in his resonant voice and felt a tinge of guilt. Thacker was the department fledgling, and the other officers would give him little time and no credit. He knew that feeling. Rory reached out and gently laid a hand on the dog's matted head.

"It's Homer," Thacker said, his deep voice almost a hush. "Homer Coot."

"You knew him? From his looks, I figured the guy was a transient."

"Everyone knows Homer. He's the town character."

At the trailer across the lot, Lloyd lowered his phone and called out, "All yours, Naysmith. Looks like you got your first detecting job."

Thacker's eyes shone. A low whistle escaped his lips as he stood.

Rory headed for the cruiser with a hundred details clear in his mind. His luck had returned. A homicide—a real case. There'd be no stopping him now.

Chapter Three

The sun had already set when Neil Wallace heard his wife, Jesse, pull the car into the garage. He picked up the TV remote and punched on the evening news. Typically, she stopped at the gym for a workout after seeing her last patient at Winterset Memorial Hospital. She was early. He enjoyed evenings alone, unwinding from his day and being the lord of the manor—no matter how fleeting. The two of them rarely spent an evening together. His real estate business and position on the city council kept him out nights. Neither complained. Theirs hadn't been a contented union for some time. Her unexpected arrival irritated him, particularly since he wanted to be out of the house without needing to use a lame excuse. He had places to go. Things to do. None of them involved her.

Jesse entered from the garage into the kitchen, dropping her gym bag and keys on the countertop. "So, you're here." Over the drone of the broadcast news, her greeting sounded like an accusation.

"Not for long," he said.

Her eyes flashed. "I had an extra-demanding day at the hospital. I'm drained." She avoided meeting his eyes, fussing with the contents of her bag instead. "What I need is a quiet evening, comfy pajamas, and a good book."

"You'll have to tackle that on your own. I'm going out."

He held the remote in one hand and a glass of whiskey in the other. She looked worn, not at all the stately, eloquent beauty he had married. Her makeup minimal, she looked washed-out. Her porcelain complexion revealed fine lines around her eyes and allowed delicate veins to show at her temples. Neil was proud his ancestors were Scots, giving him the ruddy, roguish Highlander appearance that appealed to women. In his mid-fifties, he could boast a full head of hair, perhaps more salt than pepper now, but he knew he looked sharp in his black tailored suit. He couldn't remember the last time he'd seen her in anything other than baggy sweats or white coat.

He cleared his throat, pulling her gaze his way. "Replay of my day: money, not enough money, and if only we had money. City commissioners can be demanding. They're fighting over every detail of the new senior home expansion with no end in sight." He pulled his red silk tie loose and tossed his head. "They need my expertise."

She pulled her cell phone from the bag and connected it to the charger. "Do they?"

"I have an obligation—"

She cut him off. "Esther called." Turning her back to him, she crossed to the refrigerator, opened the door, took out a bottled water. After a swallow, she recapped it, then added, "She can be so dramatic."

Naturally, her sister and mother were more important than anything he had to say. "What's wrong with your mother?"

"Not wrong, really. Marilyn convinced her to go down to the police department to file a complaint." She rummaged in the cabinet, found a power bar. "You remember when Mother caught a fellow loitering on her lawn? I guess it happened again."

Merry band of Mullins women, he thought. The three of them, Esther, Jesse, and their mother, Lydia, always into some intrigue. Marilyn Beauregard, now there was a woman who needed to mind her own business. "Bet that was a hoot. Did the police laugh when she told them all foreigners were terrorists?"

"Actually, I think Marilyn believes that, not Mother." She frowned, eyeing his whiskey. "Esther says they've added a detective to the police department. Mammoth, Weymount, something like that." Ripping the wrapper from the bar, she took a bite, her face scrunched in concentration. "No, wait, it's Naysmith. Detective Rory Naysmith. He's the one who took their complaint."

He snorted. "Great." How many policemen did a town of eight-thousand need? A dedicated detective seemed one too many.

"Did you hear about Homer Coot?"

"What do you mean?" He leaned against the door jamb and took a sip, taking in her measure. He had to admit she was still a good-looking woman, even in her sweaty workout clothes and pinned up hair. If she just wasn't so aloof, a trait he'd once thought alluring, but lately found condescending. The ice cubes rattled when he lowered the glass. "What about him?"

"He's one of the vets that lives, lived, in the subsidized housing. He was probably ten or twenty years older than us. I don't expect that you knew him. I only know of him because he lived in the apartments across the street from Mother's house and he helped out at the church. I understand he was caught in the Vietnam draft, returned from his tour not fit for much. Maybe you know him through your drinking buddies?" She jutted her chin in his direction and looked down her nose at his drink.

He lowered his head, swirled the cubes in the tumbler. "What happened to him?"

"That's just it. They don't know. The police found his body buried in a pile of leaves behind your precious care home."

He could feel the heat rise to his face. "It's not my care home. I'm working on—"

"Oh, all right." She chucked the balance of the power bar into the trash. "Marilyn said if they hadn't stumbled over him this morning, she would have known something was up when he failed to show up at the church. Apparently, he was to set up the chairs for the book club meeting tomorrow."

"Heart attack, then?"

"No, murder." Jesse shook her head slowly. "Shot. Mother had only talked to him yesterday. She's quite upset."

"Surely Lydia wasn't some place he frequents?" Jesse gave Neil a steady glare. He didn't want to invest time in a full-out argument. "I'll reserve judgment. Go ahead. Tell me what sister Esther said."

Jesse opened her month to answer but stopped as if reconsidering her response. After a pause, she said, "They seemed to think I should know him."

"The police?"

"No, Mother and Marilyn. He might have been in the veteran's group I work with at the free clinic. Poor soldiers. They are so lost and getting to the VA in Omaha is a challenge. But I can't place him. There are so many marginalized souls in Winterset. The world can be a scary place, especially if you don't fit in."

"Are you talking about the vet who does odd jobs around town?"

"Yes, that's the one, Homer Coot."

Neil drained his glass quickly, and while Jesse inspected the freezer, refilled it from the bottle he'd left on the counter. "Never talked to him myself."

"Anyway, Mother had a word with Homer yesterday concerning her rhododendron bushes. She thinks they've got some disease, and he came over to take a look before starting his shift at the liquor store. Esther said Mother's words were along the lines of, 'Why those haunted boys spend so much time with liquor is beyond me.' " She gave him a pointed look. "Sounds like something Mother would say and Esther would repeat. I'm just going to heat up a couple of pot pies."

"I hate to see your mother upset about anything. She shouldn't spend time with men you don't know. She's a good judge of character, but at her age, and in her condition."

"Mother can take care of herself. And what she can't do, Esther can see to."

"I just meant—"

"I know what you meant. You're always giving her too much credit. What is it you say? She's old, not dead. Mother offered Homer a way to improve his lot,

26

that's all. Everyone needs to feel worthwhile, even if it's just by helping an old lady out."

He didn't like the idea his mother-in-law might be connected to the murder, no matter how remote. Lydia was gracious, generous, and unlike her daughter, free of rancor. He'd hate to see Lydia dragged into a murder investigation. "What about the dead body?"

Jesse pulled two pies out and turned the oven on to preheat. "Oh, I don't know much. Esther said Mother witnessed him arguing with another man, but the police haven't asked her yet, and she hasn't had a chance to tell them about the argument."

"You think it might have something to do with the murder?" His collar felt tight, he rotated his shoulders. "How would they know to question her?"

"I imagine Marilyn will drag her down to the police station again."

He scratched behind an ear with the remote as he watched Jesse unbox the pies and put them on a cookie sheet. Marilyn had entirely too much influence over Lydia. "I only have enough time to catch the news. I'll grab something at the diner. And don't expect me back until late." He waved the remote and took another sip.

Jesse nodded at the glass in his hand, disapproval clouding her expression.

"Don't start," he said.

****

"Yes?" said the young woman who opened the door at the Elliott house.

Neil had expected Irene Elliott. This was something better. "Well, hello," he said, taking in the suppleness of her small waist and breasts. She wore a soft, pale sweater and tight black slacks. He had no trouble imaging her without her clothes. "Who are you?"

"The maid. Who are you?"

"Wallace, Neil Wallace." He offered a handshake. "Are you from around here?"

The maid ignored the extended hand but answered, "Omaha." She stepped back and allowed him to enter.

"Is the old guy around?"

"Mr. Elliott is in his office. Do you know where that is?"

"Yes, but I'd prefer you show me."

"Suit yourself." She walked him through the sitting room and down a long hallway, stopping in front of a large oak door. She signaled with an open hand for him to enter, and then she turned and headed back to some remote part of the house.

Neil watched her retreat before rapping on the door. "It's me, Neil."

He heard a muffled voice inside and turned the handle. He found Jonathan Elliott seated at his desk, talking on the office phone. Jonathan waved for him to enter.

"I need at least fifteen of them," he said into the phone. "More would be better."

The room was otherwise quiet. The walls were a dark burgundy and covered with prints and paintings. Neil imagined the room had been designed by some expensive fag decorator out of Des Moines. Jonathan was the only thing that looked out of place. His gold-to-silver hair lay just over his collar in the back, showing his contempt for barbers. His suit, always the best cut and cloth, seemed to bunch up around his shoulders and bulge out at the stomach. The knot of his Italian silk tie, out of square, shifted more to the left than the right.

"You say twelve thousand? Ridiculous," Jonathan said. "Twelve thousand is out of the question. I'm not asking you to build the damn things. I just want you to tell me you can get them."

Neil took a seat in the leather chair facing the desk. He picked up a souvenir hand-grenade lighter from the desk and tossed it from one hand to the other, killing time. Elliott was a fool, always sending for him and then making him wait. He tossed the lighter again.

"Twelve thousand, then. I don't like your terms, but I can tell you're a businessman like myself." Jonathan picked up a pen and scribbled on the tablet in front of him.

Neil's mind wandered back to the maid, and he absentmindedly let the hand grenade drop to the carpet. "Kaboom," he said in a dramatic stage whisper.

Jonathan slammed the receiver into the cradle. "Got it!" He picked up the phone again and punched in a number.

Neil got out of his chair and walked over to the window. A luxury car pulled into the drive. Irene Elliot climbed out and headed for the house while Jonathan negotiated behind him. Neil didn't miss the elegant cut of Irene's suit, the confident, feminine carriage of her body. The headlights went out, dropping the drive into darkness, and her expression was lost to him. He imagined she could see him at the window, and he wondered at her thoughts.

Behind him, Jonathan said, "I've arranged for the merchandise. Are you there? You're drifting out... Get with Neil and take possession." He listened a moment longer and then hung up the phone.

Neil returned, dropping into the chair to face him.

"Gadgets. What did we do before cell phones?" Jonathan asked.

Neil nodded agreement. His mind more on Irene—and the nicely packaged maid.

"It's arranged. I could use a drink," Jonathan said.

Neil got up and opened a liquor cupboard on the wall. He poured two glasses of scotch, neat, handing one to Jonathan.

"Cigar?" Jonathan offered and opened a desktop humidor.

"To the wheels of progress," Neil said, raising his glass and reaching for a cigar. His grin matched Jonathan's. "Twelve thousand in cash, I assume. And the usual arrangement." Neil adjusted his tie, moving it slightly more to the left than to the right.

Jonathan raised his glass in a toast.

Neil emptied his in one swallow.

Chapter Four

The morning after the discovery of Homer Coot's body, Rory set up a control center in his office. His former employer, Omaha PD, used a particular area to tack up clippings and photographs from open cases. The display encouraged investigators to speculate on connections between suspects and victims and facilitated the bouncing of ideas off one another. The Winterset PD had no such space. And WPD only had one investigator—him. Luckily, Rory had a private office with plasterboard walls.

He liked to draw broad conclusions from minute details he found in the photographs. Visual stimulation offered a different perspective from official reports, the murder book, or even the case file. Creative thinking led to deductive reasoning. After taping up Homer Coot's picture and the shots taken behind the care home, he sat, leaning back to study the wall.

The *Winterset Gazette's* write up was missing. When he'd stopped to purchase the newspaper earlier, the vending machine in front of the station had been empty. He was eager to read what the local paper offered on Coot's background. He'd already requested records from the Department of Defense and checked for outstanding warrants. Rory put in a call to the coroner and discovered the autopsy was underway across the street in the basement of the County

Courthouse. He left a message. The details would fall into place, his strategy—old fashioned feet on the ground and nose to the grindstone.

A knock interrupted his thoughts. The door opened, Chief Mansfield stuck his head in. "Good, you're in." He spotted the wall. "So, you're working the Coot's murder this morning."

What did the man expect? Naturally, he was working the case. Next, the chief would ask whether he'd solved the crime, or demand to know why he was taking so long.

Mansfield entered, crossed to the photos, and murmured, "Good, good," as he examined them. He turned to face Rory. "Officer Thacker won't be in until second shift. I've arranged to have Sunny send him in as soon as he arrives." He waved his hands at Rory, palms out. "No need to thank me. I'm taking him off patrol for the day. It's the least I can do. You will keep me informed?"

"Sure. I'll do that."

How much could the rookie add to his investigation? Thacker was more likely to hamper it. Rory wondered why Mansfield hadn't assigned a seasoned officer to work with him. Not that Rory needed someone else's skills, but wasting his time babysitting wasn't going to get the job done. Was the chief hoping to direct the investigation by planting someone to watch him and report back?

"Anything from the autopsy?" Mansfield asked.

"Not finished yet."

He frowned. "Not even the preliminary?"

Rory wondered if Mansfield's micro-managing style included second guessing, twenty-twenty hindsight, and the right to sidestep any criticism or backlash. "Preliminary is what we knew yesterday. I have a call into the coroner, and he'll get back to me as soon as it's finished.

Mansfield harrumphed, took another look at the photographs, and left.

Thacker arrived before nine dressed in street clothes, baggy sports jacket, running shoes. "Reporting for duty, sir."

"Detective or Rory will do. Take a seat."

Thacker sat, craning his neck to view the photographs. "What's that?"

"Thinking material." Rory wasn't quite sure how one sat at attention, but Thacker managed, back ramrod straight and hands folded on his lap.

"I'm assigned to the Coot murder investigation team. What's my first assignment?"

Rory grunted. "Doesn't your shift start at two this afternoon?"

"Isn't time of the essence?"

Rory scratched his forehead. "Point taken." There was an investigative team? Thacker more than a driver—*God help him.*

The rookie leaned in, his face taut with eager intent. "Where do we begin?"

"Don't know about 'we,' but I am waiting on the autopsy, would like a copy of today's Gazette, and need to find the scene of the crime."

"Wouldn't that be the lot behind the care home, sir?"

"The care home was the body dump. I need to locate where the murder took place."

Thacker nodded, licked his lips, straightened his shoulders. "Do we have a plan of action?"

Rory slumped in his chair. "I start with Homer's activities on his last day, question everyone he came in contact with, and maybe, just maybe, through luck and diligence, uncover the murder weapon, the motive, and the killer."

"Great plan, sir."

The police academy graduated cadets who were physically fit, knowledgeable of the laws, but lacking any experience that enabled them to turn book learning to honed skills, ready to serve the public. Where had Thacker received his field training? Was he even out of probation? Rory feared the need to transition the rookie from case studies to dealing with a real-live investigation. Wasted time. But he'd have to if the younger man was to be of any use at all.

He cleared his throat and began. "Working a case isn't like you see on TV where clues jump out when you enter a room. You don't trip over them. People don't blurt out confessions. I uncover the facts, build a case, and then I'll arrest the criminal that took Homer's life."

"Excellent!"

"There's nothing easy about it. It takes determination, deductive skills, and a keen nose to unearth the lies."

The rookie's expression clouded but Rory continued, "A detective develops an instinct that separates truth from fiction. You'll learn. Everyone has something to hide. Wives withhold the credit slips from their husbands, people in business chew mints after martini lunches, and the cheerleader claims she didn't attend a movie with the quarterback, even though there are eyewitnesses. The trick is not getting discouraged or sidetracked by the deceit. There's as much to learn from the reasons one lies as there is from the true accounts."

"Noted. Where do we begin?"

There would be no way around it. Thacker would be part of the investigation, and Rory would have to instruct him. He drew a deep breath. "Okay, what do we know? Was Homer close to anyone?"

Thacker squinted as if looking inward, searching his memory. "Not that I know. He was a vet, a drinker, always about town. But a particular friend? I don't think so." His expression was sad, apologetic, disappointed he didn't have the answer. He perked up. "I know he worked evenings at the liquor store."

"Good. Did Homer have a problem with anyone at work? And if he worked evenings, where did he spend his mornings? What did he do in the afternoons?"

Thacker reached inside his jacket and took out a pad. "I should take notes."

Rory sighed, picked up his hat. "How about you bring a car around, and we run out to Coot's apartment?"

****

Thacker drove down Lincoln Avenue, passed the Hometown Grocery, turned left onto 13th Street, and passed Washington Elementary, a formidable square brick building on Lincoln Avenue between 13th Street and 14th. At 20th he passed the city park where the lawns were gold and mums red. Rory noted each landmark, committing them to memory.

Shortly they arrived at the apartments. Two elderly men sat on a wooden bench by the front door enjoying a morning smoke. "Let me out here," he said. "You can park in the back, then come around to join me." He nodded at the pair, now watching them with interest. "I intend to talk with these gentlemen and satisfy their curiosity."

The men looked in their nineties, both dressed in civilian garments that hung with an unmistakable military precision on their age-ravaged bodies. The one on the left asked, "Is this about Homer?"

His friend said, "The police were here yesterday. Haven't had this much action since we landed at Normandy."

Rory smiled. "Yes, this is about Homer."

They nodded. "Good man, but younger," Lefty said. "He didn't serve in our war."

His friend added, "Still, he wouldn't want trouble. Never went looking for any." He dropped his cigarette butt into an empty can and pulled out the makings for another. "Smoke?"

Rory shook his head. "I'm Detective Naysmith, WPD. I'm piecing together Homer's movements on Tuesday, day before yesterday. Maybe you can shed some light on his daily routine?"

They didn't have much to offer. Neither remembered seeing Homer on Tuesday. Either he was up early and already off or had slept in late. After Thacker joined them, the old vets fell to telling stories. Rory and the rookie sat beside them on the bench, letting the old soldiers talk.

Not yet ten, the hour most businesses opened, Rory felt no need to move on. The weather was unseasonably mild, sun comforting, fresh air invigorating, the stories entertaining. He listened and watched as a woman emerged from the modest home on the opposite side of the street. She waved an arm in farewell to the woman inside at the window, mounted a bicycle, and road off. Rory had seen her before, but although familiar, couldn't place her. At ten, he offered his thanks, and with Thacker, they resumed their search.

****

Esther Mullins heard the phone ring as she turned down the alley and entered the backyard. Unhurried, she leaned her bike against the house, pulled the screen door open, and then crossed the worn linoleum floor to drop her bags by the table. "Mother?" The black handset was only halfway to her ear. "Hello, Mother?" she repeated after correcting its position. The dial tone answered back. Frustrated, she placed the receiver in its wall cradle. What now? She'd just left her.

She heeled off her tennis shoes. Reaching behind, she tugged the cell phone from her hip pocket and placed it on the table. From her purse, she produced a small flip phone, opened it, and checked for messages. None.

Off the kitchen, the extra room remained halfway through the transformation from spare bedroom to office. During the last week, she'd removed the faded wallpaper and cleaned the paste residue. She'd scrubbed from floor to ceiling, and yesterday she'd planned to paint the walls. Only she hadn't. She'd gone to the police station with her mother, a fool's errand, leaving her behind schedule. True, they'd met the new detective—older than she'd expected, shorter than she liked. Hopefully, the rumors were true. Winterset could use a good man.

Esther picked up the flip phone and held down the one button. She heard the electronic ring. Lowering the phone, she looked at the display, did a quick up to her ear to verify the ring continued, and then slapped it closed. Mother could wait.

One gallon of primer and two gallons of Gypsy Rose sat in the corner. Esther picked up the primer, stepped into the office, and, through the east window, caught sight of her neighbor Axel carrying an armful of papers toward the alley. His hair was tied back in a loose ponytail, his jeans hung low on his hips, and a pack of cigarettes was rolled up in his T-shirt sleeve. An unlit Marlboro hung from his lips. She hoped he didn't intend to light a fire, or the cigarette, with the wind gusting. Then again, he did what he wanted—when he wanted. Working, for instance. He was young enough, and fit enough, to work for one of the local companies, but he was always between jobs. Of course, he was good at odd jobs and usually available. He stepped out of sight.

"With a desk under the window and a few file cabinets along the inside wall…" she said. She'd better check on Axel's progress. Stepping out the back door, she called out to him.

"Just carrying stuff out to the burn barrel, ma'am." Axel stepped back into the yard between the houses. "Need something?"

"I'm wondering if you picked up the lumber for my desk? I'm painting. I'll need it soon."

"To tell the truth, I was going to do it today. Well, that was before I got called in by Elliott."

"Elliott?"

"Yeah, Elliott Construction." He took a lighter out of his front pocket and lit the cigarette. The sweatband, the full beard, brows so bushy they grew together, creating a furry ledge over small gray eyes, all complemented by the receding hairline, gave him a look only an eye patch could improve.

"No hurry, Axel, just checking." She turned and headed back to the kitchen, pausing in the doorway to see if he followed.

Axel tossed his cigarette butt into the garden patch where carrot tops still grew, and cucumber vines lay withered on a low trellis. "Hey, I can bring those storm windows up for you."

"Sure, I'll let you in through the front."

She crossed quickly through the house. With only four rooms, it was negotiated with an economy of steps—kitchen, living room, and then out the front door and onto the enclosed porch. The screen door was latched, and she lifted the hook just as Axel rounded the corner.

"I better clean your gutters soon," he said hopefully. He shook his head from side to side, adding, "If you want, that is."

Esther wondered if he'd heard something down at the VFW. People were always talking about things that weren't their business, things they didn't understand but were willing to pass on. Was he worried she couldn't pay for odd jobs now that she'd been laid off? Did he feel guilty about mentioning Elliott?

Axel studied his boots and said, "Man, it really sucks about your job. Almost thirty years, and you get what, a thank you? You got to watch out for yourself these days. That's what I do. Nobody gonna throw me out. I'd be over at the courthouse filing a grievance. Sue 'em. That's what I'd do."

Esther sighed. She held the screen door open, and he stepped in. "I'm not exactly unemployed. I'm going to work from home, keeping books for individuals. I've already lined up some clients. Really, you can't blame Elliott Construction if business moved to the city."

"But they're into lots of projects here."

"I settled into the job. I even took it for granted. You do, you know?"

Axel's eyebrow raised, and he narrowed his gray eyes as if trying to read the sincerity in Esther's face. "But thirty years? It just ain't right!"

"Poor Jonathan Elliott. He inherited me as well as the business."

"He coulda done worse."

"Jonathan and I never developed a close relationship. We were just bookkeeper and owner. And he with a young wife…" She paused a moment before adding, "Once I thought Elliott Construction couldn't get along without me. No one was ever going to know the company books like I knew them. Maybe I still believe it, but I don't blame him."

Crossing the porch to the chest freezer, Axel said, "Hey, it ain't your fault." He opened the lid and rummaged around, rearranging the contents. Then he stood upright with a Tupperware container in his hand. "Say, these are pecan cookies!"

Esther re-latched the screen door. "You're welcome to them."

"I keep telling you, you need to put a lock on this thing. Anyone can come along, break onto your porch, and steal your junk."

"You're the only one interested in my pastries." She heard the cell phone ring from inside. "I really doubt anyone would risk a night in the pokey for a cookie. Come in. The storm windows are down in the basement."

In the west corner of the kitchen, Esther opened the basement door. A whiff of damp air floated into the room. Axel descended the stairs, creating a hollow thud as each foot fell. There was silence once he reached the bottom. Satisfied he'd managed the stairs without mishap, she headed to the table and the phone.

Esther picked up the flip phone first and checked for messages. None. She noticed there were only two bars of battery life remaining.

In the quiet house, she heard Axel's progress in the basement, cardboard boxes shuffled and dragged over concrete. A muffled curse drifted up as she crossed the living room. A definite thud was followed by a clunk when she stopped at the curtain covering the bedroom entrance. She slid the curtain open, entered the room, and crossed to the nightstand serving as a charging station. One cord lay on the table, winding around the lamp base. The other had slipped to the wooden floor below.

The bed groaned as she sat on the edge and reached down. If only Mother were willing to get a medical alert system, there would be no need for the cell phone Jesse, her sister, insisted they each carry. Sure, it was a good idea, pay as you go, large display, only three numbers, but what good was it? Mother refused to leave it on, or it was dead or at the bottom of her bag where she couldn't hear it ring. It was a nuisance. Who was going to respond? Mother lived two streets over and two streets down. It was twelve miles to the posh golf-course community where her sister lived. If only Jesse would do her share instead of leaving everything mother-related for her to deal with.

"Miss Esther?" Axel interrupted her musing. He stood in the doorway, straining with a pair of heavy storm panes in his arms. "Should I put these on the porch?" He balanced the bulk on his thigh, just above his left knee. The top barely cleared the curtain rod as he leaned back with the effort to hold its weight.

The cell phone burped to life. A message illuminated its face.

—*Call ur mother*—

Esther's gaze played over the top of the nightstand. Next to the dog-eared paperback sat a framed photo. It was one of the few gifts she had received from Jesse. It displayed their mother, Lydia, youthful and happy, smiling with her whole face.

Warmed by an unmistakable feeling of love, she dialed the number.

It went to voicemail.

Chapter Five

Wednesday morning, Rory broke down the last moving box and threw it onto the mound of cardboard in the corner. The office was unpacked. Ten days on the job, and he still didn't feel at home. Perhaps it was the books piled on the carpet instead of arranged on the bookshelves. Or maybe it was the chair that hit him behind the knees when he sat. He knew it wasn't either of these things. Instead, it was the mystery of Winterset, the small-town mentality with its greater-than-homeland loyalty that refused to let him in.

Even the other officers were reluctant to accept him into their fold. Well, he'd just have to earn it—"because it was the right thing to do." Frustrated, he sat. His weight deflated the cushion, and the metal frame found his tender spot.

"Anything new?" Thacker's voice came out of nowhere, startling him until he realized it came from the two-way radio on his desk.

"Come on in," Rory said.

Thacker entered, dressed in blues and carrying a loose-leaf notebook. He immediately took the chair next to Rory's desk and spread the notebook open over Rory's paperwork. "You want to review? I got the notes organized here. Interviews. Autopsy. Suspicions."

"Sure."

Thacker had spent the better part of the week with him. He hated to admit it—the rookie had proved invaluable. The citizens, hesitant around Rory, were more than eager to spill the beans for the young, fresh-faced kid. Irritating but useful.

"Homer Coot, deceased," began Thacker. "Found last Thursday morning with a single bullet wound to the chest. Dead approximately four hours. Death occurred at an unknown place, body dumped at the lot next to the Winterset Senior Care Home by perpetrator, or perpetrators, unknown. No murder weapon found in the proximity of the body. One twenty-two-caliber bullet extracted during the autopsy performed by Dr. Peter Moss. No match found in ballistic records using the NIBIN database. The twenty-two handgun, specific weapon used in the commission of this crime, not recovered." He leaned over the notebook possessively and looked earnestly at Rory.

"Tell me about Coot," Rory said.

It didn't hurt to go over it again. It would give him time to think. Settling in, he leaned the chair back, propped his feet on the corner of the desk, and faced the hodge-podge on the picture wall. He was ready to listen, and Thacker could use the practice.

"Homer Coot, sixty-nine, Vietnam vet, turned up in Winterset with an honorable discharge at the rank of Private First Class. He lived on a military pension earned after twenty years' service. Occasional handyman for the Lutheran Church, part-time maintenance engineer at AAA Liquor. Residence is over on Maple Street in low-income housing. He lived alone." Here he stopped and said in a quick clip, "Course, he was never alone. The VFW adopted him, and so did the fellows down at the Lodge. I just don't get it. Who'd hurt Homer? And why? He didn't bother anyone. He was harmless."

It didn't help to muse. It took legwork to produce real results. Rory nodded. "AAA Liquor. We should talk to the owner again. This time we do a complete walk-through."

"Putting Triple-A at the top of the list," Thacker said.

There it was. One of the things that bugged the heck out of Rory. Everything, everybody, every place had a nickname. AAA Liquor was Triple-A. The Benevolent Order of Elk's meeting hall was the Lodge. Everyone had two jobs, usually not related. No one, it seemed, was willing to clue him in. It was as if the whole town spoke in code.

"We should conduct the interview before he opens," Thacker said. "He might be there stocking shelves already. Without Homer, he's a one-man show. Later, he'll care if we interrupt him, it being the day before Thanksgiving."

"You're probably right." Rory checked his watch. "Get a car assigned. We'll go now."

****

Thacker pulled the cruiser into a spot in front of the store. AAA Liquor was a dirty brick building sitting at the end of a row of crumbling storefronts built in the 1920s. The shop had seen better days. Litter collected against the building where Rory and Thacker found the front door ajar. A folding gate used to secure the door overnight was unlocked but not folded away. Rory shoved it to one side and entered. Thacker rushed past and into the store. An insistent buzzer went off, announcing they'd breached the threshold.

A voice called out from between the liquor stacks, "Not open. You can look around, but I can't sell ya nothing 'til ten."

"Winterset Police," Thacker announced.

Rory stepped to the counter. Pint and half-pint bottles were lined up behind it. Dust-free, they populated a chest-high wooden shelf worn smooth by constant rotation. A mountain of empty cardboard boxes stood to his right. A sign on the wall advertised, "Ice Cups — 25 cents. No Refills." He heard someone in the back at work with a box-cutter.

"I ain't got time today," Triple-A said, emerging from the aisles with an empty box in each hand. He tossed them at the foot of the mound and rubbed his hands together. "Folks will be in as soon as it's legal. Won't have time. Not today."

"We only need a moment." Rory pulled a notepad from his breast pocket. "Homer Coot."

"Coot's the reason I ain't got time."

"I realize this is a busy time for you," he said. "Last week, you said—" He flipped a page, found what he was looking for, and read verbatim "—Coot works weekends and most evenings. Extra around the holidays. That include Thanksgiving?"

"Yeah," Triple-A said, distracted by a newcomer who tripped the buzzer and entered the liquor store.

"I have here that he worked last Wednesday evening," Rory said. "And I quote, 'Homer left at nine, before stocking the shelves.' "

"Yup, like I told ya last week, I made a mistake by cashing his check. He took two bottles of Jack and headed out before I intended to let him go for the night."

"That unusual?" Rory asked.

"What? To leave early or taking two bottles?"

"The bottles."

"He don't mean no harm, but he's got a drinking problem." Triple-A's ruddy complexion colored. "Two bottles is one more than normal."

"You pay him with liquor?"

"No, not usually. He's got demons. I try not to add to his problems. Tried."

"But last Wednesday…"

Triple-A opened the ice freezer, took out a bag, dropped it to the floor twice, and then emptied the contents into an Igloo cooler. "Funny thing. I didn't think about it at the time, but when I hauled the trash out, there was one of them bottles."

"What bottles?"

"I was thinking two was one too many, and sure enough, there was one full bottle sitting beside the dumpster. I just brought it in and put it away for him. Course, Homer didn't come back to work. The accident and all. But funny."

"Nothing funny about losing your life," Rory said.

"I didn't mean that. I meant Homer taking two like he was expecting company. Even Homer can't drink two bottles alone."

"You know who his friends were?"

"Guys down at the Lodge. Maybe some of the other vets in the apartments. I don't know, really. I just use him for odd jobs. Not like we was friends or anything." Triple-A put the cooler into the ice freezer and slammed the door. "Look, I don't know anything.

47

I'd help if I could, but…" The newcomer set a bottle on the counter, and Triple-A turned at the noise. "I got a business to run."

Both men looked at the clock above the freezer. It was fifteen minutes to ten. "Sure. Mind if we look around?" Rory asked.

"Help yourself."

Rory stepped into the back room, where Thacker stood in the doorway leading to the alley. "We need to take a look at the dumpster." He crossed gingerly through the room, avoiding boxes stacked haphazardly against the walls. At the door, a tattered Army sweater hung from a nail by a row of rusty metal lockers. He caught the scent of burnt wood as he stepped through the doorway. "Triple-A says Homer left with two bottles, and later, he found one unopened by the dumpster. A man with a drinking problem doesn't leave a bottle. Not unless he's distracted or interrupted."

Thacker looked confused. "There wasn't a bottle with the body."

"No. And I suppose the trash has been collected." Rory lifted the lid and shrank back as ripe odors released into the air. Except for wet cardboard and a few scraps of paper at the bottom, the container was empty. "Looks like it was emptied yesterday. Is there a burn barrel?"

"Over here." Thacker crossed the alley. Rory followed.

The empty lot they entered was abandoned and had been allowed to turn wild. Thick brush and a few scrawny trees separated them from a set of railroad tracks. A makeshift fire pit sat on the alley's edge. Cinder blocks formed a semicircle at its perimeter, and the ground, packed hard, was littered with cigarette butts.

"Looks like the break room," Thacker said.

"Yeah, and possibly Coot's after-hours lounge."

Thacker stepped toward the rail bed. "Look how close we are to the tracks. A front-row seat to Homer's leisure moments."

"No one rides the rails these days. Too dangerous. You'd be surprised to know there's no caboose, either."

Thacker gave him a puzzled look.

Realizing the rookie had never known the joy of trading waves with a caboose operator or signaling the engineer to blow the train whistle, Rory felt old, but shook it off. "If there's no empty bottle and no blood pool, we need to look elsewhere."

Thacker pivoted smartly. "The apartments?"

Frustrated that he still hadn't identified the actual murder site, he snapped, "Someone knows Coot's movements that night," then added in a calmer tone, "who better than those who shared his history and his drink?"

Thacker clicked his heels. "I'll bring the unit around."

Rory closed his eyes and drew in a deep breath. *God, grant me patience.*

Chapter Six

After a quick breakfast, Rory left his apartment above the old Hillard Department Store for the police station. Hilly's, as the locals refer to it, had been closed for a decade. Once used for offices, a corner of the top floor had been sectioned off and converted into comfortable living quarters. The apartment location was convenient and the rent reasonable in exchange for daily patrols as live-in property security agent. Using the private stairs on the outside of the building, he descended to ground level across the street from the station's back lot.

Instead of walking directly across the street, he made a detour down Front Street, enjoying the extended Indian summer weather. He passed the hardware store, where a nativity scene crowded the sidewalk, then a huge Christmas tree on the county library's lawn, and noted holiday streamers hanging from the streetlights. Black Friday sale offerings and the mild weather would encourage a flurry of holiday shoppers. Winterset was ready for a festive Christmas season, and the only thing missing to make the town postcard-perfect was a good snow.

Entering the station through the garage, he heard Sunny in the dispatch office but had no desire to poke his head in to announce his arrival. Expecting a quiet day with most citizens taking advantage of the four-day weekend, Rory unlocked his office and worked undisturbed, entering his notes from Wednesday's visit to Triple-A into the computer. Finished, he sat back to muse. Why abandon a full bottle of Jack Daniels? By all appearances, the alley separating the building from the wooded lot behind was used as an outdoor lounge. Cigarette butts were scattered like used wicks of dental cotton beneath a large spreading oak. Styrofoam cups like those sold by Triple-A had been found among the litter, and the ground had been trampled, indicating its popularity. Had Homer shared his bottle? If he had, with whom? Not with the vets from the apartments, he'd established that already.

Rory made an initial visit to the apartments the day after they'd discovered Coot behind the care home while working to establish the man's movements on his last day. A second visit on Wednesday was necessary to learn more about Coot's living environment. Rory learned that, along with the veterans, Winterset's subsidized housing contained a large population of Mexican immigrants. Many were crowded into two-room apartments, full families of seven or eight, and even larger if the household included multiple generations. The vets living among them were a small, tight-knit group. A retired army sergeant managed the property. Rory closed his eyes and replayed the scene.

He and Thacker arrived at the complex as the Lutheran church ladies carried in a Thanksgiving meal. Marilyn Beauregard had greeted him, wearing a ring on every finger, bright colored garments, and a flowing scarf. His mother would have suggested she was a woman who still sang in the choir although her voice had gone flat with age. He smiled at the imagined assessment.

In her arms, Marilyn carried a turkey roaster. He offered to take the pan from her.

"Please"—she handed it over—"there's plenty more in the van."

He tipped his head, indicating to the rookie that he should oblige. "Officer Thacker will bring them in."

He followed Marilyn into the community room and placed the pan where she indicated on the table. Residents lined up in the wings as a dozen church ladies assembled the feast, most in aprons and brandishing serving utensils. As a group the women looked matronly and frumpy, but one woman stood out because she was younger and dressed in an attractive sweater set and flattering slacks. Cheerful and grandmotherly, she was not.

When Marilyn handed him a serving pan of mashed potatoes, he took advantage of the moment. "Who is the lady in the green sweater?"

She lowered her voice. "Irene Elliott. Trophy wife to the local construction company owner. They think they're royalty."

"She's not one of your regular church ladies?"

"Hardly. Her idea of charity involves money. Lots of money. And usually, in her favor. I was surprised when she showed up this morning. Jonathan must have insisted. He supports the community, and his first wife chaired most of our charitable events. This one"—she gave Irene a glower—"Her favorite charity is closer to home. She married him for his money. Oh, her demeanor and manners are gracious and graceful, but I wouldn't look too closely at her motives."

He raised a brow in question. "Not your best friend then?"

"Keep your friends close and your enemies closer," she advised and handed him a ladle. "I'll be back with the gravy."

He'd meant to ask Thacker about Irene Elliott, but the thought got away from him once the meal got underway.

It had been a pleasant afternoon. He and the rookie shared in the meal after manning the potatoes and green bean casseroles. Then, while sitting with the vets, he learned a foot path ran from the apartments, followed the rail tracks, and ended at AAA Liquor. You can step off behind the VFW or the Lodge, they'd said, and a lot of the downtown businesses. But none had used it to join Homer for a drink on his last day. They used it often, they said, no one had a car and it was a convenient shortcut.

Today, he planned to follow up on those curiosities—the young trophy wife, and the foot path.

Sunny's voice came through the intercom and broke in on his ruminations. "Detective Naysmith, you ain't busy. I can see you just sitting there."

Not for the first time, Rory thought about hanging his jacket over the closed-circuit camera. "It's called thinking."

"I need help with the Christmas decorations. Think on your feet."

Grudgingly, he went to lend a hand. Beads spilled from a lopsided bag, and the dispatcher's desk was piled high with garlands and bulbs. Sergeant Powell, shameful blush clouding his rough face, stood with his arms extended, hands bound in a tangle of Christmas lights.

Sunny pulled a string of beads from the bag. "A little color. That's all I'm after. Red and green and silvery twinkling things to distract the citizenry from their plights."

"What plights would those be?" Rory asked. "Plight to remain silent?"

"Plight from wrong?" offered Powell.

Sunny put a hand on her hip. "I don't need no lip from the likes of you two. The town already has its decorations up, and here we are without a speck of holiday cheer. What kind of statement is that? And the children's Christmas party only a week away."

"We were just having some fun, Sunny," Powell said.

"I think the Santa suit is just your size. How's that for fun?"

"You wouldn't!"

With an evil-sounding chuckle she reached for another strand of beads. "I might."

****

Beware what you wish for—the flakes started on Sunday morning. Rory spent the day at home, studying a book titled *The Manly Art of Tomahawk Throwing*. It was his day off, and he kept an eye out, mindful of the descending storm. He made a second pot of tea. He longed for coffee, but his doctor advised against a midday mug.

By afternoon, he'd weighed the benefits of a polished competition tomahawk against that of a blue steel custom ax, and the roads were snow-covered. After a light supper, he decided on the tactical tomahawk, logged on to the Amazon website with difficulty, and, using the skills of the technically challenged, typed in his two-fingered order.

By nightfall, the roads were impassable. Each hour brought a colder wind and another inch of snow. At midnight, he went to bed and didn't give the snow another thought—until the ringing phone woke him. "Naysmith," he said and squinted at the bedside clock—two-forty-seven.

Powell's rumbling voice said, "We're gonna need you to come down."

What was Powell doing at the station in the middle of the night? Rory rubbed his eyes, trying to wake. "What time is it?"

"Time to get up."

"I'll be in at nine."

"We need every man out on this one, Naysmith. The roads are treacherous. Guys can't get in from the country even though the road crews have been out for hours. We're short-handed and losing the battle to the weather. Those who made it in are on their second shift and going into their third. This storm caught everyone by surprise. We've got a mess."

Rory shivered as he rose to look out the window. His rumpled lounging pants hung from thickening hips, and fabric pooled on his bare toes while he looked out over the flat roof of the Winterset police station. Outside was a wonderland with snow still coming down. The police station back lot was covered in white, making it impossible to tell where the street ended and pavement began. A single car sat in the lot. He scratched his head and said, "Looks cold."

"Damn right. It is cold. Look, I wouldn't ask, but there are more problems than we can handle. People didn't plan right. They left after a Thanksgiving weekend at grandma's and got stuck in the storm. Just pull on a pair of pants and give us a hand."

"It'll mean overtime."

"Look, Naysmith, it's not my idea to call you. We're stretched thin, and even the chief is out. Course, if you think you're exempt, too old to be of any help, well, that's a different thing."

Rory scowled. "Nah, I can do it. Just give me a minute."

"I ain't going nowhere."

Chapter Seven

Esther lay beneath two corduroy quilts whose weight held her a willing captive. Muffled by the overnight snow, the world was silent as if wrapped within a cocoon. She burrowed into the feather pillows and pictured the snowflakes floating down to blanket the house in a serene glow of pristine white. She drifted back to sleep.

A shovel scraped cement, the unmistakable reminder of life even in winter. She woke slowly, stretched, and glanced at the clock on the nightstand by her head. Bolting upright, she reached for the alarm clock while simultaneously throwing the covers from her body and swinging her feet to the floor. Nine o'clock? It had been six only moments ago.

She gazed around the room, disoriented. The phone lay by her bedside, the paperback had fallen to the floor, and beside an empty glass tumbler sat the youthful face of her mother, smiling. Mother! She had slept through their early-morning ritual of exchanging phone calls. She reached for the phone and flipped it open. Holding down the number one, she dragged her free hand over her forehead, raking back the strands of hair to lift them from her face, and slowly sank back into the hollow her body had left in the bed, resting her head on the pillows. No answer. She unconsciously tugged the quilt up over her breast and covered her flannel nightshirt, seeking warmth. Well, it was Monday morning, after all. Mother's day out. She closed her eyes fondly at the thought.

****

"Esther? Esther, are you there?" Jesse's voice sounded impatient. "Are you still in bed?" Esther was surprised to find the cell phone at her ear. She listened to a pencil tapping on the other end, then, "Good Lord, Es, it's after ten. I've forged my way to the hospital and might need a sled to get back home again. Granted, Neil can break out the snowmobile. It's terrible out this way. How's it look there?"

Esther lifted her head and arched her back to look at the window from her prone position. Through squinted lids, she noted a slight ribbon of light peeking below the edge of the window shade. She strained, listening for street noise, heard a low moan—the whisper of winter. Rolling over, she eased out of bed and crossed to the window, pulled the shade out from the bottom, and released the cold air trapped between pane and covering. Through the frosted glass, she watched the flakes drift down from a murky gray sky. The yard sat silent, drifts formed over the evergreen shrubs, and the willow branches hung low enough to touch the blanketed ground. Looking toward the street, she said, "It's pretty deep. The snowplow hasn't made it this far."

"But you have power?"

Esther hesitated, reached for the lamp pull, and tugged. The bulb lit. "Sure. You?"

"There are a lot of houses without electricity." Esther heard the scratch of a pencil hitting the desktop. "Listen, I tried to get Mother, but her phone is off."

58

There was a slurp and a ceramic clunk before Jesse continued. "I tried her home phone, but there's no answer. I think maybe her power is out."

Esther slipped her feet into floppy blue slippers. "It's her day to play bridge." She reached for the red fleece robe hanging on the brass hook by the doorway. The right arm went in smoothly, but she circled west as she tried to find the left armhole and still keep the cell phone to her ear.

Jesse said, "She wouldn't try to drive in this, would she?"

"There's not much slows her down. Marilyn probably swung by and picked her up. Her big boat gets better traction than most four-wheel drives. You know what Marilyn and Mother are like. Together, nothing stops them."

Through the connection, Esther heard an office phone buzz. Jesse quickly added, "I'm just trying to touch base. I know you'll take care of her, but I want her to know we are okay." Esther heard the persistent buzz and the frustration in Jesse's voice. "I've got to go because we're short-handed. Tell her to call." Before Esther could reply, the phone went dead.

In the living room, she clicked on the television. It came on too loud, halfway through an episode of Law and Order. She quickly changed to CNN. "The storm continues to press the Midwest, producing heavy snow and ice across most of Kansas and Missouri." She clicked again. "The area sustained blizzard conditions, and Chicago picked up sixteen inches overnight." She punched in the number for the Weather Channel. "Hundreds of schools, colleges, and even workplaces are closed today as the first winter storm of the season moves across the midsection of the country."

Esther slumped back in the recliner and watched the screen transfer from one snow-covered landscape to another. A ribbon of Omaha closings crept along the lower edge of the screen as she sat mesmerized. She slipped her hand in her pocket and found the phone. Why wasn't Mother answering?

She finally made it to the kitchen and put on a pot of coffee. Maybe she should call the church to see if Mother had made it that far. The television was playing in the living room, the Weather Channel following the storm, but she had lost interest in the trials of others and listened only halfheartedly for new developments. She filled the sink and put last night's dishes in to soak before taking her coffee mug to the table. She tried her mother's cell again. Nothing. Something was wrong. She reached for the wall phone just as it rang.

"Esther, what a morning"—Marilyn's voice sounded far away—"Let me talk to Lydia."

Esther clutched the phone. "She's not with you?"

"It's treacherous out. You can't imagine what I had to do to get out, and then I had to follow a snowplow from my corner all the way down to the church."

Esther's volume rose as she realized the implication. "And Mother's not with you?"

"No, the weather and all. That's why I want to talk to her."

Her heart sank. "But, Marilyn, she's not here."

"I'm sorry. I thought Lydia... Well, she told me last night... Well, maybe I misunderstood..." Marilyn cleared her throat before she continued. "Lydia wanted to see you today." She hesitated and added, "She was upset about something, and I just assumed, when she didn't turn up at cards, she meant to come straight to your house this morning."

"I don't understand. Upset about what?"

A definite crunch, grunt, and swish came from the other side of the back door. Esther stepped close, stretching the phone cord across the kitchen behind her, and nudged the curtain aside to peer out. Her neighbor in a giant, snow-encrusted parka hunched over a shovel by her stoop. As she watched, Axel stood and pitched a scoop of snow out over the snow-covered yard. He had finished a thin trench from the alley to the house and appeared to be working on uncovering her door.

Marilyn continued. "About? Well, I don't know. I'm certain Lydia wanted to tell me, but she didn't explain in detail, just that it involved one of you kids and an argument."

"You think I argued with Mother?"

"I think it was something she saw. You know how she likes to watch the neighbors. Maybe upset is too strong a word."

What argument could she mean? Jesse and Neil? She didn't have time for Marilyn's meddling. She needed to locate her mother.

"Marilyn, she's not here," she repeated. Even to her ears, her voice sounded harsh. "When I talk to her, I'll tell her you called."

Finished with Marilyn, Esther dialed her mother's home number. The phone rang, but no one answered. She thought about her mother's answering machine. Puzzled, she decided it could only mean the power was out. She tried Jesse. The call went to voice mail. She hung up without leaving a message and immediately headed for the bedroom and a change of clothes.

****

Esther held the back door open and called to the back of the winter-encrusted figure shrugging down the path toward the shed. "Axel, come in from the cold."

He turned and trudged back. Stepping into the kitchen, he stomped his galoshes, and snow clumps fell onto the throw rug just inside the door. "Sorry, ma'am," he said, kicking the small pieces back onto the rug. Then, slipping feet out one at a time, first boot, then sneaker, he stood stocking footed. With his left hand, he pulled the string that tied his hood and, with the other, brushed it back, exposing sweat-soaked hair and cheeks that glowed red. His mustache and eyebrows, heavy with ice, began to thaw.

"Don't be silly. Get out of your coat and warm up." Esther set a fresh cup of coffee on the table. As Axel struggled with the rest of his winter gear, she took cookies out of a plastic bag and arranged them on a plate. "I would offer you pie, but the last piece went home with Jesse and Neil on Thanksgiving." She picked up his coat, crossed to the basement door, opened it, and hung the garment on a hook to dry. She stood his boots by the wall before she joined him at the table. "Thanks for the help. We had quite a storm last night."

"Yeah, started early and went late. I was out after midnight, pulling a car out of a ditch on County Line Road. I guess they hit some ice and just slid right off." Axel picked up two cookies and started to chew on one while swinging the other in the air for emphasis. "Sure weren't ready for a storm. Not this early in the season."

He took another bite and said through a mouthful, "Why, I haven't put chains on your tires yet."

She watched Axel's face anxiously. "From what I hear, there are some power outages."

"I heard that, too, but it's mostly over on the west side of town. The snow got a little heavy, and combined with the wind, it pulled down the lines. It'll take a while for the crews to get out and repair them, considering the condition of the roads." He sat back and contemplated the situation. "Sure is funny. First four-day weekend this year, and now it's stretched to five or maybe even six. Wish I had a job so I would get the day off." He laughed at his own joke.

"I'm concerned about my mother." Esther set her cup down. "I haven't talked to her this morning. She doesn't answer the phone, and I think her power is out." She looked at Axel.

Over his coffee cup, he looked back.

****

Country western wailed from the speakers. The heater fan, turned up full blast, blew unheated air full force onto the inside of the windshield. Esther huddled in her warmest winter coat, navy wool hanging down to her calves, with a burgundy scarf over her head and wound around her neck. She shivered as the old Ford pickup made its way through the snow and held her purse tightly on her lap. Four blocks had never seemed so far.

As they pulled to a stop in front of Lydia's house, the pickup belched a dark cloud of smoke and died. "Look okay?" Axel leaned forward, hugging the steering wheel, and looked around Esther to survey the house.

The lawn was untouched. Snow sat twelve inches deep on the rose bush hedge, and the roof looked frosted by a wild baker who'd gotten carried away with the marshmallow icing. The chimney was hidden and silent. Esther gripped her purse tighter and hugged it to her chest. The garage door was closed, and the driveway looked untouched. A small snowdrift had settled where the metal garage door met cement. The curtains on the front picture window were open, and inside, the house looked numb, shadowy, and sinister.

Though she hesitated, Axel threw his door open and bounced out. He slammed the driver's door, and an avalanche fell from the truck's roof, passed through Esther's line of sight, and landed against the passenger door. The door handle gave way when she tugged, but she didn't have the strength to push it open against the mound. She watched through the windshield as Axel sank to his knees in the powder, which covered the ditch edging the front yard. He windmilled his arms and gyrated his hips, raising one knee almost to his chest before planting it in front of him and then raising the next. Slowly he managed the climb back to level ground. "Hold on, Miss Esther. Let me get the door."

Not waiting, she scooted to the driver's seat and exited. Stepping in Axel's footsteps, she rounded the pickup. "Doesn't look like she's home. I hope she's all right." Axel made it to the front door and huddled there, waiting for her. She plowed through the drifts, leaving a furrow in her wake, to join him. "It's never locked. Go on in." She nodded at the front door.

Still trying to catch her breath, she paused and held it while Axel knocked soundly on the door. He pushed it open and called out as he cleared the doorway, "Miss Lydia? It's Axel and Miss Esther."

Silence met them. The house was gloomy and still. "Miss Lydia," he called. There was a groan and then a whoosh of warm air as the furnace kicked on, circulating heat through the room. "Miss Lydia," his voice echoed as he crossed the foyer, ignored the living room, and headed for the kitchen. Small nuggets of snow dropped with each step.

The kitchen was empty. A single china cup and saucer sat on the drainboard, a used tea bag embracing its side. Axel threw the light switch, and the room flooded with light. He crossed to the small maple table and picked up a stack of envelopes resting against the napkin holder.

Esther went down the hallway, checking room by room. She gingerly stepped into her mother's room, stepped out again crestfallen. "Mother's not here," she whispered, her panic rising. A large orange tabby circled her feet, brushed the snow from the hem of her coat, and purred loudly. Esther absently reached down and scratched him behind the ears. "Commander, where is your mommy?"

"The garage is empty," Axel announced. "And the phone is dead." She pulled the flip phone from her pocket, held down the number three button, and willed her sister to answer.

Chapter Eight

A slender blonde opened the door at Lydia Mullins' house. Rory held his shield up for her inspection. "Detective Rory Naysmith, ma'am, WPD. You filed a missing person report?"

"Yes, yesterday." Her voice carried a detectable amount of peevishness. The white lab coat she wore over navy blouse and slacks shouted professional, no-nonsense.

He kicked the snow from his feet as she held the door open for him to enter. "Come into the kitchen. We are about to make coffee." With an abrupt turn, she headed into the house. "I'm Doctor Jesse Wallace, the younger daughter."

"Yes, ma'am," he said, and swiped the fedora from his head as he followed her.

"The police are here," she called out.

Rory stepped into the kitchen and found two more women waiting. They stared back at him with deer-in-the-headlights expressions; the room felt cold, matching their mood. "It's about time," the tall brunette said. "We reported her missing yesterday."

As Rory recognized the woman, his heart gave a sudden leap. He was more tired than he realized. Mullins. The mother and daughter with the terrorist complaint. The name should have jumped out at him; it had only been last week. It certainly felt longer ago.

Standing in the kitchen, she appeared taller than he remembered from their first meeting. He straightened to his full five-foot-seven stature before answering. "Yes, ma'am. That's why I'm here." He tried to make his voice calm and reassuring.

Jesse introduced him. "Detective Rory Naysmith, this is my sister, Esther Mullins, and Mother's dear friend, Marilyn Beauregard. We are beyond concerned."

"I've met Mrs. Beauregard." Rory struggled out of his overcoat. "And your sister." He took a chair, joining Esther at the table. Sitting across from her, he noticed the auburn tint in her hair and dark circles under expressive eyes. Her wrinkled shirt made him wonder if she'd slept in it or gotten any sleep at all.

He noted that Marilyn moved confidently around the Mullins kitchen. He retrieved his notebook as she scooped coffee from a canister into the brew basket. She pulled a carton from the back of the refrigerator, opened it, and put her nose to the opening. Satisfied, she set it near the sugar bowl on the table in front of him.

Jesse opened three cupboards before finding what she was after. "Ah, that's where she keeps them." She moved four mugs to the counter and impatiently pulled the half-full carafe from the machine to pour one, which she handed to him. "Cream? Sugar?"

"No, just black. Thanks." He took a pen out of his shirt pocket and opened his small spiral notepad. He jotted a single word, *Mother* and underlined it. Looking up, he found all three women watching expectantly.

"Don't detectives usually wear decent clothes?" Jesse asked.

Rory looked down, his clothes were rumpled and more than a little worn. Called out in the middle of the night Sunday, he'd pulled on a pair of old jeans and hadn't found time to change, much less sleep, in the last thirty-six hours. "Yes, well, budget shortfalls and sudden snowstorms alter the dress code." Resenting the need to defend himself, he added, "I spent Sunday night and all day yesterday patrolling in a cruiser. A lot of people found themselves stuck in the storm, and the department did everything it could to help. In the midst of it all, we got the report about your mother and expected she'd turn up. A lot of people were missing and are not yet accounted for. It seemed reasonable at the time to assume..." He let his excuses fade, realizing it wasn't making the situation better. "Well, the point is she is still missing." He looked apologetically at Jesse. "I need additional information."

"She's seventy-five but not a young seventy-five," Jesse said, impatiently crossing her arms over her chest.

"She means Mother can be a little forgetful," Esther added. "She was wearing a green wool coat and black shoes. We don't know what else." She looked down into her coffee cup. "We didn't notice anything specific missing from her closet."

"She's five foot two and wears eyeglasses and weighs about a hundred and eighty pounds," Jesse said.

"One-eighty?" Esther asked, looking askance at her sister. "Surely not that much?"

Jesse made a hand motion at Rory, indicating he should write it down. He did. "We've given the police the identifying information on the car. You have the number of the plates on file." Her timbre indicated she'd resent repeating any piece of information.

Rory let the sisters wait while he decided on the best tone to use in addressing them. He decided on "detached-all-business" and said, "True enough, but it helps to go over things again. Can you tell me when you last saw your mother?"

"Thanksgiving," the two sisters said at once.

"And I talked to her Sunday night," added Esther, her voice barely audible.

He watched her eyes fill with tears. It made him uncomfortable and guilty for adding to her distress. Rory, who never thought of himself as a comforting person, switched to his "calm-reassuring" voice. "That's good. Did she say whether she was going out?"

"She wasn't going out. She sounded as if she would stay in, and we talked about the storm, and she didn't say anything about going out."

Rory looked at Jesse. "Did you speak to your mother yesterday?"

"No." Jesse made a motion to pick up her coffee mug, her hand trembled before she stopped herself and waited for his next question.

"Dr. Wallace, do you have any idea where your mother might have gone yesterday? Was there anything she said to you on—" He flipped back a page in his notepad. "—Thursday that might indicate her plans for Monday?"

"None," Jesse answered.

Marilyn helped herself to a second cup of coffee and topped off Rory's. "I haven't seen her since Friday. As you probably already know, we do most things together, unless the girls have plans."

"The car is gone, and the garage door is closed but not locked," Esther said. Rory jotted it down, judging that Lydia had gone on her own initiative and planned to return shortly, with no need to close up the house. Good signs in his estimation.

"She is forgetful," Jesse said.

"I already told him that," Esther said, flipping a hand dismissively in Jesse's directions. She fingered the lip of her mug and added, "She used to work at the grocery store. She was a wiz at the cash register, and people liked to come in and talk to her. Last year, she started to make mistakes, and Mr. Clark, that is, the boss, said maybe it was time she retired."

Rory watched as Jesse looked pointedly at her sister, squinting and flaring her nostrils. Might be something there, he thought and jotted down *dementia* as Esther continued. "She was a little scatter-brained but managed around the house well enough."

"We should tell you Mother liked to carry a lot of cash," Jesse said.

Rory held his pen poised above the notepad. "Oh? What kind of cash?"

"Maybe as much as a thousand dollars at a time. She didn't trust ATMs, didn't carry a checkbook, and hated going to the bank. Sometimes she'd just get money out of the bank and stuff it all in her purse, carrying it around until it was gone." She nodded toward Esther. "We both tried to talk her out of it. We could see it made her a potential victim. Anyone could see she had a lot of money."

"Everyone knew she didn't like going to the bank," Esther added.

Marilyn nodded in agreement.

Rory turned his attention to the tall sister. "Ms. Mullins—"

"Call me Esther, Detective."

"Well then, Esther, do you have any idea what direction your mother might have gone when she left?"

"I have no idea. Her comfort zone is limited to downtown, the church, the grocery. If Mother headed to church, that would be south." She stretched out an arm and pointed toward the back door. "If she headed to the store, she would have passed my house going north." She dropped her arm as if the statement had drained her of energy.

"We'll do a thorough search in both directions," Rory said.

"We don't know that she headed to either place," Jesse argued. "I can't imagine what possessed her to go out into the storm."

He didn't have any more questions and started to stand. "That's it for now, ladies. WPD will step up their efforts and we'll let you know when we have something to report. Do you have any questions for me?"

The room grew quiet as they sat with their thoughts.

"What now?" Esther asked. Her lip quivered as her eyes once again filled with tears.

Detached-all-business, Rory reminded himself. "We'll be searching and expect to be able to find something as the snow clears. Snowfall Sunday hampered our progress. Keep in mind, she may already be somewhere safe. If she left any indication where she headed, that would give us an advantage in locating her. Did you say she gets confused? Maybe she got confused and found someplace warm but hasn't contacted you yet. Does she have a cell phone?"

Jesse answered, "Yes, she does."

Esther shook her head. "I've tried and tried that number. There's no answer."

"We've checked the hospitals," Jesse added.

Rory nodded, the police had managed that as well and with no success. "I'd like a recent picture of your mother." He sat as Esther left the room in search of a photograph.

Returning, Esther handed him a small snapshot. It showed a picnic in the park, perhaps the previous Fourth of July. Rory could see flags and banners behind the women, who were seated at a picnic table. "She's the woman on the right," Esther said. "Marilyn is the one on the left. I have a better picture of Mother, but this one is more recent."

He looked pointedly at Jesse. "I'll need the names and addresses of her friends and any relatives she might have gone to visit."

"There's only Marilyn. No relatives. Our dad's sister lives in Seattle, but they only communicate at Christmastime. Other than that, her parents are gone, and she is an only child. So, it's Esther and me. And Marilyn, naturally."

"What about your father?"

Jesse answered, "He died when we were teenagers. Mother's been living here on her own for decades. I look in on her when I can."

With that, Esther stiffened. Enough to make him wonder what he'd missed. There was definitely tension between the sisters.

Jesse took a smart phone from her pocket and referenced it as she wrote on a pad. She ripped off the top sheet and handed it to Rory. "This is our contact information." He saw it contained the phone numbers and addresses for Dr. Jesse Wallace, Esther Mullins, and the friend, Marilyn Beauregard. He tucked it into his pocket.

Esther asked, "If she is stuck in the snow somewhere, do you think she'll be okay?"

"Oh, more than likely. It was a bad storm, but the temperatures weren't that low. Your mother had a coat, and someone will see something. She'll turn up." He cleared his throat, hoping it wasn't a lie. Esther might be perceptive, and he'd told her something she wanted to believe. His experience told him that no matter how sharp her mind, perspective and common sense took second place to emotion and fear. She'd grasp at straws, and then hold him accountable for his promise.

Time ticked by as he sat there, doing nothing more than thinking how he'd feel if his own mother was suddenly not where he expected her to be?

"Is she…" Esther hesitated. "Do the police… Do you consider her an official missing person?"

"Yes," Rory answered. "Missing children and the elderly are an automatic need for concern. Why do you ask?"

"I found a search and rescue center manual online. I printed it out, and I wonder if we could, well, if we could set up a center for Mother."

Rory tapped his pen on the open note pad and looked at each woman in turn. Online? Lord, help me. "Can I see it?"

The women waited while Esther went into the other room and returned with a bundle of paper. She handed the pages to Rory. He flipped through them and said, "We have an abbreviated version of this at the station. We can talk about doing some of the items listed here, but in a small town, a lot of stuff won't work."

Marilyn leaned in. "I could completely handle doing a door-to-door canvas. There hasn't been a baptism, bar mitzvah, or funeral I haven't attended in this town. I've drunk from all the punch bowls, and believe me, everyone knows me well enough to open the door. I could get them to come to the church for a meeting, and we could set up a search and rescue center there."

"That is, if Pastor Mark is okay with it," Jesse said.

"Why wouldn't he be okay with it?" Esther said sternly. "I put the church bulletins together every week. He lets me do the bookkeeping. There is a dedicated phone line in the basement, and they have a fax machine." Now that she had a mission, she became more animated. "It's the perfect location." It was evident to him that the women had been discussing just such a possibility before his arrival. Oh, boy, small-town America.

Marilyn saluted him with her coffee cup, sending the dozen silver bracelets on her wrist jangling. "We can be ready by tonight."

Rory ran a palm over his balding head. "Let's use the next twenty-four hours to get organized. I'll call in additional help while you rally the troops."

He didn't think he'd ever miss the city, but Winterset wasn't turning out to be the quiet little town he had hoped for. With an unsolved murder, pressure from the mayor via the chief, and now a missing mother, when would he find time to sleep? He clicked his pen closed and placed it and the notebook back in his pocket. He leaned back in the chair.

"The first thing you'll need is flyers," he said. Their heads bobbed. "There are a dozen details. You'll need to devote yourselves to the task and separate your emotions from your actions."

Determined faces met his. He felt the bulldozer begin to roll. He shifted his eyes to Esther. "Are you sure this isn't too tough for you to handle?"

Marilyn answered, "No, and yes we'll be ready," Esther looked resigned but willing. Dr. Wallace, he noticed, had gone as pale as the snow that covered Winterset.

Chapter Nine

Clutching the phone to her ear, Esther paced in tight circles in her mother's kitchen. "Yes, I'd like to speak with Detective Naysmith." She stopped in front of the sink to glare at the snow through the window. "No, it's about my mother." Distracted, she turned on the hot water, immediately turned it off, and leaned over the sink. "No, it's not an emergency. Well, yes, it is. You see, she's missing."

The tabby jumped onto the counter and stepped between Esther and the window. Commander nudged her with his head. When she didn't respond, he patted her arm with a furry paw and made a soft rattle in his throat. She gently picked him up and put him on the floor.

"Yes, he knows. He was here earlier. That's why I'm calling." She opened the cupboard and took out a can of cat food as she listened. Commander circled her legs as she one-handedly pulled the tab top from the can. "Yes, Esther Mullins, he has the number. But I thought. Well, I… Oh my…" She tossed her head back, clutched the phone tighter and too quickly added, "I thought I could talk to him now." She heard the panic in her voice and reined herself in with a deep breath. More composed, she said, "Please, have him call me as soon as possible." She hung up the phone as her eyes once again filled with tears.

"Oh, Commander." She spooned his meal into the food bowl and the cat made a grunt of enthusiasm.

She cleaned up the few dishes left from Detective Naysmith's earlier visit. *It's only been one day, there's no reason to go to pieces. Not yet.* But her mother called every morning, left word any time she went out, and checked in as soon as she returned. Mother hated shopping alone and never dined out without a friend or daughter.

After the detective's visit and while Marilyn prepared the all-hands-on-deck search, Esther and Jesse drove the route between the house and the church. They'd cruised down alleys, motored through empty neighborhood streets looking for the car in parking lots, and tried to guess where their mother had gone. But truthfully, they didn't know where to begin. They'd found no sign of Mother, and no sign of the Pontiac.

She put the last mug back in the cabinet with growing anxiety. There was something dreadfully wrong. Detective Naysmith had assured them that she was probably warm and happy. She hoped he was right. Jesse had returned to work. And while Marilyn distributed flyers, Esther couldn't just sit and do nothing.

Her gaze landed on the envelopes sitting on the kitchen table. Shuffling through them, she recognized utility bills, gas, electric, phone, and water. There was a Hallmark card addressed to Marilyn and an entry for a sweepstakes. Neil's name was scrawled across the front of one sealed envelope. She turned it over. It was a standard business envelope, white, and with no other markings, just thick and a little heavy, as if it contained a pamphlet. Curiosity gnawed at her, but she repressed the urge to open it then and there, and slowly returned it to the pile. Why would Mother address something to Neil? Esther tapped the envelopes even and set them back down thoughtfully.

A search of the small roll-top desk revealed a stack of Christmas cards, addressed but not sealed, twenty-seven in all. Esther recognized a few names, but the majority were made out to people who were strangers to her. There were stubs from money orders and a business-size check register, the kind that allowed three, high-fraud-security hologram checks per page and made carbonless copies. She flipped through the last couple of pages, but the carbons matched the envelopes on the table. An old cookie tin held dozens of pictures, but most were taken at the church or luncheons her mother had attended, or landscape shots of distant mountains and empty fields, people and places unfamiliar to her. Considering all the time they spent together, Esther was ashamed to discover she knew so little about her mother's life.

Nothing held a clue, not even the half-finished letter to Aunt Celia describing their wonderful Thanksgiving. Esther guessed that it was going into the Christmas card. But, if Mother had meant to share her plans for the weekend, she hadn't gotten that far. The letter ended after describing the zest Neil had shown for her homemade pumpkin pie. Esther's hands trembled as she systematically worked her way down through the remaining drawers, knowing her mother would be furious when she found Esther had rifled through her personal things.

Yesterday, she'd phoned the police. The sergeant at the WPD duty desk had been impatient and had only agreed to listen when she broke into tears. They'd driven down to the station to fill out the official missing person report. The sergeant was annoyed that the sisters couldn't wait what they, the police, or maybe it was just the sergeant, considered a reasonable time—there was severe weather, after all. Well, wasn't that the reason they were concerned? Irritated or not, he'd filed the paperwork and sent them home to do their due diligence. She and Jesse had gone back to mother's house and looked: For signs of violence? Proof that Lydia wasn't there? Hints of where she might be. Did she have her purse? What was she wearing? Did the doors and windows look normal? Was there evidence of foul play? However, not wanting to disturb their mother's home, they had scanned only for the obvious, believing she would be home as soon as she was found.

The sisters tried to assure each other that if they just let the police do what they were trained to do, things would be all right. Esther had gone home after midnight, alone, and distressed. Unable to sleep, she'd ended up on her old friend the Internet, Googling "missing person," "elderly missing," and "search missing person."

****

Having volunteered to stay at her mother's house, Esther feared she wasn't doing everything she should. The silent house added to her feeling of abandonment, and she wasn't any closer to finding Mother than she'd been the day before. She settled into the recliner in the living room. The shades drawn over the front window made the room dark and gloomy as she brooded about her next move. Commander soundlessly crept over the back of the chair and settled in her lap. She tried to picture her mother dressed and leaving in the middle of a blizzard. It just didn't seem possible, yet her search failed to find evidence proving Mother hadn't done that very thing.

At the sudden pounding on the front door, Esther bolted upright. The knock was so unexpected she hesitated, her heart pounding in her chest. The door opened.

"Anybody home?" sang Irene Elliott as she poked her head in, making a crane-like swing from left to right. Her normally spiky hairdo covered by a fur hat and her body bundled in a floor-length designer coat, she entered without invitation. "Hello?"

Esther struggled to stand but got tangled in the recliner, which hadn't retracted any quicker than she had responded to the knock.

The open door flooded the room with light. Irene said, "Oh, there you are," and rushed to hug Esther. "I came as soon as I heard."

"Heard?" Esther croaked, trying to find her voice as she stepped out of the embrace.

"Yes, I thought something was wrong yesterday when Lydia didn't show up for bridge club, but then many didn't make it because of the snow. I told Marilyn that something was up. We should have reacted immediately." She paused expectantly, staring at Esther.

Unwilling to add to gossip and speculation, Esther offered, "No, Marilyn told me Mother wasn't at cards yesterday."

"Who knew the storm would come in with such force? Never would have dreamed on Friday—"

"Friday?" Esther interrupted.

"Yes, Friday. You know, all the sales. Great prices everywhere, up at five, out on the streets, fighting for carts at Walmart, the usual Black Friday, day-after-Thanksgiving shopping."

"I don't think Mother would be interested in that."

"Well, normally, she isn't, but this year, I convinced her to join us. I guess it was silly, but Lydia and Marilyn said it might be the last time. You know, the last time they would be healthy enough to handle an outing like that independently. Lydia said it made her feel young and it was as good as playing hooky."

Esther could picture her mother up for something that would make her feel young. But to go with Irene Elliott didn't make much sense. "Who went?" she asked, indicating a seat for Irene as she sat down herself.

Irene unbuttoned her coat and took a seat on the sofa before she answered, "Why, Marilyn and Hattie." Esther knew Hattie was Irene's sister-in-law who they carried around with them so they could throw together a foursome at any given moment.

In her search for her mother so far, she'd talked to everyone she could think of, including Irene. "Why didn't you tell me yesterday when I called?"

"You didn't ask. Besides, it wasn't anything much. We were through by noon because we started early. We did stop for a salad at that new place in the mall but were home shortly afterward. Then played a hand."

Esther just stared at her. Was Irene teasing her? Mother had gone all the way into Omaha with a car full of women? Shopping and fighting the crowds?

"Marilyn drove. She has the biggest trunk, and…well, your mother's car…" Searching for the right word, Irene paused, and ended by saying, "You know your mother's car."

"But I talked to her on Friday morning. She didn't say anything about shopping."

Irene gave her a tight-lipped smile.

Impatiently Esther demanded, "Did you see Mother on Saturday or Sunday?"

"I stopped by on Saturday afternoon to borrow her copy of that hot new book on the Top Ten list." Irene tilted her head to the right and looked at Esther innocently. "I didn't stay long. They were predicting snow, and I wanted something to read just in case the roads got bad."

Esther didn't say anything. It wasn't the first time she'd wondered why her mother bothered with this much younger woman. What could they have in common?

"I saw her at church on Sunday morning. Jonathan and I noticed you weren't there."

Esther closed her eyes and leaned her head back. She thought, Damn it! but instead asked calmly, "Did Mother say anything about her plans for yesterday?"

"Just the usual card game." Irene looked contrite. Then, almost with contempt, she added, "They talk about a lot of things, Marilyn and Lydia, but they don't always do them."

Wide-eyed, Esther wondered what kind of things she meant. And who was Irene Elliott to judge someone else?

Irene was in no hurry to leave and they were in the kitchen, making yet another pot of coffee, when the call came. Irene sat at the table, fingering the envelopes, and Esther was setting up the Mr. Coffee. Esther jumped at the first ring. By the third, she was breathing again, crossed to the desk, and picked up the receiver.

"Yes?"

She turned to look at Irene, her eyes narrowing as she listened. "Okay," she said and hung the phone up. "That was Detective Naysmith, the detective assigned to Mother's case. He's on his way over."

Irene sat forward and licked her lips. Esther didn't like her eagerness and broke eye contact. Her mother's cozy kitchen, once a place of comfort, felt cramped and airless. A lump formed in her throat, and she swallowed. Fingering the flip phone in her pocket, Esther lowered her voice to a whisper. "They've found my mother's car."

Chapter Ten

Rory stood inside the doorway to Lydia Mullins' home, hat in hand, and looked at Esther. He wore his sincere face, the one he used to deal with a bereaved family. It had served him well in the past, and he hoped calm sincerity would advance the situation to the next phase.

"Yes," challenged Esther, barring his way.

To the right he saw the darkened living room. Over her shoulder, framed photographs hung on the floral papered wall leading back to the sunny kitchen. She didn't invite him to join her in either room. He had no alternative but to deliver his news under a picture array that documented the family's happiest moments.

"One of the deputies found your mother's car down at Al's Auto Repair. You know, the yard out back of Al's is one of the town's impound lots? A lot of cars were towed during the storm, some because they were parked on the snow routes, others because they were abandoned after the roads became impassable." He knew he was rambling but couldn't help himself. "Who knows how all the other cars came to be there. Anyway, we've been checking all the impound lots, and during the check at Al's, we found the car."

Rory looked around for a place to lay his hat. Not finding anywhere convenient, he plopped it back on his head and retrieved a small notebook from the inside pocket of his coat. Flipping it open, he read, "Pontiac. Model Grand Am, four-door, the year 1990. White, plates Nebraska twenty-nine, F, six, five, eight. Does that sound right?"

"Mother's car was towed?"

"Not exactly."

"What are you saying?"

"The car in question is at Al's Auto Repair. Not in the impound lot, but in the repair shop."

Esther's eyes filled with tears. "I don't understand." She cocked her head to one side. "Are you sure?"

"I'm not doing this very well. Let me begin again." Rory slipped the notebook back into his pocket, pulled the hat off his head, and slowly fingered the brim. "While searching for your mother's car, we checked the impound lots, parking garages, parking lots, and side streets. We ran across her car at Al's Auto Repair Shop where she had left it for repair."

"Where is my mother?"

"Not there." Rory noted the tear that slipped silently down her cheek. "The problem is that we want to get into the car. Your mother left keys, but we can't search without your permission."

"I still don't understand. Unless you think..." Her eyes widened.

"No. But I thought you'd want to be there."

"Of course." Esther nodded. "I'll get a coat and call my sister."

****

After a brief phone conversation between the sisters, they agreed to meet at the repair shop. The drive was made in silence and with Esther sharing the front seat of the city-issued car. Her eyes searched the neighborhood and then the businesses as they passed through town. Rory endured the silence, glad that she held off on the questions he couldn't answer. The roads were clear, and traffic was unusually light, indicating that life was taking its time getting back to normal after the storm. Rory couldn't think of anything consoling to say. He was thankful that Dr. Wallace would join them. It would be easier to deal with both sisters together than dodge their emotions one at a time.

They pulled into Al's just as Jesse's black luxury sedan rounded the corner. She was parked and out of the car before Rory could maneuver into place.

"What's this about?" she demanded, stepping right up to the driver's door and shouting into the window. "Why are we here if Mother is not?"

Rory recognized the frustration and understood her anger. Esther unbuckled her seat belt and exited the passenger door. Jesse rounded the car to throw her arms around her, and as the two sisters silently embraced, Rory stepped out and waited.

"What do you want us to do?" asked Jesse. She gave her older sister a solid squeeze, then released her. The two women stood hand in hand, looking at the detective.

"The car is inside," he said and headed for the service department door. The sisters followed.

Officer Thacker stood at attention just outside the door. "Detective Naysmith," he said. He spoke without hesitation in a resonant and full voice. "The car is in one of the service bays, sir. I spoke with Al Shuler. That's Al of Al's Auto Repair. It appears that the car was left outside on Friday night. There was an arrangement to service the car after the weekend. It was locked, and the keys were dropped into the night box by the door. The investigation has discovered that the lot is left open until around nine, when a security guard checks for anything fishy, pulls the gate closed, and padlocks it. Routinely an opening man unlocks it the next morning. On weekends, that would be Monday morning, only this week, they didn't open on Monday. It was Tuesday morning before they brought the car in."

"This morning," Rory said to clarify the situation for Esther and Jesse.

"Affirmative. This morning, they opened the dropbox and matched the keys to the few cars left overnight. Well, over the weekend"—Thacker looked sheepishly at Rory—"and moved them into the service bays for work."

Rory nodded. "Good work. There couldn't have been many cars left over the weekend."

"Actually, more than you would expect."

Mechanics, their tools, and hydraulic lifts sounded behind the doors. Rory said, "Are we ready to inspect the interior of the car?"

"Affirmative." Thacker turned and entered the service department with crisp, clean movements. His heels didn't click together when he pivoted to face the doors, but Rory wouldn't have been surprised if they had.

The Pontiac sat in the bay at the far end of the room. Large heaters hung from the ceiling, blowing warm air down on the service mechanics working diligently on other cars. Esther, Jesse, and Rory followed the young officer across the floor. The men, hard at work, ignored them. Two additional police officers stood with the Pontiac. Together they stepped forward as the detective and sisters approached. The men looked like a set of bookends, dark Irish, ruddy-cheeked, dressed in navy wool-blend pants, commando sweaters, and full utility belts. They were identical save the fact one was tall where the other was not.

Rory nodded to each man in turn. "These are the Mullins sisters, Dr. Jesse Wallace and Ms. Esther Mullins. Their mother owns the car. What can you tell us?"

The taller man answered, "The outside of the car is clean. Except for the rust, a few dings, and the missing paint, it looks good. No new dents or signs that anything unusual happened to the vehicle recently. We had the servicemen put it up on the lift, and there is nothing impressive about the undercarriage. We also took samples of the dirt from the tire treads and shot a couple of photos." He stopped and looked at Jesse before he added, "That's as far as we wanted to go." He looked at Rory. "We're waiting for your instructions."

"I think we can open the inside and see what we see." Turning to the sisters, Rory added, "The serviceman has already been inside. There aren't going to be any big surprises. We need to see if we can find anything that will help us understand where Mrs. Mullins might be."

As the two patrolmen started to inspect the interior, Thacker stepped away from the group. Jesse and Esther stood by Detective Naysmith and watched as they found the front seat empty except for paper mats that lay on the floorboards. The back seat revealed a year-old church bulletin, ninety-four cents in change, and a bag containing the pie cozies Lydia had used at

Thanksgiving. The glove compartment contained the original Grand Am owner's manual, a copy for proof-of-insurance for every year dating back to 1996, and a cell phone charger still in the wrapper.

Rory realized that the task would be a slow affair since the men were doing a thorough job. Just as his cell phone rang, he thought perhaps the women didn't need to witness the whole process. He stepped away to take the call but kept his eye on the sisters.

Dr. Wallace shifted from foot to foot, the concrete floor not helping her legs or her feet in what Rory considered impossibly high heels. She was visibly uncomfortable, while Esther stood calmly in her sensible, sturdy loafers. Although they had been in the garage for over thirty minutes, the women still had on their heavy winter coats. Jesse had unbuttoned hers, and it hung open, exposing the business attire underneath. Rory imagined that she wore a white jacket over her fashionable clothes when she worked. But he wondered at the shoes. Esther looked like a sensible, albeit worried woman dressed in her blue jeans and wool sweater and bundled in her pea coat. The sisters were a surprise. Their temperaments were different, and their demeanor, polar opposites. There was a family resemblance, but Dr. Wallace was lithe and willowy, a worked-at beauty. While Ms. Mullins, in his opinion, had a healthy, substantial look that he'd call handsome.

He listened to the report from Lloyd and learned Lydia Mullins' MasterCard showed a charge from Thrifty Car Rental. The transaction was entered on Saturday, but the clerk remembered it was a late customer pickup, transpiring after Friday's books were closed, but definitely part of Friday's business. *Could*

Lydia Mullins have driven it all weekend without anyone noticing? There was nothing new on Homer Coot.

He stepped back to the sisters as Jesse turned to Esther and said, "This isn't helping. Did you know Mother planned to leave the car here?"

Esther lifted one shoulder. "No. But she mentioned trouble with the Pontiac."

"Right. Thanksgiving. We advised her to make an appointment to get it looked after. I can't figure out how she left it here." Jesse flattened her lips, gave him a forced smile. "How long will this take? I need to get back and do rounds."

"Really, Jesse?" Esther sounded exasperated. "Aren't you concerned about Mother? Isn't there someone else who can take on some of your duties?"

"Don't go there, Es. I am as concerned as you are. I missed rounds this morning to meet with this detective and this"—she nodded at the Pontiac—"isn't leading to anything useful. I can spend my time more productively, and you can watch while they search. I'll only be a phone call away." As if to punctuate her point, her phone rang. She glanced at the screen guiltily, and then she, too, stepped away.

The sound of the trunk popping open brought Rory's attention back to the car. The lid didn't swing fully open but hovered two inches above the latch. The shorter policeman lifted it to reveal a small pile of shopping bags among the usual things that accumulate in a trunk, which, in this case, consisted of a spare tire, jumper cables, old shoes, and shopping bags from Macy's and Sears. The policeman lifted the bags out one at a time and sat them in a line behind the car.

Esther moved forward to inspect the contents. Without opening the bag from Sears, tools were evident, and the others undoubtedly contained spoils from Friday's shopping trip.

"There's activity on her MasterCard," Rory said, stepping behind Esther and unintentionally startling her.

"What?" she asked as Thacker rushed up to join them.

Clearly proud of himself, he started speaking immediately, his deep voice overtaking the conversation. "The night guard doesn't come on duty for a couple of hours yet, but I spoke with him." Thacker referred to a scrap of paper in his hand. "One Mr. Franklin P. Larsen, one-o-one Elm Avenue, apartment nine. He clearly remembers Mrs. Mullins leaving her vehicle on Friday evening. And he says that he witnessed her leaving in a dark sedan."

"Good work," Rory said, taking the scrap. "That coincides with the information I just received." He turned to Jesse. "Can you see that your sister gets home?" And then addressed Thacker, "Let's talk to Franklin P."

****

Freedom Arms at 101 Elm was a three-story brick building with apartment nine on the second floor. They took the elevator up. Franklin clearly wasn't ready for work as he let Detective Naysmith and the young officer into the apartment. The security guard wore baggy flannel pajama pants and a ratty T-shirt. The living room contained a matching sofa and over-stuffed chair, a rental more cardboard than plush, which sat proudly facing a sixty-inch flat-screen TV playing a recorded episode of Hawg Quest. The coffee table, cluttered with a pizza box and empty beer cans, blocked access to the sofa. A pile of unopened mail sat on the floor beside the chair, Franklin's obvious seat of choice.

He muted the volume on the TV and said, "Yeah, I worked Friday at Al's Auto. It's an easy gig, and they pay pretty well. I'm just waiting for something better, but the guard job pays the rent. I do it and then go down to the club on Front Street and watch the door. Makes for a long night, but my days are free." He shoved the beer cans onto the pizza box and pulled the table out from the sofa to allow space for Rory and the officer to scoot behind and take a seat. Franklin took the chair for himself.

Thacker nodded and pulled a small spiral tablet from his jacket. He opened his mouth just as Rory shot him a look. He closed it again.

"Officer Thacker here," Rory said, indicating the young officer, "spoke with you earlier about the elderly woman leaving a car at Al's?"

"I don't know how elderly she is, but I remember the car."

"Why's that?" prompted Rory, retrieving his notebook.

"Well, the shop closes down at about eight, depending on the volume of work going on and how many mechanics are on duty. Sometimes it runs a little bit after, but it always gets quiet by eight thirty. On a Friday in late November, you can count on those guys punching their timecards right on time. They drive all the vehicles they can into the building for protection overnight, and head out. I have to wait for the stragglers, and sometimes their conversations drag into the parking lot. So, last Friday was pretty cold, and the guys were eager to get home, but two of the fellas were discussing plans to stop for a drink and didn't seem in any hurry to make a decision where."

"So, it was after eight."

"Yeah, even later. You see, after the others finally left, I went around back to have a quick smoke. Al doesn't like employees to smoke where it's visible from the street." He scratched at his chest through the T-shirt, a sure indication that he was embarrassed and added, "I needed to relieve myself as well."

"And?" prompted Rory.

"Well, like I was saying, I have to wait for the lot to clear and then make a sweep checking and get everything locked up."

"So, you swept the lot after eight."

"About eight forty-five. I came back up to the front yard, and there she was. Three new cars had appeared. The owners didn't make it before the doors went down, and the cars would be sitting on the lot for the weekend. I recognized the older model because my gram has one. And it was Mrs. Mullins' because she locked the car and headed for the building just as I came around."

"Did you talk to her?"

"No," Franklin said defensively.

"Why not?" Rory entered a note in his book.

"Uh, I might have, but she was going to the dropbox when I first saw her, and before I could make a move to intercept her, she was at the building. You know women get a little jumpy in the dark in an empty car lot. I've learned that it's best to make a little noise and let them see me first, maybe even see and recognize the uniform and then approach."

"I can understand that," Rory said. "So, you didn't talk to her or get close enough to identify her."

"No, but I'm sure it was Mrs. Mullins, bundled in a shaggy winter coat and that woolly scarf around her head, even though I didn't see her face, I recognized her. She was a checker at Hometown Grocery for years, and I've been going to that grocery with Mom and Gram all my life. I'd know her anywhere." Franklin paused to watch the TV. Glen Hall had a fish on. Rory noticed that Thacker was watching as well.

Rory pushed the fedora back. "Let me make sure I've got this right. At eight-forty-five p.m. Lydia Mullins was at the front doors of Al's Auto Repair Shop, having dropped her car off for the weekend. You didn't approach her or speak to her, but you are confident that it was Lydia Mullins." He looked down his nose at Franklin waiting for a retraction. Surely, this wasn't correct.

"That's about it," Franklin said.

"What happened next?"

"Well, I scuffed my feet and cleared my throat, you know, calling attention to myself, when this black sedan, a muscle car, pulled into the drive and stopped in front of Mrs. Mullins. The driver got out and said something to her. Then they drove away."

"Did he threaten her?"

"Oh, no. He got out, walked over to Mrs. Mullins, talked a minute, and then they got in the car and drove away."

Rory scratched his head. "She just got into the passenger door, and they drove away?"

"Nope. The man got in the passenger door, and she got behind the wheel. I can still see it. She's so short that behind that wheel, she looked about twelve years old. She drove off with her nose peeking over the steering wheel. It took her a while to adjust everything, but then she drove it away."

Thacker fidgeted in his seat. Rory added a note.

"Can you identify the car?"

"Sure, it was a brand-new black Dodge Charger, hemi, V-8 with a 470 HP engine. I know because I've been looking at that model myself. Sweet."

"Uh, huh. Well, that agrees with the information I have from the Thrifty Car Rental."

"I didn't notice which way they went. I watched Mrs. Mullins jerking and gunning the engine until she had the car at the gate, and then I checked on the other cars. Didn't notice if she turned uptown or down."

"Uh-huh. We can get that information from Thrifty." Rory jotted one last note, put the book back in his pocket, and stood. Thacker hesitated a moment and then followed suit.

As soon as the door closed behind them, Thacker said, "So the victim in question left willingly with an unidentified man in a muscle car after a late-night rendezvous at the local mechanic shop." His deep voice sounded earnest in the apartment hallway. "What do you make of it, Detective Naysmith?"

Rory rubbed his balding pate before placing his hat on his head. "The unidentified man works for Thrifty and their rendezvous, although late, was not clandestine. We have more to do than search for one woman. We better cancel the APB on the 1990 Pontiac." He buttoned the front of his winter coat and added, "This snow made a mess of things." Three days lost to the snowstorm, and another searching for a car.

The Coot investigation already lagging, had been sidetracked by the elements—his priorities rearranged for him by Mother Nature.

As they stepped into the apartment building elevator, Rory said, "And we need to update the description of Lydia Mullins to include a woolly headscarf and a shaggy coat." The sooner he found Lydia Mullins, the sooner he could resume his murder investigation.

Thacker scribbled a note as the elevator doors closed solidly behind them.

Chapter Eleven

Across town in the dark, smoky Elks lodge, Neil sipped a cocktail biding his time. The afternoon hours crept forward like a trek through tar—slow and blistering. He had a business, an errand, and a missing mother-in-law. The Jack 'n' Coke passed the time but not the worry.

The only patron seated at a table, the bartender brought him a fresh drink, then returned to wipe down the mahogany bar that curved out from the wall in a horseshoe shape. Behind the bar, an equally smoky mirror displayed the image of the regulars hunched over their beers. Neon beer signs, accented with strings of Christmas lights, flashed in syncopated rhythm. The Kaulburg cousins sat on red imitation leather barstools as red, green, and yellow reflected in the bar back mirror and off their pale faces. When the side door opened, it drew Neil's attention. Axel Barrow appeared in the doorway.

"Close the door. You're letting the ambiance out," Freddy yelled.

Vision-impaired from the plunge from bright afternoon sun, Axel slowly entered and took a position at the bar. Max, the bartender, set a beer in front of him. Axel didn't sit, but leaned against the bar, his left foot resting on the foot rail, the stool nestled against his butt. He dropped his keys and a pack of Marlboros on the polished wood and grabbed the longneck. After the first slug, he tipped the bottle at the man to his left. "Thanks, Sarge." Then picking up the cigarettes and pounding the pack against his palm, he looked around the room, spotted Neil, and said, "Wallace. Any word?"

Neil shook his head, lowered his gaze, and picked up the drink in front of him. He wasn't surprised that Axel knew Lydia was missing, he lived next door to Esther. He wondered how far the grapevine had carried the news of his mother-in-law's disappearance. Axel turned back to the bar and Neil listened as the men resumed their discussion.

"I tell you it's not true. If you eat five pounds of potatoes, you can only gain five pounds. Think about it," Sarge said. He was clad in overalls, red flannel shirt, and work boots. A navy watch cap sat on his head. His nose momentarily glowed green and then turned its normal red. "You can't say you gained fifteen pounds over Thanksgiving. It's not scientifically possible."

"Nope." Ed took a slurp of beer in agreement.

"That's why I start with the desserts," Freddy said. "I want my calories to count. Give me five pounds of Nadine's pie any day over five pounds of celery." He nodded at Max and twirled his finger in the air, ordering another round. Neil declined.

Max took a bill from the pile on the bar in front of Freddy, returned a one, and slapped down a quarter. After flipping a drink token down in front of each man, he scooped up the empty bottles and returned to his task of polishing.

Freddy picked up the quarter and dropped it in the tip jar. The jukebox, prominent in the front corner, and four illegal slot machines against the south wall were silent. It was happy hour, and beer was two for one. Max poured a bucket of ice into the sink, his makeshift cooler, and quickly began shoving longneck beer bottles into the man-made rime. "Some storm," Axel said, starting the conversation up again.

"You don't need to tell us. We were out working the streets," Ed said.

Neil knew Ed, Freddy, and Sarge were cousins on their mother's side. They worked for the county, mowing in the summer and plowing in the winter. They would have been assigned spots on the road crew, helping to locate motorists stuck in the storm or in need of assistance. They had probably worked straight through until the end of the storm. He wondered where they'd been when Lydia went missing.

Freddy said, "Took the Henderson woman out of the ditch on County Line Monday morning. She was near froze to death, wearing only her fall jacket. You'd think people woulda had better sense."

"Twenty-eight cars," Sarge said, shaking his head.

"Yup," agreed Freddy. "Twelve that just drove off the road when they couldn't see the lanes, seven down in ditches, one with a flat tire, and a six-car pileup. The rest just plain abandoned." They sipped their beers, undoubtedly reflecting on the stupidity of drivers in general and twenty-eight in particular.

Neil took a five from his wallet and ambled over to the jukebox, fed the bill in, pressed buttons, and then flipped through the selections as Faron Young began to croon "Hello Walls." He was still making selections when Shelley West burst into "Jose Cuervo." Finished, he took a position at the end of the bar that gave him a view of the entire room.

Axel shrugged off his parka and let it drop on the barstool behind him. "Quiet in here today," he said. "Really something about Lydia Mullins." Axel lifted his bushy brow and looked at the mirrored reflection of the cousins.

"Yeah," Freddy said. "Lots of people without power and phones."

"Plenty of lines lying in the streets after the blizzard blew through," added Sarge.

Axel picked up his bottle and continued. "No. Not that. She's gone missing." He tipped the bottle up and drained it.

They all hesitated and then picked up their bottles as if to make one last toast to her memory. Freddy and Ed had their swallow, but Sarge asked, "What do you mean, 'gone missing'?"

"Just that," Axel said. "Ask Wallace. Monday, she didn't check in with the family. When they went to see about her, she wasn't there. They haven't heard from her yet." He looked pointedly at Neil. "She hasn't turned up."

Neil swallowed hard. Did Axel think he knew something? He was just as concerned as anyone else. Lydia. Trusting, understanding, Lydia. But before he could respond, Ed said, "Probably off shopping. You know how women are."

"Or gone off to the Bahamas, out of this weather," offered Freddy.

Although each man had a full beer and a couple of tokens in front of him, Neil did the finger-twirling thing for another round. "I don't think so. Axel was there when Esther went to check on Lydia. The place was closed up tighter than a drum. Didn't look like she'd slept there the night before. The girls still don't know where she is."

"What day was this?" Sarge asked Axel.

"Just yesterday."

"Monday? They won't do a missing person in that short of a time. Not an adult, anyway."

Axel set his bottle down hard on the bar top. "They better."

"What is this world coming to?" Sarge said. "First, we lose Homer Coot, and now we've lost Lydia Mullins."

****

The discussion went on for some time. Neil heard noise in the hallway outside and imagined the new arrival entering the Lodge through the front entrance, coming down the hall past the trophy case and the wall of Lodge sweetheart pictures. He noted when she stepped into the rear of the bar room. In the dimly lit area, she crossed the dance floor and made her way to the slot machines against the wall and took a seat. The other men missed her entrance into the cavernous room behind them. Neil suppressed a sly smile.

"Wasn't old-man Mullins a lodge member?" asked Freddy.

"Yeah, seems like he was," offered Ed.

"Yup, good old Roscoe Mullins. I think he was chaplain in 1980."

"Gone missing," mumbled Axel. Neil watched them closely.

"Women don't just disappear, not in this town," said Freddy. "I bet she went off to her kin. How old is she, Wallace? Maybe she just forgot to tell the daughter her plans, and there you go, off to Toledo without a note."

"Maybe," agreed Axel. "But Esther Mullins seems real upset. The car's missing, but the house looks normal. Geez, even the suitcases are there. They called everyone they could think of, hospitals, the police. They even called the bus station. Someone should know something. Gone."

"Probably got in the car when it started to snow and just drove south."

"Maybe." Axel fingered the label on his beer.

"Yeah, that makes sense, drove until she was clear of the storm. It was late, so she stops at a motel or a hotel and gets a room, falls asleep, doesn't call anyone."

Axel looked at Neil, then Freddy, pointed his longneck bottle at the latter, and said, "And when she woke up, she didn't call?"

"She could have done her shopping and then got back in the car and drove home. It takes one day to get there. It takes one day to return. You should see her tonight." Sarge set his empty on the bar and flipped a token at Max for a replacement. "I wouldn't worry, Wallace."

"Don't be silly!" The voice came from behind Axel and the cousins, so unexpected that all four lurched forward and stared into the mirror at the girl's image. Lacey McKenna was dressed in her work smock, the nametag proudly displayed at her breast. She was a little messy after her shift at Hometown Grocery, the starched uniform wrinkled, with a small spot of blood on the sleeve. She smelled faintly of sour milk. Her hair, blue-black that didn't come from nature, was pulled up into a tail and then wound around and skewered into a bun on top of her head with a number two pencil, allowing the tattoo behind her ear to show. Her pale Irish skin glistened. In the dim bar light, Neil found her appealing, even in disarray, a young woman with a satisfied, tossed look of just having climbed out of bed. "Don't be silly," she said. "No woman takes off without her makeup and her girlie things."

Sarge swung around to face her, and she stepped between his knees, holding a fifty-dollar bill out toward Max. "I'll need to break this. Is there money in the till?" Lacey leaned into Sarge as she held the money forward.

Max nodded and reached under the counter and pulled out a zippered moneybag.

Axel said, "I don't think there was any makeup missing. The Mullins sisters couldn't tell about the clothes, just that the suitcase was still there."

"Well, there you are." Lacey took the bills from Max and slipped out of Sarge's reach. "There'll be an explanation that doesn't involve voluntary leaving. No woman, nine or ninety, goes away without her goodies. I'd look at the storm or an unexpected visitor." She moved away from the bar and back into the shadows. The jukebox finished playing the last of Neil's selections, and in the silence, he heard the dings from the eight-liner as she fed in a bill.

"All-righty," stated Ed. "Here we have a deceased brother Elk, and his bride of, let's say, eighty goes missing."

Neil looked at him over the rim of his glass.

Ed continued. "We should launch an investigation of our own. You know, maybe get the Ladies Auxiliary involved. Make some phone calls. See if we can find someone or something that will solve this mystery."

While the others talked, Neil slipped away from the bar and into the oversized room, satisfied there was nothing new to learn. He stopped behind Lacey and watched the slot machine reels as they rolled.

Without acknowledging him, she reached down to the giant handbag sitting at her feet and took out an envelope. She held it over and against her left shoulder.

Stepping between the girl and her reflection in the mirror, Neil kept his arm tight against his body, taking the envelope. Then he turned slightly, and with his back to the men, slipped the envelope into the inside pocket of his jacket. Smoothing the coat over the package, he turned and headed back to the bar.

"Round's on me," he said and took a position next to Axel. "Another Jack 'n' Coke, Max. Get the boys whatever they'd like."

Chapter Twelve

The sun had set by the time Jesse finally left the hospital and headed home. So much had happened since they had discovered her mother missing, yet nothing had happened. She needed to go by Esther's but just didn't seem to have the energy. Her sister was right—she needed to focus. Jesse turned the sedan through town past the shops dressed for Christmas. She drove soberly, not noticing the life-size nativity scene in front of Best Hardware or the lamp posts draped with holiday decorations.

She turned left at the old department store and slowly passed the police station, a one-story white building trimmed with blue and lit from the inside. The Winterset Police sign illuminated the empty parking lot while four of Winterset's dozen patrol cars parked diagonally, noses out, at the curb. Jesse let herself pretend the other cars were on patrol. Perhaps it was foolish to think they were out searching for her mother, but she hoped it was true.

As she turned down Lincoln Avenue and neared the park, her thoughts ranged from guilt to disbelief. They had been a family at Thanksgiving, sharing and forgiving, all of them on their best behavior. Even Neil had joined in the game of Password after the dishes had been washed and put away. He acted contrite and humble, as he should, his best and charming self. Jesse saw to it that Lydia and Neil had no time for a private conversation. Esther was Esther, not questioning the fact that they had arrived hours late and empty-handed. Thursday seemed like a month ago.

She stopped the car along the slender drive that ran around the lake, let the engine idle while she stared out at the landscape. Covered with a sheet of ice, the lake was as still as a pane of glass. On the playground, the teeter-totter looked like a giant in the darkening night, and the swings hung limply from their frame. The shore, piled with mounds of snow just days before, looked undisturbed, lonely, and barren. The sky was already dark and twilight crowding in as she slid the car into park, sat back, and leaned her head against the headrest. Mother, she thought, where can you be?

When her phone rang, she took it from the cradle on the dash as her husband's face filled the screen. She tapped the icon and raised it to her ear. "Yes?"

Neil's voice didn't match the smile in the picture as she listened to his latest excuse. She heard country music in the background and the unmistakable milieu of a barroom. It was barely seven o'clock; his speech was slightly slurred, and his sentences fired in a staccato to hide the fact that he'd once again started the evening early.

"Neil, do what you want," she answered and pressed the off button.

Her mother was missing, and she needed his support. Instead, he was out drinking himself numb. Some things she understood. Others she overlooked. But this, this was something else. She didn't see how she could ignore the fact that he just didn't give a damn.

Idling by the lake in the quiet as the sky over Winterset turned to night, despair pressed down on her. Jesse wondered what had happened to her young Scot. When had they lost their dreams? Was it last year when she became head of Internal Medicine at Winterset Memorial? Ten years ago, when the real estate market bottomed out? Neil's obsessions and her career had taken over, and now they were scrambling hard to validate their lives.

She slowly pulled away from the curb. She followed the drive around the lake. The sedan was on top of the wooden barriers marking off the new boat ramp before she was aware of it. She was lost in thought and almost missed the jog to follow the detour. Nothing stayed the same. Expansion, improvement, encroaching, even Winterset wasn't immune. A slight excursion into the neighborhood brought her back to cradle the shore.

The phone burped to life. This time the picture of A.A. Milne's Piglet filled the screen. Even in her gray mood, she smiled at Dad's childhood nickname for her sister. Esther hated it, but Jesse thought it fit. "Hey," she answered as she lifted the phone to her ear. Her smile faded as she listened.

"I don't think I can make it," she answered softly, hating herself for being a coward. "There are some things I need to take care of." Esther didn't push, but Jesse knew she was letting her sister down, leaving Esther to manage the search effort alone. When she clicked the phone off and placed it back on the dash, her hand trembled.

The vehicle left the park and followed the streets on the outskirts of town, aimlessly meandering through neighborhoods. Jesse snaked her way past homes with curtains drawn and cars cooling in the driveways. She needed time to think, and before she knew it was slowly creeping down Front Street. The businesses had closed for the day. The grain elevator outlined behind the Post Office stood a stoic sentinel. Christmas lights and lamp posts bright on Main Street didn't reach the buildings on Front. There was one business open, the Benevolent and Protective Order of Elks. The B.P.O.E. sign lit a beacon to the fact. Jesse backed into a curb spot across the street and a block down from the Lodge front door. From there she saw Neil's car parked next to a dented compact model. She turned off the engine and then the lights.

What am I doing here? I can't just go busting into the bar and demand that Neil pay attention to his family. He had to want to do these things. She unfastened her seat belt and reached into the passenger seat for her bag. Or can I? A figure emerged from the Lodge door just as she was about to open the car door.

The woman headed toward Jesse's parked car. Halfway between the Lodge building and the sedan, she stopped. Fumbling with a giant bag, she searched for something in the bottom, pulled a key chain out, and tucked the bag under her arm. She turned to the parked compact and unlocked the car door. In the dark, it was hard to make out who it was, but as the door opened, the interior light threw a glow into the night, exposing her face.

"Lacey McKenna," Jesse muttered and watched her wiggle into position behind the wheel. The compact roared to life, the brake lights came on, but the car didn't back out.

The front door of the Lodge opened. In the light spilling out onto the sidewalk, three men loudly exited the building. Together they weaved to the right then to the left as behind them Neil strutted out. Jesse watched him, tall and lean, with his drinking swagger, a bravado which he now exploited. Jesse scrunched down in the car. The windows began to fog with condensation, and she needed to wipe the glass to clear the view. It was dark, but still, she feared the movement would call attention to her position. Neil continued to Lacey's compact. The Kaulburg cousins rounded the corner and were lost from view, leaving his tall silhouette standing at the compact's door.

"Damn you," Jesse muttered into the night.

The phone bleeped in its holder on the dash. "Don't ring, please don't ring," she whispered as she grabbed the phone and held it under the dashboard in preparation for the incoming call.

It didn't come. Jesse glanced at the scene before her, saw her husband standing over the compact, and pushed the power button to activate the display. Tapping the settings icon, she slid the brightness toggle as far to the left as it would go. The light wasn't out but dim enough that the glow wouldn't reflect off her face or the windshield.

"Call Neil," she said into the quiet interior of the car. She stared out through the muddled glass, watching her husband.

Neil bent forward to poke his head through the driver's window. Jesse couldn't see into the compact and imagined Lacey purring there in the driver's seat. The phone rang in the sedan. As she watched, Neil stood, and through the night, she heard his phone ring, an echo of the ring inside her car. He didn't answer but patted his chest pocket, where it usually rested. Just when Jesse thought he would let it go to voicemail, he didn't.

"Hon," he turned, leaned against the compact, and sloughed down to rest his back against the door frame of Lacey's car. "I thought you were meeting Esther tonight?"

"And I thought I should check to see what time you thought you might be home."

"Can't say. These meetings can go on for hours."

Jesse watched the vapor rise from his lips and dissipate into the night. White. Funny, she thought, it should be colored, a flag to denote lying—scarlet or burgundy perhaps. "I wonder if you could pull yourself away and go to the church with me. We are organizing the search for Mother."

"Jesse, normally I would jump at the chance to do something to help Lydia, but I've got a Council meeting. You know how it is. I have a position to represent, and there isn't anyone I can trust to carry my message to the others. You know how the Council is full of self-serving bastards."

She didn't answer. *Maybe a purplish red.*

"Well, all right. My best guess would be around ten. I should be home soon after. You don't need to wait up."

You wish.

Neil stood and stepped away from the compact. As he left the car, Lacey reached out and caressed his sleeve. He turned back and smiled.

Jesse heard it in his voice when he added, "You've had a rough couple of days. You need your sleep." Too bad, the smile wasn't for her. If she hadn't been watching from across the street, she might have thought it was.

In her mind, she screamed, "How can I be so stupid?" But, into the phone, she hesitantly added, "I'll try," and clicked off before he said more.

Neil looked at the phone's face, then gently put it back in his pocket. He moved to his car and slid in without an effort. The door closing seemed to echo in the empty night. Moments later, the compact backed out and rolled down the street. Neil backed out soon after.

Jesse sat for a while staring at the empty parking spots. Should she follow? Did she really want to know? Then she, too, started the engine and eased her foot onto the gas. Gravel crunched under her tires as she slowly pulled out and made her way toward home.

Chapter Thirteen

Across the train yard, Neil saw the night operator in the control tower. The solitary man hunkered in front of his computer screen, backlit by a fluorescent glow. The yard moaned with night sounds. Rail cars whined as they were pushed up the hump and uncoupled. Gravity pulled the freed cars down toward the waiting trains as the retarders let out a pneumatic hiss and the metal wheels screeched on the rails. The squeals and whines were followed by a series of clanks as each car passed through the appropriate switch and climbed down through the ladder to settle at the end of the building train with a clang. Each clang was followed by the final hollow echo of an empty car.

Beside a massive crane, Neil waited, exhaling puffs of white vapor. The crane loomed overhead, its load suspended but silent. He listened to the clank of metal on metal and the deep groan of heavy weight on rails. A solitary night owl called out his name. He leaned against the wire mesh cage where cylinders of welding gas stood in a silent tribute to the night. Coat collar flipped up, he pulled the woolen scarf tight against his throat and hunched his shoulders against the wind.

Neil pushed up his left sleeve, high enough to expose his watch, checked the time, and confirmed what he knew. Branch was late. He shoved the sleeve down and his hand back into his pocket. "Goddamn cold," he said.

His car sat beside the construction trailer. From his position at the cage, he could barely make out its bulk behind the small rectangular structure. Where was Branch? The trailer was almost invisible in the shadows, a nondescript box without windows, fronted by a set of concrete steps that led up to the single padlocked door. Overhead, a canvas sling suspended an awkward load of rebar, casting an eerie shadow as it swung gently from the steel hook. In red, the company name was painted on the side of both crane and trailer, *Elliott Construction*. Neil huffed into the neck of his coat and stomped his feet to throw off the chill.

He heard the crunch of tires on gravel and stepped back into the shadows as he watched the truck follow the chain-link fence and turn at the access gate. Without headlights, it made a U-turn and came down the gravel lane to stop next to his car. He heard the locks click inside the black dual-cab pickup and waited impatiently for the driver to emerge. In the dark, he heard the ping of the cooling engine and tried to look through the tinted window at the man he knew was seated behind the wheel. Branch, he thought, about time, and with relief, he started toward the truck.

The driver door opened, and the man stepped out. Branch Dubois straightened to his full six-foot-six height, shook his two-hundred-ten-pound body from head to toe like a dog throwing off a coat of water, and headed across the lot and up onto the concrete stoop to lift the lock and insert the key. Over his shoulder, he said in a muffled voice, "In here." He threw the door open and stepped inside, leaving Neil to stumble forward after him.

Branch flipped the light switch on and entered the cluttered office trailer. He picked up the remote control from the foreman's desk and pushed the power button. The portable heater started with a snap, and cold air blew out into the room. In a moment, the smell of burnt dust filtered into the small space, the currents stirred the stale air, and the interior began to warm. Branch stood before the desk and said, "Have they found her?"

"No."

Branch was a good four inches taller than Neil, but with his regal bearing and broad shoulders, Neil gave the appearance of a taller man. Taking command of the situation, he shoved the tubes of architectural drawings off the desk onto the floor, pulled out the desk chair, and sat down. He pulled his gloves off one at a time, making a show of placing each on the desk.

Branch hesitated only a moment. Then he cleared the clutter from the chair on the visitor's side and took a seat. "Simpler if they don't find her. Better for us, having the authorities focused in other directions."

Neil winced. It wasn't the first time he wondered if Branch knew something about Lydia's disappearance. "There is a police investigation underway, but no leads. A community group led by my mother-in-law's friend, Marilyn Beauregard, is organizing a search party out of the church basement. And her daughters have talked to everyone in town."

"Good," Branch said, not really listening.

"My wife has offered a ten-thousand-dollar reward."

"I heard talk," the younger man said.

"Her idea of leaving no stone unturned."

"I see." Branch draped his long arms over the armrests and settled his bulk back into the chair. He lifted one foot and placed it on his knee.

The men sat facing each other. The silence grew. From outside, Neil heard the whine and clank of the rail cars as they were shunted through the yard and the muffled voices of the yard crew calling out to one another.

"So, why the urgent meeting?" asked Branch.

"Nothing urgent, just business. I got the envelope from Lacey, and everything is taken care of." Neil held eye contact with Branch, who finally lowered his lids. The older man didn't miss the moment Branch looked away, and the left side of his face lifted in a knowing smirk.

"These little tokens aren't peanuts, you know," Neil said firmly. He let the statement hang until he saw Branch shift in his seat. "The snowstorm was inconvenient, but you put us behind." He hoped Branch heard the menace in his voice.

"Threats won't be necessary. No one predicted the snow. Trucks weren't rolling."

"If you want more money, do what you're paid for without excuses."

Branch leaned back in his seat. He opened his mouth as if to argue but then snapped it shut without complaint.

Neil knew he could demand whatever he liked, Branch was arrogant, but he was well paid. "And Branch, where were you?" He said his name as if it had two syllables. "Spending time with hoodlums in a bar?

The boss isn't happy. We need you to hold up your end of the bargain."

Neil could feel his cheeks flush. Man, he could use a drink. He patted the breast of his coat over the bulky envelope stowed in the inside pocket.

"So, that's it, then?" Branch asked. He sat in silence, studying Neil's face.

Neil slowly reached into his breast pocket. "A small task list from the powers that be." He extracted the white envelope, held it in his right hand and smacked it against the open palm of his left.

Branch eyed the envelope. In the stillness, the heater clicked off, dropping the trailer into silence.

"Nice sum of money your wife is willing to lay out." He kept his attention on Neil. "I suppose your sister-in-law came up with the reward idea."

"She might have," Neil agreed. But he knew perfectly well that Jesse had offered the money on her own without consulting Esther, or him, for that matter.

"Esther Mullins likes to get into things that don't concern her," Branch said.

Neil pushed his chair out from behind the desk and stood. He was worried about Lydia. Did he need to worry about his sister-in-law as well? Rounding the desk, he held the envelope out to Branch. "See that you take care of things. I don't like these meetings. And the boss doesn't like the mess. See to it," he warned, keeping a grip on the envelope just a moment too long before finally relinquished it to Branch's greedy hand.

Branch stood, dropped the padlock on the desk, and left.

Neil turned the heater off for good and straightened the desktop, placing the architectural drawings back on top and checking all the drawers. He heard Branch's truck back out to crunch down the lane as he took one final look over the trailer interior. Jonathan would have something to say if he mistreated company assets. Satisfied everything was in place, he picked up the lock and exited the trailer.

The wind was up, and the mercury down as he scurried from structure to car, getting out of the weather. The suspended load overhead swayed, and glancing up, he had a fleeting thought about balance but lost the concept to more urgent concerns. The load looked unbalanced. So what? It was none of his business.

Neil was well clear of the trailer when the rebar broke loose from the canvas and careened toward Earth. In his rearview mirror, he witnessed the first bar land on the cylinder cage and roll off. The second broke through, struck an oxygen tank, and sent out a spark that ignited a blaze, followed by an explosion. He turned in time to see the construction trailer go up in flames. The crane followed immediately afterward, the flames growing from the bottom up until it, too, was engulfed. Before he cleared the yard, the fire alarm and the yard horn screeched into the night.

Chapter Fourteen

It took a full day before the community search effort got organized. Rory spent the time spinning his wheels on the Coot murder though, according to the chief, the missing woman took priority. That evening, he joined Marilyn Beauregard at the door to St. Matthew's Lutheran Church, accompanied her in and down the stairs, and waited while she flicked the light switches. She lifted them in sequence, lighting the church basement from the back of the room to the front. She walked up to a single table in the front. Shifting an overstuffed bag from her shoulder to the table, she carefully removed bulletins, flyers, clipboards, and maps, lining them up across the tabletop.

"Got everything you need?" he asked, thinking Marilyn cut a crisp image in her navy pinstripe pantsuit against the backdrop of white-painted cinder-block walls. She jogged a stack of flyers into a neat pile and pulled out a sheet of paper.

"Hope so," she said and began to read her notes.

At a sound coming from the back of the room, she looked up. Rory followed her gaze and saw Axel moving about, snapping folded table legs into a locked position and lining tables up in columns. Esther appeared with a chair under each arm. The next time Rory looked, the room was ready, and Esther had moved to the church kitchen and was opening and slamming cupboard doors, like she was searching for something. Axel stood at the back of the room, close to the door, holding an unlit cigarette in his hand.

"Go on out and take your smoke break," Marilyn called back to him. "I got some stuff to set up here, and Esther can manage the coffee and tea alone. The tables look just right." She looked over at Esther. "The urn is in the broom closet. It's too big for the cupboards."

Marilyn went back to looking at her notes, and Esther continued to bang in the kitchen. A few moments later, people started to arrive. "Harold Eaches and his wife, Ruth," Marilyn whispered to him.

Rory saw the older man push his wife's wheelchair into the room and noticed Marilyn's grimace. "Ruth uses a wheelchair because of her rheumatism and apparent dementia, but Harold still talks to her as if the situation has never changed between them. Watch," Marilyn said.

"Where do you want to sit, Ruth?" Harold asked. "I would like to be in the back, but if you prefer the front, I don't mind." Ruth stared out into the room and didn't seem to hear a thing. "Good, we'll sit here. Oh, look. They're making coffee." He parked the wheelchair at the end of the last table and walked over to the kitchen. As he approached Esther, he asked, "Can I help?"

Esther had finished filling the coffee pot and was on her hands and knees under the table trying to plug it in. With her backside turned toward Harold, she looked awkward and somewhat foolish. "I think I got it, but thanks for asking," she called back over her shoulder. Rory suppressed a smile.

"Bob and Joe Price," Marilyn said, her voice stronger now that two young, fit fellows had arrived to help. "Eloise and Filipe Gonzalez, they're the young couple that lives close to Lydia's."

Rory noticed Jonathan Elliott when he entered and took a seat beside Harold in the back. Thinking it unlikely the distinguished gentleman would partake in the search he wondered why he was there and went to greet him. "Good evening, Mr. Elliott."

"Detective Naysmith, you have a nice crowd gathered. I take it there's been no progress."

"Not yet. An organized civilian search is the next step."

"I won't be searching."

Rory was taken back and again wondered why Jonathan was there.

"Lydia Mullins is a prominent member of our church and I thought I would support the search effort."

"Always appreciated," Rory said. "And your wife, Irene, is it? Will she be joining you?"

"Irene has other commitments this evening. Naturally, she is concerned for Lydia. Do I speak to you or Ms. Beauregard about donating to the effort? I can have walkie-talkies and snowmobiles at your disposal."

"Marilyn is coordinating the search, it'd be best if you spoke to her."

"Good," Jonathan said and headed in her direction, stopping at every table to speak to the volunteers.

At precisely seven-thirty, there were thirty-five people in the room by Rory's count. "Let's get started," Marilyn said over the din of conversation. Everyone in the room stopped talking and faced her. "I appreciate y'all coming to help. This is Detective Rory Naysmith. He will be assisting us." She indicated Rory, and he nodded at those collected. Marilyn stopped a moment and held up a flyer with a picture of Lydia and "$10,000 REWARD" printed on it. "Lydia Mullins has been missing since Monday. A search and rescue center will be here in the church basement. We will ask you to sign up for the search using one of the clipboards. I'll pass out maps and ask you to provide cars, snowmobiles, bicycles, whatever it takes to cover all the areas. We would appreciate if some of you would help by answering the phone here, volunteer to feed the search teams, or use the phones to reach out to others in the area for information.

"Dr. Wallace is offering a ten-thousand-dollar reward for information leading to the discovery of her mother," Marilyn said. There was some murmuring in the room.

Joe Price leaned into his brother's ear, but he spoke loud enough for everyone in the room to hear. "Jesse Wallace? Why, she hasn't spent more than five minutes in Winterset in years. She is the real missing person."

Marilyn turned her back to the group and wrote, "TURN YOUR CELL PHONE OFF," on the whiteboard. She pointed to the words. "I forgot to mention this at the beginning, but I need you to check your phones right now and turn them off. I need your complete attention."

Rory leaned toward Marilyn's ear and whispered, "I'd like to say some things."

"Okay, go ahead."

He scanned the faces, then cleared his throat. "As Ms. Beauregard said, I'm Detective Naysmith."

Harold Eaches said, "I heard a rumor you were in town."

There was laughter for a few moments, and Rory felt his balding head turn red. "I want to make sure we have a couple of things clear. The police have searched as best we can. We don't have the manpower to cover every inch of Winterset. We will use the search center here at the church as a central place to communicate information that will aid us in finding Mrs. Mullins and returning her safely to her family." He watched as heads bobbed. He noticed Jonathan Elliott was no longer among them.

"Since it is already late and too dark to do any good with what's left of today, we'll start in the morning. Walkers and drivers should be here in the church basement for breakfast by seven-thirty. You'll report back no later than noon, then lunch for an hour, and again by five tomorrow evening. If you find Mrs. Mullins and she is compromised in any way, I don't want you to move her. Make sure you have your cell phone charged and with you at all times. Call the center with any information, and all information, as soon as you receive it. I can't stress how important your role is and the importance of canvasing your entire assigned area—"

A ringtone, AC/DC's "Highway to Hell," broke in on Rory's instructions. Axel, standing in the back of the room, looked around, but he quickly understood as everyone looked back to where he stood. He retrieved the phone from his jeans pocket and turned it off.

"I hate that," Ruth Eaches said, and everyone laughed.

Rory brought their attention back to the front of the room by saying very loudly, "This is a serious search project, and I want everyone to know what to expect and how to do it. Are there any questions?"

Marilyn stepped forward, placing herself slightly ahead of Rory. "Any information anyone can give. Ask people when they saw Lydia last, what was she wearing, where was she headed, who was she talking to." She glanced at Rory and stepped back. "That sort of thing." From her answer, he was confident she had read the entire search and rescue manual.

"And, posters need to be everywhere, the more, the better," he added. "We located Lydia's Pontiac this afternoon at Al's Auto Repair and are certain she is driving a black Dodge Charger. Ms. Beauregard has posters of the car as well as the reward poster for Lydia. When you leave, take a handful, dress warmly and—"

Rory's cell phone started to vibrate. It jumped and oscillated halfway across the table. Everyone looked at him. He looked down at the phone display and held up his hand. "Sorry, got to go. We'll see you here for breakfast, seven-thirty sharp."

Chapter Fifteen

Being summoned to the rail yard meant Rory spent another night without sleep. The fire had been contained, but the trailer was a complete loss. He'd been an onlooker, not part of the operation. He hated the feeling of being an outsider but had stuck around until the fire trucks departed. After a few minutes in a hot shower removing the smoke and soot, he assigned Thacker to get the search underway at the church. By eight, he arrived at the station feeling exhausted. He sidestepped a worker and tripped over an empty box. Heavy black cables stretched across the floor and a line of electronic monitors fenced off the hallway in front of his office. He stepped into the dispatch office. "Sunny, what's going on here?"

"New equipment. We've got to stay up with the times."

"What's wrong with the old equipment?" He looked suspiciously at the monitors on the wall above the pay window. They were dark, thank God. For once, Sunny hadn't watched him walk over from the apartment.

"Watch out for those cables," she warned. "We're updating to the twenty-first century."

Rory rubbed his head. "Six CCTV monitors aren't enough? Now we'll have dueling displays? We already had five too many if you ask me."

"No one's asking. It's a software upgrade, anyway, and these new ones are going in the chief's office." She waved at the line of monitors. "But if you have to know, they're not for surveillance. They're backup. You know, instead of uploading to the cloud when the cruiser comes into the lot at night, it will first upload to our in-house server when they're within Wi-Fi distance and then into the ether. Or we can watch, live stream, on-demand, at our fingertips, regardless of where they are." Her lacquered nails formed air quotes. Rory hated when Sunny's voice conveyed glee.

"Wi-Fi distance?"

When was the last time someone actually looked at a surveillance video? No one ever looked at them. Sure, they recorded automatically when the unit's siren was engaged—outside view to capture the scene and inside to document the actions of the officer and anyone else inside the vehicle. But even in Omaha, they didn't bother to look at them. Too much trouble. Too much footage.

"We're getting those body cam thingamajigs, too," Sunny said. "No act goes unseen. Might as well get used to the idea. No scratching. No gouging. No nose p—"

"I thought the videos were used because eye-witness accounts weren't always accurate. Used only to substantiate actions, not to spy on our men?" He also hated that the public couldn't take a man's word anymore.

Before Sunny could respond, they were interrupted as someone opened the vestibule door and entered the station from the street. Rory looked up at the monitors out of habit. They were still off.

"Yo, Naysmith, got something for ya." The scent of Aqua Velva made its way through the payment window before the dispatch door opened, and the visitor stepped in. Negotiating around the black coaxial cable that snaked across the floor, he said, "You must be redecorating." He stuck a hand out, clasped Rory's, and pumped vigorously.

"Glad to see you again, Doctor Moss—"

"Make that, Petey." He winked at Sunny and made a small bow in her direction. "Looking efficient as always, Señora Gomez."

Rory noticed she had the decency to blush and made no effort to challenge his observation. Petey's gesture couldn't have been an easy one, considering his girth. "Do you have something new on the Coot murder?" he asked.

"I brought the official, final, and completed autopsy report. I tried to send it electronically, but it seems your Internet connection is down."

"I wouldn't know about that," Rory said, glancing at Sunny.

"I thought I'd bring the report in person. We didn't have much opportunity to get acquainted last week, dead body and all. I'm using it as an excuse to drop in."

"You don't need an excuse," Rory said. "Come on back to my office, where things are…somewhat better organized."

As the two men dodged beige-clad workers, Sunny called after them, "You can even stream it on your phone!"

****

"What going on out there?" Petey Moss asked, nodding toward the outer office.

126

"Sunny's on a mission. If you're not here to help, it's best to stay out of her way."

Petey gave him a puzzled look; Rory explained. "The department's upgrading the CCTV system, adding some new features, and granting the chief Big Brother permission. Anything new in the official report?" He took his chair and waved Petey into the other. "Cases are piling up. I sure could use a break in this one."

"I fixed the time of death. The cause was definitely the twenty-two wound. I'm afraid my autopsy doesn't disclose anything about Homer that wasn't obvious from his lifestyle. His liver was playing out, but no illegal drugs in his system."

"Time of death?"

"Close as I can give you, it was between two and four that morning."

"He was off work at ten. Drank a bottle of Jack and ended up at the senior home by two," Rory mused. "Four hours. Six hours, if you agree with the theory he was the prowler the neighbor reported." He scratched his balding head. "Even a heavy drinker might have a hard time downing a full bottle in four hours. The term 'drunk as a skunk' comes to mind. Would he have enough hand-to-mouth coordination to drain the bottle? I wonder if someone helped him drink it." Rory took the report from Petey and glanced at the back page. "A fifth of anything in a single evening, if it didn't put me to sleep, would absolutely turn me into a borderline-blackout, crazy-stupid drunk."

"Been there," Petey said. "Back in my misspent youth, I did a fair amount of drinking. When I turned twenty-one, I had a run at a dozen margaritas. I drank the first eleven just fine, but about four sips into the twelfth glass, the tequila smell threatened. Let's just say I credit divine intervention with saving me from greater stupidity." Petey's smile lit his cherub face. "Now, I'm older and wiser."

"But could a man do it without help?"

"Let's see. One ounce of eighty-proof alcohol is roughly equivalent to a twelve-ounce beer or a six-ounce glass of wine. A fifth, if memory serves me right, is twenty-eight ounces, could be thirty-two ounces, let's call it thirty. In what amount of time could you drink five six-packs or thirty glasses of wine?" Petey looked expectantly at Rory, who returned what he hoped was a look of disbelief. Petey kept on talking. "Keep in mind that beer takes longer to drink, for most of us, than a shot of booze. So, if he could polish off thirty beers in six hours and still be conscious, then he could probably handle a fifth on his own."

Rory would have pooh-poohed the whole idea, but he thought about his ex-wife, whose father had fought in Korea. According to her, he came home from war a big guy, six foot three and two hundred pounds of mean. For about a year, he'd return from work each night and open a bottle of Jack Daniels, chug it, and put it down empty. She said he was an everlasting, mean, nasty drunk toward his family though he'd always seemed pretty mellow to Rory. Up till then, he hadn't thought it was even possible to drink that much, not unless you wanted to die.

"But your question is—is it possible?" Petey said. "For the average non-drinker, no. For a moderate-to-regular drinker, it would depend on the overall time, body mass, metabolism, food consumption, health, tolerance, you know. For a heavy drinker, it might not affect him at all. But it would eventually kill him if he kept it up. Ergo—Homer's liver. I'd say he was a functioning drunk, and again say he could have done it on his own."

"I was hoping to find someone who shared that bottle with him," Rory said.

"He was known to drink at the Lodge. Had some VA buddies in the apartments."

"Nothing else, huh?"

"The bullet wound was made from up close. Probably no more than two feet away."

"That would suggest he knew his killer."

"He had enough alcohol in his system that he wouldn't have put up much of a fight. Senses probably compromised. So, it'd be easy to get next to him without being noticed. I did find this"—Petey opened a soft-sided valise and withdrew a photograph—"in his stomach. People swallow strange things." He handed the picture across the desk to Rory.

"Huh? This looks like a key?"

"It is a key. A standard, run-of-the-mill luggage key, as the boys say."

Rory raised his eyebrows. "Luggage? As in suitcase? Briefcase?"

"Or could be a diary key. You know, those little pink frilly books with unicorns on the front that adolescent girls use to record their private thoughts. They always have a strap with a lock—moms and brothers can't be trusted not to snoop. Anyway, it was there with his stomach contents. I thought you'd find it interesting."

"Can I get a duplicate made?"

"If you could find the right item, a bobby pin would spring the lock. Or a bolt cutter would cut through the strap. The trick would be locating the correct item. Petey reached into his shirt pocket and produced a duplicate key. He wore a sly grin as he handed it to Rory.

As soon as Petey left, Rory checked the Homer Coot evidence log. No case, valise, lockbox, or diary listed. He hadn't expected to find one. As he recalled, they'd turned up a duffel bag in the apartment search but not a single suitcase. The spartan room had been simply furnished, no wall safe, plenty of dust bunnies under the bed. Nothing that required a key to open. Where would the old vet put something he wanted to secure? If not home, his home away from home? He called Thacker's cell. "When do you come on duty? I want you to run by Triple-A Liquor again."

The autopsy gave Rory something new to worry over. He could count on Thacker to report in as soon as he'd scouted out the lockers at Triple-A. But right now, he had to check on the search for a missing mother. He grabbed his hat and left the chaos at the station.

Chapter Sixteen

Transformed from the night before, the church social hall looked almost shabby. Rory stopped in the basement entry to catch his breath. At this time of day, sunshine streamed through the high-mounted windows, flooded the room with light, and exposed every blemish. Esther Mullins stood at the front table with a clipboard in her hand. She placed a tick, paused as if visualizing the face that matched the entry, and then moved to the next. It was quiet in the room, but he could hear pots and pans banging in the kitchen and the noise from the children in daycare overhead. The searchers were gone, and the trash bins full. He checked the phone at his hip and looked up to see Esther place the clipboard aside and straighten the notepad lying on the table, a lost look on her face.

"They just left, Esther," Marilyn said. Rory had missed her standing in the other side of the room, where she transferred names and grid numbers from a sheet to a whiteboard. "Give them time. If they find your mother or anything helpful, we'll get a call."

They didn't seem to notice him, and Rory held back, listening.

"I know," Esther said. "I feel helpless—as if it's hopeless."

"It can't be hopeless with all the concern and effort that's going on."

"Oh, Marilyn, what if we don't find her?"

"I'm not even thinking that." Marilyn stepped back from the board to survey her work. Crisp, even lettering angled slightly uphill and filled the top half of the postings. "It's Thursday. Things always looks better on Thursdays."

Esther took a flip phone out of her jeans, held down a button, and placed it to her ear. A moment later, she lowered it, tucked it back in her pocket, and began to wander around the room. Rory stepped through the doorway. She had her back to him as she straightened a chair, then slowly made her way to the head table and looked down at the phone. "How long before the next call?"

Rory asked, "How long have they been out?"

Esther gasped and put her hand on her heart. He cringed.

Marilyn looked over her shoulder at him, scowled, and said, "Esther, why don't you use this time to set up a phone group? We have the complete list with everyone's cell phone numbers, and you'll be ready to make a global broadcast when we find her. You know, blast it to all the searchers at once." She pivoted, walked to a refreshment table, and adjusted a box of donuts slightly, making the arrangement on the table symmetrical, pastries, coffee pot, and napkins evenly spaced. "There, we're ready for the boys in blue." She winked at Rory.

"The *Gazette* comes out in the morning," Esther said, still watching the phone. "I typed up something last night. You said yesterday it might help to put a notice in the newspaper."

He'd wanted to give her something constructive to do with her time, intending to limit her worry and needless speculation. Not that it actually would, but he wanted to help lessen her misery. "We shouldn't underestimate the citizens of Winterset, Omaha, or Sioux City."

"Yes, widen the search parameters or scope or something." Esther's hands hung loosely at her sides. Still lost, he thought.

A laptop computer sat on the table and an attached printer spit out sheets of paper. As Marilyn picked up a page, he struggled out of his coat, folded it across his arm, and waited.

"Detective Naysmith, join us," she said, looking pointedly at his hat.

Swiping the fedora from his head, he said, "I had a few details to attend to at the station." He handed the hat and coat to Marilyn. "I trust Officer Thacker got the search crews organized and out." From their earlier call, he knew the rookie had covered for him, but he wanted to give Marilyn a chance to demand an apology, if she expected one or wanted to voice a greater concern. She didn't seem to, and he added, "I had a late night and an earlier morning. I see you've been busy."

He stepped over to the whiteboard and read through the postings, examined the posters of Lydia Mullins and the Dodge Charger taped prominently at the top and the rows of neat entries. In his opinion, Marilyn Beauregard was doing a splendid job, keeping things recorded and organized.

"There was a fire at the train yard last night," he called over his shoulder.

Esther and Marilyn waited as he systematically read over the board and then crossed back to the table, picking up the clipboard to review it as well. News of the fire didn't seem to be news to them. He was learning that in Winterset word traveled fast. Pulling out a chair, he took a seat at the table. He'd returned to wearing dress slacks and a sports jacket instead of the blue jeans he'd worn for the last few days—days of unexpected storms and rescues. If Esther noticed he looked fresher and more professional, she wasn't giving it away. He hated to think he'd wasted the Irish Spring soap.

"We've had one set of searchers call in so far," Esther said, handing Rory a printed page. "They found nothing from Mother's house down to Fifth Street. I told them to go on to the next block. Did I do right?"

"Yup. Just keep them moving. There are a lot of areas to cover, and the in-town area is the easiest and can be completed the quickest." He checked the page as Marilyn collected a cup of coffee and selected a glazed donut for him. When she held it out, he looked at her with an expression he hoped said, "I shouldn't," but he knew his stocky body said otherwise, and accepted them graciously.

"This is good," he said to Esther, returning the printout. "I think you've covered it all. Can you fax it to Sunny at the station? She'll put the appropriate media jargon in and send it on to the presses."

Not much later, Thacker called to report the metal lockers at AAA Liquor were empty. Triple-A, the owner, had admitted Coot liked to put his "sippin' toot" in the one closest to the back door and he'd never seen a lock on any of them. It would take him considerable time, Thacker said, to go through the whole place, and they had permission and wouldn't need a warrant. Rory filled him in on the search progress and then asked him to swing by Coot's apartment just in case.

When the phone on the table rang, Marilyn picked it up before it rang a second time. Esther and Rory watched as she scribbled something on the tablet, then hung up. Before they could comment, the phone rang again.

"Any word from your sister?" Rory asked Esther, taking a second donut. She ignored him, watching Marilyn intently. He persisted, "This situation is trying on all of us, and I hoped to see her this morning. I suppose she's already come and gone?"

"Good." Marilyn put the phone back on the cradle. "We're making progress." Esther perked up and followed Marilyn to the whiteboard, where she added some lines to the bottom of the list. From where he sat, Rory noticed the new lines angled slightly downhill. He pulled a sudoku from his pocket and smoothed it out on the table.

At eleven o'clock, the Price brothers came back from their search of the city park, the baseball diamond area, and the trees on the east end of the lake. They had found nothing and were ready for their next assignment. Marilyn complied, and Rory gave up the sudoku to ruminate on the subject of keys—small keys, loose keys, and what they might unlock.

Reports drifted in, but no discoveries. The team who had signed up to cover Main Street phoned to report they had started at the west end of the street after parking behind the police station. They didn't expect to find Lydia shopping or dining but were pleased to say every window and every single light pole displayed a poster now. Unfortunately, after talking with the business owners, they'd learned zilch.

When Rory's phone vibrated on his hip, he checked caller ID—Axel. Surprised to find he had his cell number, he answered hesitantly, fearing the worst. "What's up?"

"Constable! How goes the hunt?" Axel's voice came through the connection. Unfortunately, a country singer's raspy voice came as well, almost overpowering the inquiry.

"Nothing new here at the search center," Rory said.

"What? Can you speak up? I'm over on County Line Road, hoping to spy something amiss."

Rory raised the volume of his voice, "I say, we are still searching." Marilyn gave him a glare. "Turn down the radio, Axel." The radio noise disappeared, and in its place, Rory heard the window rolled down, and the wind rush. "Have you found something?"

"The road is clear, there's a slushy mixture of sand and grit along the edge, probably the county boys doing. Most of the snow is gone from the fields. If I see anything fishy, I'm prepared to stop and snoop around."

"No sign of Mrs. Mullins then?"

"I've got my eye out for the black Dodge Charger. I just hope it isn't in a million pieces, in the back of a big rig, and headed for the Mexican border."

"U-6 is complete," Marilyn said, hanging up the phone at the same time he disconnected with Axel.

It was a long afternoon. Calls came in, assignments went out, and the basement filled with preteen Scouts who had searched from the new school over to the church with no success. Even Marilyn seemed to give up hope.

Pastor Mark grabbed the Scout hat that sailed past, effectively ending a game of keep away as he turned to the troop leader to receive his debriefing. Findings consisted of one lost and muddy sneaker, a left-hand leather glove without a thumb, and an assortment of candy wrappers and empty soda cans. The boys had obviously confused the missing person's search with trash pickup.

Rory crossed to the whiteboard. As the day had grown, the entries had kept pace. The whiteboard filled and a sheet of poster board had been hung next to it to accommodate the expansion. A map of Winterset hung from masking-taped corners, grids marked with indelible ink and the completed areas colored in with magic markers. Esther stood there, shading in U-6 with an orange high-lighter pen. There was little left unmarked.

Esther lowered the pen. Rory could see her face was set in a bewildered frown, her eyes sad. "I really thought we'd find something." Her voice was so quiet that at first he thought he was reading her mind. Then she said, "What happens now?"

"Don't give up."

She searched his face. "I'm not hopeful anymore. I can't jump back and forth between wondering, fear, hope, disappointment..." Her voice trailed off, and she looked back at the map. "I appreciate all the effort, I truly do. But I just want to go home." She smoothed the curled piece of tape on the upper-right corner of the map, her face changing from pale and sad to wan and bleary-eyed. "I picture myself sitting in my kitchen and

Mother dropping in. She'll scold me for hiding behind my computer, coax me into a game of two-handed canasta, and tell me the latest gossip. I want things to go back to normal."

"It's too early to think they won't."

She looked at him through tear-flooded eyes. "She's dead, isn't she?"

Chapter Seventeen

The night was cold but clearer than Rory's thoughts as he drove down the street. What a day he'd had, weepy women, unruly teens, discouraged volunteers. Emotions were running high in Winterset. The search effort wasn't inspiring optimism. Maybe that was a good thing, and the town wouldn't harbor false hopes. But it sure wasn't good for the family. Slowing to a stop, he shot the beam of his searchlight out to illuminate the area around Esther Mullins' house, then down the gravel drive between her house and the next.

A figure shot straight up. Axel Barrow had been lying on the hood of his pickup.

Rory pulled the city car into the driveway and effectively blocked the truck. He turned off the engine and then the headlights. He got out and walked up the drive.

"Cold night, sir," he said as he approached.

"Yep," Axel said. He swung his legs over the side of the hood and sat hunched over, weaving his fingers together between his legs, facing Rory.

"You keeping an eye on things?"

"Sure." Axel pulled his feet up to sit with booted heels tucked against his butt and knees spread. His fatigue jacket looked warm enough to keep the chill out, and he wore a stocking cap pulled down over his ears. His fingerless gloves made Rory suspicious that they might keep his hands warm, but also let him work on engines, or handle wire, or easily roll joints without taking them off. After searching all day, he was surprised Axel wasn't inside, and said so.

"The day was lousy," Axel said. "I wanted to see for myself that Miss Esther got home. She's in there typing on her computer." He jerked his head at a window where Esther could be seen sitting at her desk. "It's quiet. I'm watching. Thinking. Making sure things stay that way."

Rory nodded—he was on the same mission. "And staring at the stars?"

"And staring at stars."

"I wonder if you have any insight into Mrs. Mullins' disappearance."

"What? Are you asking if I'm hiding something? Do you think I'd hurt Miss Esther? You think I like seeing her cry, I mean all-out broken hearted? Man, I'd give anything to know who did this."

"Did what, exactly?" Rory asked.

"I mean… I don't know anything."

"Do you have any theories? You should know Lydia Mullins pretty well, living next door to her daughter like you do. Maybe you have an idea of where we should look."

"You mean a theory like she might be kidnapped or robbed and murdered and her body thrown out in some cornfield or hidden in some haystack?" Axel reached into his pocket. Rory lifted his brows, but Axel pulled out a crumpled cigarette pack.

"Geez. I can't even think about the things people are saying. People talk about Miss Lydia like they're talking about a missing shoe, not like they remember they're talking about Lydia Mullins, a real, live, honest to gosh person. She might be just some police report to you, but she was a good friend to me."

"Is," Rory corrected. "You mean she is a good friend to you."

"Is," Axel admitted. He lit the cigarette. "Did you hear them talking about someone killing Miss Lydia for the money in her pocketbook? Why, when I heard that, I just wanted to, well, I wanted to..." He shook his head like he was trying to bounce an idea loose. "I just want to find out who did this." He flopped back, supporting his body on his elbows, his steel-tipped boot toes pointing at Rory.

"We don't actually know what happened," Rory said, "but something did, and we'll all feel better when we can make sense of it."

"Damn straight," Axel said. "Shouldn't you be checking out some of these rumors?"

Rory shifted on his feet, kicked some loose gravel, and watched the stones roll off the driveway. Esther Mullins, a citizen he'd hoped to defend, a person who deserved shelter from harm, her mother missing over forty-eight hours and the chances of discovering her whereabouts diminishing with each hour. He couldn't let his mind go there. Not Esther. He swallowed hard. He didn't have a clue. "She's crying? Do you think Miss Mullins is okay in there by herself?" He glanced at the house. "Maybe I'll check on her."

"I've been watching," Axel admitted. "She's in there typing away. I haven't seen anyone around, and I think she's settled in. I can't imagine what's going through her head. She heard what people were saying, too. I just want to tell them to shut up. I mean, if they have something helpful to say, why don't they say so? But not this—not stupid, crazy rumors. This is crap."

Rory tipped his hat back, scratched his forehead. "You believe any of the crap?"

Axel looked at the sky and let out a heavy sigh. "Nah."

"So, other than rumors, the things you've heard, do you have an opinion to share?"

"Well, I've been thinking about that boy Juan"—he sat straight up—"the one who lives over in the apartments across the road from Miss Lydia's house."

"Juan Alvarez?" Rory asked.

"Yeah, that's the one. He's a known shoplifter."

"That was when he was ten, and he's eighteen now. I spoke to Juan, but I don't think—"

"Listen, he was hanging around Miss Lydia's house. Did you know that? I saw him myself a couple of times. Have you taken that into account?"

"He's a good kid," Rory said.

"See, there you go. You ask for my ideas, and then you just shoot 'em down without checking 'em out."

Rory nodded. Axel was right, if he asked for an opinion, he should be willing to consider its value. He'd responded too quickly, and there was nothing wrong with being diplomatic, even if he knew he'd already eliminated Juan as a possible suspect in Lydia's disappearance.

"Look, I appreciate the information. Let me know if you get any other ideas. And in the meantime, let's stick together. We're both looking for the same woman."

Axel curled his lip. "You mean Lydia Mullins."

Too late, Rory realized he should have used her name. "Keep your eyes and ears open, sir," Rory said, backing away, heading for the car. Well, at least Esther wasn't alone.

He drove around for another half hour, then found himself in front of Esther's house, again. Axel's truck was parked in the drive, but the hippie had gone. Her lights were still on. He parked, walked around to the back, and knocked at the kitchen door.

A moment later, the light over the stoop came on. Rory looked through the pane at her, his hand raised, his fingers folded in mid-knock. He lifted his brows in a question.

"Detective Naysmith," Esther said, opening the door. "Is there something new?"

She looked harried. Rory had no intention of adding to her worries. "No," he said and felt unsettled in the dim glow of the bulb, his hat in hand. She stepped aside to let him in. "No, I saw your light. It was a rough day, and I wanted to see that you were getting along all right."

"Why wouldn't I be all right?"

He'd worded the statement wrong. "It wasn't an ordinary day," he amended. "I thought maybe you would like some company."

She looked at him through stern eyes. "I've been alone a long time, Detective Naysmith. One more night isn't going to drive me batty."

"I didn't mean that. I thought perhaps you'd need to talk it through with someone. I noticed that your sister didn't come to the search center today?" He said it as a question, hoping that he'd missed Jesse's coming and going. "Maybe you and Dr. Wallace aren't as close as I thought?"

"What did you think?"

"I don't mean any offense, but when a mother goes missing, usually, the children, family, whatever, rally around each other. You know, for family support. Your sister seems to be missing as well."

Rory stood at the door as she moved to the cupboard by the sink and removed two glasses. She set them on the counter, opened the cabinet under the sink, removed a bottle, and turned to Rory. "Will you join me?" she asked, adding, "My sister isn't missing, Detective. She's hiding."

Rory shrugged out of his overcoat and pulled a chair out from the table.

Esther took the coat and hung it on the hook in the stairwell before pouring them each two fingers of bourbon. She took the seat across from Rory, staring at the hat he'd returned to his head.

"Hiding?" Rory prompted, swiping the fedora off.

Esther rose and placed the hat over his coat in the stairwell before rejoining him at the table. "Yes, Jesse doesn't do well with emotions. She can't be involved. I guess it was our upbringing. We never were a huggy-kissy family. Well, maybe Grandma was. But Dad was untouchable. Oh, we loved him, and he us, but any outward sign of affection, that wasn't done in the Mullins household. We took our cues from Dad, so Jesse hides when there is conflict."

"This isn't just some conflict."

"It doesn't matter. Jesse has always overscheduled, overachieved, and overdone life. She doesn't attend family conferences because she has hospital rounds. My sister will miss a christening because she has volunteered at the homeless shelter. She even misses family outings if she can think of a minor obligation that exists in the same time slot. Jesse is great at offering to coordinate an event, but when the time comes to spend any time on the project, she's nowhere around. But you can count on her to make a phone call or two, and she is great at texting and email."

"You didn't expect her at the church today?"

"I hoped. But I wasn't surprised that she only called between rounds. You know, yesterday was extremely hard on her. Too many command performances, mother's house, Al's Auto, but she was a real trouper in the morning. I've learned not to count on her."

Esther set the glasses on the table. Rory looked at his but left it untouched. "I can't imagine her shy."

"She's not shy." Esther took a seat and fingered her glass. "Jesse's the social sister."

"You do all right." Rory took in the exhausted expression on Esther's face, the sleek brown hair with the hint of auburn, the doe eyes, the sad turn of her lips, and wished the situation was better. He wished he had some news. Good news, something that would calm her fears. He thought that even in despair, she spoke and moved with gentleness. He felt the need to help—a leftover knight-to-damsel impulse that he didn't know he had.

"So, what of the fire?" she asked, changing the subject.

"Accident. Carelessness. Negligence. Elliott Construction has had its share of bad luck in recent days. The crew left a defective sling on a crane holding a load of rebar at the rail yard construction site. The wind and the weather played havoc with the load, dropping it onto some gas tanks. The result was the fire. The worst part is that their whole project is compromised. I spent some time with the arson investigator this afternoon, and it appears that there was no foul play. But a whole lot of used and abused equipment. What didn't get damaged in the fire is pretty much useless. All that's left of that investigation is for the insurance company to wade through the debris."

"Elliott Construction?"

"Yep, your old boss."

If she was surprised that he knew about her connection to Elliott Construction, she didn't show it. She watched his hands as they held the tumbler. Feeling awkward, he set it down. When she didn't respond, he wondered if she resented his investigation of the construction site fire as well as handling the missing person case involving her mother—that and the truck stop hijacking. There were a lot of other cases, all of them requiring his attention. He didn't have to wonder long.

"Detective Naysmith, I don't like the idea that you divide your time between cases. I'd like to think Mother is more important."

What could he say? There was a division of time.

"It's late. Shouldn't you be home with your wife and children?" asked Esther.

Rory hadn't seen that coming.

"The job is pretty much my mistress these days," he answered automatically. Then he decided Esther deserved more of an explanation. "My wife left for Des Moines while I was still with the Omaha PD and our children were small. Today the kids are grown and scattered. I'm not sure where my ex-wife lives. Although they, my sons, keep me updated, and more often than not, we avoid the topic." He picked up the glass, but it never went near his lips. He held it in his hands and slowly turned it between his fingertips, finally setting it down again. "I guess I've been alone a long time, too."

The glasses sat on the table between them. Rory kept his eyes on the amber liquid, not sure what response he expected from Esther.

"You're right. I couldn't settle down," she said. "It was almost too much at the church today, too much activity and too much earnest desire to help. And not one clue. I wanted something to happen that would point us in the right direction, any direction. It's the not knowing. I think about her lost in the countryside, hungry and cold. Or wandering around the city, not knowing where she is or even who she is. I close my eyes, and I see her lying in a ditch, wrapped in her green coat. Perhaps she has crossed into Mexico with a band of drug dealers like they say. Maybe she's locked in a trunk, frightened, with her hands bound and her eyes wrapped, struggling for air. I'm mad at her. Why would she carry that much money around? Why couldn't she stay at home? Then I realize it's not her, but the not knowing that haunts me. A hundred thoughts run through my mind, each worse than the one before. If we don't find her, or a trace of her, I don't think I'll be able to stand it."

Esther sat for a long time, staring into her glass. Seeing her eyes flood with tears, Rory let her have the moment. She was incredibly brave, stoically facing the unknown. Words of comfort came to mind, but he knew they were useless, platitudes that wouldn't stop her worry and perhaps make her think less of him as a result. And somehow that seemed to matter.

In the ensuing silence, the orange tabby found its way into his lap, and he stroked its back, thankful for the chance to comfort someone, something, even a lost woman's cat.

"I haven't eaten today," he announced. The cat jumped down. "There's the all-night diner out by the interstate. I'm headed there for an early breakfast. Maybe you will join me?"

Esther looked at him. Perhaps she saw the wrinkled shirt, the unkempt hair matted by the hat he perpetually whipped on and off, and the chin in need of a razor—he didn't know. She stood with her untouched bourbon, reached for his, and took both glasses to the sink.

"Not today," she replied, dumping the contents. "I haven't had much of an appetite. But I'd be glad to make you something to eat." She began the process of making a pot of coffee. The brew underway, she crossed to the refrigerator and removed a pack of bacon and a carton of eggs.

There was silence while she worked at building a breakfast.

Bam!

Rory shot to his feet, the chair scooting out behind him. "What's that?"

Esther's look was one of bewilderment. Together they crossed to the office and stopped. They heard a thump on the outside wall, followed by a muffled shout. The outline of a man appeared in the window and disappeared just as suddenly. "Stay here," he commanded, and headed for the back door. Esther was right behind him.

Two strides and they were outside. Clear of the house, Rory could hear Axel's voice. "Bugger. Don't even think about it. Hold still." He could see the tall man trying to hold a smaller, wiggling fellow, the effort hindered by the slippery fabric of the smaller man's ski jacket. "What you doing? Huh? Trying to take another one!" Axel wrestled the man to the ground.

"Axel." Rory's voice was a command. He stood with his hand at his chest, poised over the revolver in his shoulder hostler. Esther was snug against his back and he could feel her breath against his ear, where she peered over his shoulder.

"Sheriff, grab your cuffs!" Axel shouted.

"Detective," corrected Rory. "I don't think that will be necessary." He relaxed his stance and stepped forward. Reaching down to the figure lying beneath Axel, he tugged back the hood to reveal the face.

A gasp escaped into the night.

"Juan?" Esther whispered.

Chapter Eighteen

Esther pulled the table away from the wall to accommodate four chairs. Rory took one and waited for the plate of eggs she prepared on the stove while Axel, still muttering, leaned against the door jamb into the living room. Juan perched on the edge of one chair.

"Just let him get away with it," grumbled Axel, eyeing Juan.

Bacon frying, anticipation of a hot meal, and sharing the cramped quarters gave him a warm feeling, Rory said, "Nothing to get away with, son."

Esther filled a plate and set it down in front of him. He dug in.

"Then ask him what he was doing sneaking around in the night." Axel had removed his jacket, but the evidence of the scuffle was still visible on the collar of his red wool shirt and the mud clinging to the frayed hem of his jeans. His heavy brow folded into a scowl, his gray eyes intent, and the set of his jaw tense. "Geez, what possible reason does he have for stalking Miss Esther?"

Moving his gaze between Rory and Esther, his cherub face full of innocence, his dark eyes, shining, Juan said, "I'm not stalking. Who thinks stalking?"

"No one thinks stalking." Rory set his fork down. "But I think you better explain yourself."

"Who will believe me?"

"Try us," Rory said. Axel shifted his weight from one leg to the other and snorted.

"I come to see if she has papers," Juan said.

Esther at the stove, looked over her shoulder and asked, "What papers?"

"The papers that Mrs. Lydia prepares for me," Juan declared.

"Why not come to the door and ask?" Rory asked.

"Yeah, answer that one," Axel demanded.

"What paper was Mother preparing, Juan?" Esther placed a plate of bacon and eggs in front of the young man. "I didn't know the two of you knew each other."

"We are friends from last fall."

Axel snorted louder, and Rory gave him a practiced look of disdain. It had silenced stronger men and seemed to do the trick.

"I go to the clinic to see Doctor Jesse," Juan said.

Axel grunted. "Geez, why don't you bring in the whole family? What about Ms. Beauregard? I suppose Ms. Beauregard was there as well?"

"*Sí, sí*, the lady with the jewelry. How do you say in English? *Mujer gitana*."

"Gypsy woman," stated Rory.

"*Sí*, she is the one with many rings."

Axel snorted louder, and Rory gave him the eye.

"I go to the clinic on Tuesday with my brothers. Shots are free on Tuesday, and they need them for school. *Mi abuela* is sick, she goes, too. While I wait, I talk to Mrs. Lydia. I tell her about my family and my father and my mother still in Mexico. I talk about the crops and our work in the fields. She asks about the apartment and *los niños*."

"That makes sense, Mother and Marilyn volunteered at the clinic last fall." Esther set another plate on the table and indicated to Axel it was for him. "Jesse is at the clinic regularly. So, what were the papers, Juan?"

"She asks about the border crossing. I talk about the long trip and the dream in Nebraska. I tell her about the money we send home to Mexico, where there is no apartment and no crops. I tell her about the need to bring my family together and the need for work papers. Already, my uncle, he is sent back. She listens, and she will help."

"How will she help?" Esther asked.

"Blah, blah, blah, get to the real question. Why is he in your yard?" Axel took a larger-than-human bite of eggs and ogled Juan as he chewed.

Rory looked at Axel. "A better question would be—why were *you* in the yard?"

"Geez," Axel grumbled as he shoveled in another mouthful.

"There is that law concerning immigrant children brought to the U.S. too young to know and make the decision on their own," Esther said. "I think you can file for a work visa or a green card or something without fear of deportation. Would Mother know about that? Maybe I can find something on the Internet. If she has the papers, I should be able to find them at her house."

"*Si*, Mrs. Lydia has papers," Juan insisted. "I am to come on the Monday, and we will file them. I can work at a better job and not be afraid to be sent to Mexico."

"And Monday…there is no Mrs. Lydia," added Rory.

"*Si*, yes, this is true."

"I'm sorry, Juan. I don't have the papers. I don't have Mrs. Lydia, either," Esther said.

"I can help you, Juan," Rory offered. "Come down to the station in the morning, and I'll see what I can find. But no more lurking in yards for you, and especially, not in the middle of the night."

"That's it? That's all you're going to do?" Axel croaked. "I catch him sneaking around the house, and you offer to help him? Man, that's not right. What about the other times? What about lurking in Ms. Lydia's yard and terrorizing her?"

"Apparently, they are friends," Rory said.

"Check his pockets. I bet he has her money on him."

"Give it up, Axel," Rory said, narrowing his eyes. Esther finished her work at the stove and started to draw water to wash dishes. "You're not joining us?" he asked her.

"I'm not hungry. It's been a long day." To Axel, she added, "You can't guard me every second of every day. I appreciate the thought, but you have a life, and it doesn't revolve around me. We will find Mother when it's right. In the meantime, we can't invent reasons for her disappearance. You are a good friend and a good neighbor, but I think it's time you gave Juan a ride home."

"Aw, Miss Esther. He could be—"

"No, he's not," she said. "I don't know where Mother is. I don't know what has happened to her, but this doesn't seem likely—his having anything to do with it."

Axel grudgingly pulled his jacket from the stairwell. As he slipped his arms into the sleeves, tufts of dried mud fell to the floor, he said to Juan, "Saddle up, amigo."

After the two younger men left, Rory heard truck doors slam and then the old pickup crank up. He stood, placing his fedora on his head. "Do you think that was wise?"

Esther held a dish towel out in his direction. "What? Sending the two of them off together?"

"Yeah. He seemed a little more than irritated." Taking off his hat, he crossed to the sink, took the towel, and picked up a plate.

"Axel wouldn't hurt a flea. He's a lot of bluster but has a big heart. Like the rest of us, he wants to be useful and feels helpless."

Rory shook his head and set the plate on the counter. "I hope Juan gets home in one piece."

Before Esther could answer, the pickup roared down the alley. Rory heard it squeal around the corner and into the street, immediately followed by the blare of the truck's horn. "Aw geez."

Chapter Nineteen

Friday brought additional frustration. Thacker's report on his second trip to the liquor store contained news that the employee lockers were empty. Triple-A, the man, told Thacker no one used the cabinets except the evening girl who put her purse in one to keep it safe while working the cash register. She had a digital padlock and carried it home again when she left. Homer hid a bottle occasionally in the top locker but drank the contents before the end of his shift, and never bothered to lock the door.

Impatient to catch a break in the case, Rory grabbed his hat and headed for the Maple Avenue subsidized housing where Coot had lived. He'd check for himself. The property manager sign hung beside the door to Apartment Ten. He knocked. A bald man wearing a freshly pressed T-shirt and loose-fitting camo pants opened it. "Looking for... Oh, it's you, Detective Naysmith. I thought I'd answered all your questions last week."

"And you did." Rory looked past him into the neatly kept apartment. "Just a few follow-up details, Corporal Richards, if you can spare the time."

Richards, a compact, physically fit man in his sixties, grunted and stepped aside to allow Rory entry. "I don't know anything more."

"Is the Coot apartment still empty?"

"There's a waiting list, and we turn them over pretty fast, but in this case, murder and all, it hasn't been touched. I understand it isn't the crime scene and therefore the police don't have the authority to keep us from renting it out. Your boys went through it last week."

"That's right." Rory had overseen the search, but that was before the autopsy and the key discovery. He knew only too well the difference between looking in general and looking for something specific.

"So, I'll probably start the clean-up on Monday," Richards said, "and it'll rent out by Tuesday night."

"Then you've already removed his belongings?"

Richards shrugged. "Everything your officers left behind."

Rory nodded and then pushed his fedora back to rub his forehead. "Did you find a satchel?"

"Huh? What kind of satchel?"

"I don't really know, maybe a bag or a briefcase. You've seen those soft-sided valises men carry. Ever seen Coot with one of those?"

Richards scoffed at the idea. "These aren't girlie-men, detective. We house veterans on limited incomes, men who fought for their country, love the American flag, chew nails for breakfast, and spit tobacco. They would rather die than carry a purse."

"Where are his things now?"

"There wasn't much left after the guys divvied up his clothing and appropriated his boots. I put a few things in a box for safekeeping. "

"I'd like to see the box."

Richards gave him a look like he was going to refuse, then said, "Sure, why not."

He disappeared into a backroom, and Rory took the opportunity to check his phone for messages. UPS was holding a package for him. He tucked the phone into his pocket as the corporal returned carrying a cardboard box the size of a nightstand drawer. He set it on the coffee table. "Help yourself."

Rory sat on the sofa and looked through the contents: a packet of letters, yellowing DoD documents, rusty Zippo lighter, trenching tool, campaign patches, tarnished cufflinks. They all were from Homer's Vietnam days. No purse. No bag. No diary. "Not much here."

"Homer Coot didn't seem to have any family," Richards said. "But if someone comes around, I'll give them these."

Rory picked up the letter packet, fanned through them. "Postmarks are mid-sixties. Mind if I take them for a couple of days?"

"Sure. Anything else?"

"It was a long shot, but I once knew of a homeless guy in Omaha who kept a bank book in a zippered pouch the size of a legal envelope. He was homeless, but he wasn't penniless. He'd found one of those locking money bags like Woolworth's used in the sixties to transfer the day's deposit to the bank. He carried the pouch tucked into the small of his back and secured with a rope belt. The key, he hid in the heel of his sock. It was a good hiding place. Then one day—it wasn't."

"I'm pretty sure Homer Coot didn't have a dime."

Rory stood, offering his hand to Richards. "Thanks."

"Any time." Richards walked him to the door.

Yeah, it had been a long shot. Rory fingered the duplicated key in his pocket.

****

The UPS Store was on the way back to his apartment. Rory stopped to pick up the package from Amazon and arrived at Hillard's shortly after noon. He needed to think and that wasn't an option with the commotion in the police station.

Using the door off the alley, he let himself in on the ground floor, a single room the size of a high school gymnasium, with twenty-foot ceilings to match. Desks, display counters, and store mannequins were piled in one corner. Plywood hung over the show windows, and without electricity, the open area was lit only by the sunlight spilling through the open door and across the marble floor. In the center of the space, an elaborate staircase led to the second story.

When Rory had moved in, he'd turned one section of the ground room into a home gym that included a weight bench and a rowing machine. He kept a weighted jump rope and a medicine ball in an empty dressing stall. Rain or shine, he ran sprints from one wall to the other, building endurance and giving his heart a workout, although walk-run described his style better. Rory exchanged his fedora for the strapped headlamp hanging on a hook beside the door. He flipped the lamp on and pulled the door shut.

On an abandoned display cabinet, he opened the Amazon package containing the leather half-finger gloves and the tactical tomahawk. According to the manufacturer, the throwing ax was twelve and a half inches long, with a razor-sharp stainless-steel hatchet blade and built to swing fast and true—lightweight yet heavy-duty. Perfect. He lifted it out, admired its heft, and then smacked the flat side of the blade against his palm, enjoying the play of light the miner's lamp created on the steel. Ax throwing, a manly sport, how hard could it be? He needed a wooden target and eighteen feet to use as a throwing lane.

He pulled out his phone, found Thacker's number. "I have a job for you," he said when the rookie answered.

Thirty minutes later, Thacker pulled into the alley with a dozen two-by-fours, a handsaw, a portable drill, and a can of spray paint.

"I've heard about this sport," he said, unloading the ten-foot boards. "They have leagues."

"If I wanted a league, I'd join a bowling team."

"I mean it has gotten extremely popular." Thacker looked around. "Aren't there any lights in here?"

"Nope. The building's only service is on the third floor."

"I've got a hazard spot in the cab. The battery should be good for a couple of hours."

"Great, I'll use it."

Thacker came back with the spotlight in his hand and a hatchet tucked through his belt. Rory frowned. So, it was going to be a team sport after all.

They built two targets and then pulled desks from the discard pile and set them side by side against the east wall. Placing their handiwork on top, Rory stepped off eighteen paces and spray-painted a line on the floor. "There," he said and took out the leather gloves and the tomahawk. "Let's try our luck. You go first."

Thacker lined up at the starting line, took a step, and heaved the hatchet. It made a graceful arc, hit the wall, and clattered to the floor.

After a half-dozen tries, Rory finally sank one into the soft wood. Wiggling it out, he said, "There wasn't anything at Coot's apartment. Maybe the key doesn't belong to him."

"If it didn't, why swallow it?"

"To keep from giving it back. Or to keep from being discovered with it in his possession."

"Then it could be the key to anything. And that anything could be anywhere."

"Exactly." Out of the line of fire, Rory waved the younger man to take his shot. "How do we narrow the search down? There's the church where he did odd jobs. Is there a soup kitchen in town?"

"Not that I know of." Thacker hesitated, then said, "VFW, the Lodge, VA hospital in Omaha, and the clinic at the senior center. It would help if we knew what we were looking for. And what's in it."

"Let's assume it contains a secret."

They threw for twenty minutes with mild success, neither man managed to sink a bullseye and only occasionally hit the boards.

"Crap!" Rory said when his tomahawk, once again, bounced off the wood and clattered to the floor.

Thacker wiped his brow. "I guess it takes substantial practice."

"Ya think?"

Rory put the tomahawk back in the box and tucked it under his arm. "That's it for me. Want to come up for a beer?"

Thacker checked his watch. "Nope. I just have enough time to run home and clean up before I go on patrol."

"Rain check, then. And if you come around tomorrow afternoon, we'll try again."

They agreed. After Thacker drove away, Rory locked up the department store, climbed the outside stairs to the third floor, and made room for the tomahawk in the gun safe. Settling into the recliner, he flipped to the first blank page in his notebook and made two entries. *Check with VA* and *Esther—church storage.*

Chapter Twenty

A little after eight a.m. Rory sat at his desk at
police headquarters, lost in thought. He had moved to
Winterset to leave the big city and all its crime, a plan
to slow down and remove himself from the strife in the
city. Sure, Winterset had an occasional theft or a stolen
car, but he hadn't expected a murder, a kidnapping, a
hijacking, or anything akin to that. Some days were
better than others, but recently, they all fell under the
column labeled Bad. And he hadn't expected to fall
prey to personal involvement. But here he was, once
again, encumbered with guilt.

Guilt wasn't a new feeling. He'd learned it at an
early age from ruler wielding, knuckle-whacking nuns.
He knew everyone experienced contrition at some point
or another, especially once they reached an age of
reason and became aware of shame and remorse. With
the possible exception of the sociopaths, who never
suffered regret or remorse. Well, maybe remorse, when
they were caught. But for a normal guy, excessive guilt
created a stumbling block. Personally, he believed folks
should accept their shortcomings. Rory never denied
responsibility for his failures, instead accepted life's
challenges, forgave himself, made the necessary
adjustments, and moved on. Compunction kept him
grounded, made him try harder. And because, if he

didn't move on...well, he'd be hamstrung by good, old fashioned Catholic guilt.

On the institutional gray metal desk in front of him lay the folder containing the details on Lydia Mullins, missing person. She had been healthy and happy on Sunday, November twenty-fourth, and gone the next morning. After a week without discovering a single clue to her whereabouts, Rory closed the search center and transferred all the documents to the station. Closing the center had been a sound decision, but still, Rory felt guilt. Ashamed that in Winterset, of all places, the disappearance had happened to one of their citizens, and on his watch. Guilty that he didn't have a clue. He eyed the folder. Seven days of organized search and ten days after she'd last been seen, it didn't amount to more than a skimpy pile of paper.

He picked up the newspaper and read through the news release once again.

Crime Stoppers and its law enforcement partners are urging members of the community to make an anonymous call and provide information about a missing person's case.

Lydia Mullins, 75, has been missing since November 25th. At the time of her disappearance, Lydia was driving a 2013 black four-door Dodge Charger. After an exhaustive search and investigation by officers from the Winterset Police Department, Lydia Mullins remains at large.

Anyone with information leading to the arrest or the filing of felony charges in the disappearance of Lydia Mullins will be eligible for an increased reward of up to $20,000. Contact Crime Stoppers at (308) 555-TIPS (8477).

Maybe this will do the trick, he thought, but he didn't believe it.

Thacker poked his head through the open doorway and caught Rory rubbing his head. "Detective Naysmith," he asked in his deep and solemn voice, "anything new?"

Rory folded the paper in half and tossed it to the corner of his desk. "Yep, the Penguins beat the Flyers, the weather is returning to normal, and the mayor has called a meeting for Monday to discuss the paint color for the lobby at City Hall." Thacker picked it up and took a seat. There was a colossal rustle of paper as he opened the *Gazette* by holding it at the edges and shaking it out in front of him. He leafed through the extended pages to the human-interest section and then made more noise as he folded and refolded the paper to get it to the perfect size. He creased the edge and began his inspection of the newspaper articles.

"Wow. Imagine that."

"Humph," replied Rory.

"Spiro Agnew's real name was Spiro Anagnostopoulos. No wonder he changed it."

Rory remained silent while the rookie read on. "On this day in 1973, Gerald R. Ford was sworn in as the vice-president of the United States after Vice-President Spiro Anagnostopoulos resigned. That's forty years ago. Imagine that."

"Yep, and tax evasion and bribery are still with us today."

"I heard there was a call about sighting Lydia Mullins," Thacker said over the top of the newspaper. "This time, she was seen at the Mall of America. You think it's anything?"

"No. Activity is stirred up because the reward was increased. Winterset will ask for local help from Minneapolis or Bloomington, and they'll dispatch someone to the Mall. No doubt we'll hear later that it was a six-foot albino Winnebago princess in a green coat."

The phone on the detective's desk rang, and he picked it up. "Naysmith," he said. He listened for a moment and then added, "We're on it."

He hung up. "Grab your coat, Thacker. There's been another hijacking."

****

A half-mile before the truck stop, Rory spotted the squad cars at the side of the road and had Thacker pull over. The boys were huddled around the victim, and Rory took a position at the rear, signaling for the rookie to stand quietly beside him.

"It was a Mustang with a flat tire," the man explained. Maybe forty, in frayed and faded Montana big-sky overalls, he mopped the back of his neck with a kerchief and then tucked it into his bib pocket. Red welts, turning a shade of orange-yellow, covered his flushed face. "I'm pulling in for a cup of joe," he said, "and just as I'm shifting down, I spot this young thing. The car's at the side of the road, and she's looking abandoned and helpless. Well, I'm stopping anyway, so I think, what the heck, might as well help. Can't unload until after ten." He pushed a mangled straw hat back on his head and grinned sheepishly. "That's when I lost my little pony."

Officer Garth snorted, looked over his shoulder, and caught Rory's eye. His smirk froze, and he turned back quickly, taking a step that widened his stance and placing his linebacker body between Rory and the driver.

"That's what I call bad luck," Officer Nguyen said in Rory's ear.

Over Garth's shoulder, Rory saw a bullet hole in the crown of the driver's straw hat. The driver rubbed his wrists, winced, and looked past the officers toward the highway. Rory followed his gaze, and lifting a brow, said, "Where's the rig?"

"Well," Nguyen said, "he stops for a break, sees the girl in trouble, and decides to help. Before he can get two words out, she pulls a gun, and some guys descend from out of the trees. They tie his wrists behind his back, punch him a couple times, get his keys, and then drive kit and caboodle away."

"Caboodle?"

"Yup, the whole shebang, the flatbed, the girl's broken-down car, and whatever the bad guys had come in." He nodded at the poplar grove running parallel to the highway. "We found their tire tracks over there."

"How'd we get here?" asked Rory.

"That's a story, too." Nguyen chuckled. "Somehow this cowboy here—" He flipped his hand at the driver. "—manages to get up to the truck stop. But he couldn't open the door, his hands are tied behind his back, he pounds his forehead against the glass instead, and shouts at the people inside. Can you imagine? Finally, someone hears him and lets him in. The cook takes a butcher knife and cuts his hands free." Nguyen's face beamed. "Industrial tie wraps! No one's going to believe this one."

Rory cleared his throat and held his expression steady.

Nguyen paused a moment and then added quickly, "The waitress, Emma Jean, she notified the department."

"Thanks," Rory said, stepping into the circle of officers. "Who called for the ambulance?"

"Don't need one," the driver said. "I do need that truck. Can't believe this—just can't believe this." He stuffed his hands into the bib pocket over his chest. "I'm just making a simple run up from Wichita. Got loaded yesterday and planned to deliver today. I have another haul out on Friday. Don't want to miss it. But I guess I can't make the trip without the ol' pony, can I?"

"Did you see the men who did this?" Rory asked.

"It happened too fast. I was concentrating on the tire, and the girl. The men blindsided me. All I saw was a guy dressed in black like a ninja, and he wasn't alone. Don't know how many there was, but more than one."

"Tell me about the load. Anything unusual about what you were carrying?"

"Can't say that it was unusual, but yeah, I had four front loaders on the back. I can't imagine getting busted up just for that. Hell of a note. How am I going to make a living? You've got to get my rig back."

"We'll try. Where was your delivery?"

"Up the road. I'll need to call dispatch for the exact address. It's all in the paperwork. The paperwork is in the truck."

"Okay, we'll get that later. Can you describe the girl?"

"Young, pretty, inked. Short skirt and leather jacket. Oh, and she had a blue streak in her black hair."

"Local?" asked Thacker, snatching a look at Rory. Rory grimaced.

Thacker revised the question. "Did she indicate that she was local? Maybe say something that made you think she was from Winterset?"

"She didn't say much of anything, 'Shut up' a couple of times, not much more."

Rory asked, "Could you describe the tattoos? Give us something more than boots and jacket?"

"No, I noticed a tat on the neck of gun girl. But her jacket was covering the better part of it. I'd say it was an eight, a figure eight with a...like a...heart inside it. It was running up her neck and behind her ear. To be honest, the barrel of the gun was obstructing my view."

"Is that what happened to your hat?" asked Thacker.

"Yeah, treated me like a sack of flour—girl kilt my hat."

Rory cleared his throat. "What about the car. Mustang, you say? Any model year or license number to add to the description here?"

"It was red. *Really red.* New or fairly new, but I didn't really look at it. I have to admit that I was more interested in the girl than the vehicle. Then more interested in the gun than the girl."

Thacker nodded as if he understood the hierarchy of such things.

"Then you can identify the weapon make and model?"

"Huh? I don't know nothing about handguns. It had a big barrel—looked the size of a freakin' cannon when she pointed it at me."

"We'll need your hat," Rory said.

The driver flinched as he reached for it. If his ribs weren't broken, they were certainly bruised. His battered face paled, and it looked like he'd just begun to feel the pain.

"Look, I think you need to go to the hospital," Rory said. "Thacker, let's take this gentleman into town."

So far, he knew the car was a really red mustang, the truck yellow, the girl quirky, and the perpetrators gone. Front loaders? Construction equipment. Rory didn't miss the similarities to the unsolved hijacking cases he was working.

As the officers started their tasks, he and Thacker headed for the car. Rory opened the passenger door, and the truck driver climbed into the back. It would be a fifteen-minute ride to the hospital. From there, it would be a twenty-minute drive to the police station. Rory's mind worked in overdrive. Get the details of the truck delivery, pull out the mug books, hunt for similar incidents, put out an APB on the truck. With any luck, he'd have this crime solved by supper. Maybe all three cases, even.

The battered trucker slumped in the back seat. As Thacker turned on the left blinker ready to merge into traffic a tractor moved slow and steady up the highway. Thacker let the farm equipment pass. Then he pulled out and u-turned back toward town. Once underway, he turned to Rory and said, "This is the same as the other hijackings, only different."

"Thanks, Yogi," Rory said.

Chapter Twenty-One

Thacker entered Naysmith's office and took a chair, tossing a newspaper to the floor. "I put him in the green room."

Rory looked at him over the report he was reading. Momentarily lost, he had to focus on the rookie's face before he realized he was talking about the truck-less driver. On the ride to the hospital to patch up the bruised ribs, they had discovered the driver's name, Arlo Chuckey. His great claim to fame was to have once hauled the Capitol Christmas tree from the Bitterroot Mountains of Montana to the west lawn of the Capitol Building in Washington, D.C., a tale that spanned the ride from the crime scene to the hospital and the short wait in the emergency room.

After taping up three broken ribs, the telling wrapped up on the journey from the hospital to the station, ending when Chuckey realized that the maiden voyage of his rig was the best there was ever going to be now that the truck, in Thacker's words, "had been lost to the criminal element."

"Right," Rory answered. The minute they'd returned to the station, he had been bombarded. First, with questions from the sergeant, then with paperwork, and finally, the call from the chief. Not that the call wasn't a welcome interruption from the paperwork, but the chief was looking for results. Rory hadn't had time to reach any resolutions.

He slipped from hijack sole-focus mode back into juggling-multiple-issues detective mode, his attention on the hi-jack for the moment. "Right. Is he looking at the mug shots?"

"I set him up with the extra computer in the Water Works office. I thought I should leave my desk open to research the missing equipment." Thacker pulled his notebook out and turned to a page halfway through, where a pen had marked his latest addition. "I talked to the equipment yard where he picked up the load. They aren't new to this kind of problem. It seems that they record the identification numbers off the units as soon as they hit the ground."

Thacker checked his notes before continuing. "Big money on the black market. The theft of construction equipment adds up to millions, maybe even billions, of dollars in the U.S. alone. These guys have been burnt one too many times. Now they register all units with the NER, that's the National Equipment Register. They filed the paperwork on Monday."

"Good. And how goes the quest?" Rory half-listened as his eyes returned to his report.

"Slow. I'm checking the NER, cross-referencing the National Insurance Office and Associated General Construction databases. And that's only the beginning. I've got rental agencies and building associations as well. Stolen this morning, they might be in someone's yard today or traveling across the country. Even if the equipment shows up, there's no guarantee that we'll spot them. The perpetrators could be anywhere. The NER is a place to start."

"Keep on it. It strikes me that these hijackers aren't randomly finding their prey. I'd like to know how they know the supplies and equipment are moving through Winterset."

"I will look for a common thread."

"Do that. And let me know when the men return from the truck stop. I want to know what they found in the poplar trees."

Sunny Gomez stuck her head through the office door. Christmas from top curl to toe, she had a strand of silver garland around her neck, Christmas bulbs dangling from her ears, and a sweater displaying three reindeer seated at a table, playing poker, with a mouse serving them eggnog from a tray. "Heads up," she said. "The children are here. We're firing up the tree."

Sunny ducked back out as quickly as she had appeared. Thacker looked askance at Rory.

"Go ahead. Bring me a cup of punch on your way back."

Thacker scurried from the room, and Rory returned to his reading. Moments later, a cheer rose from the front lobby and drifted down the hall to dissolve his concentration. Hoping that the chief stayed in his office, Rory decided to wander out and see what was going on.

A seven-foot Christmas tree stood center stage, complete with garland, bulbs, and lights. The girls from Water Works crowded around its base, and the few patrolmen in the station had joined the throng. Children dressed for the holidays were seated cross-legged on the floor in front of the display. The door to dispatch was propped open, and cookies and punch had been set out on the sergeant's desk. The mood was one of merriment. Rory raised his eyebrows at the wisdom of

172

this, but then he decided it was the season after all, and he ambled over to collect a glass of punch.

En route, he passed a cluster of men by the tree. Arlo Chuckey was among them. Must have been brought to the lobby by Powell, Rory thought, and looked around for Thacker. He quickly spotted him standing behind the evergreen with a pair of elfin ears on his head and a sugar cookie in each hand. Rory chuckled to himself, the ears actually looked like they belonged.

Sunny bustled in with a boom box under her arm and set it down by the punch bowl. As Rory picked up his cup, the room erupted into a chorus of "Rudolf, the Red-Nosed Reindeer" that would have made Burl Ives proud. The voices of the toddlers mingling with those of the department's finest, and along with a few giggles, they filled the room.

"Bravo!" a young woman called out. She had come in with the group of children from the daycare and stood against the far wall. Rory took a position beside her as there was limited space in the lobby—at least safe-to-stand-in space. She held a pile of children's coats and scarves draped over one arm. "I have to hand it to the police this time," she said, "giving these children a chance at Christmas."

"Glad to do it, ma'am," Rory said, accepting her gratitude for the department as a whole. It hadn't been his idea, but he agreed with the concept that all children should have a chance to experience holiday joy. And well, damnit, it felt good to do an unselfish act. He'd been first in line to donate so that the children identified as disadvantaged or underprivileged could have this simple pleasure.

"Which one is yours?" he asked.

"Oh, no, I'm not ready for the whole you-me-and-baby-makes-three commitment. I'm just helping out a neighbor by performing my one good deed for the year. God knows I could use one."

The station house front door opened, and the media stepped in: reporter, cameraman, and crew. As if on cue, Chief Mansfield entered the lobby from the hallway. Rory took it as a signal to get back to work.

The men were back from the truck stop shortly after three. The interviews were filed, and the small number of evidence bags collected was logged in. There were no eyewitnesses. Rory hoped that Thacker was having more success with the database search. He headed down the hallway toward the city offices, past the chief's office, and around the corner from Water Works. The clerk sat at her desk, and a computer sat at an unoccupied desk in the alcove, the same one that they called the green room.

"Where's our man Chuckey?"

The clerk looked up at him and then tilted her head toward the green room.

"Out for the count," she said. "FYI, he didn't find anyone in the mug shots and complained that he needed a set that included men wearing dark hoodies. He's waiting for his wife to wire him money. I don't know why he told me, but just so you know, he said he'd hang around for a couple of days to see if you come up with his truck. But if you ask me, I think he's going to bus it back to Wichita." She had a napkin with four Christmas cookies on her desk. She picked them up and offered them to Rory.

He shook his head and stepped over to where Arlo Chuckey lay on a wooden bench. His hands were tucked into his overall bib, and there was a light sheen of sweat on his brow. The cuts on his face were turning a flamboyant purple. Sound asleep, flat on his back, belly to the ceiling, he snored like a bull moose.

"Oh, look! Detective Naysmith," the clerk called, "she's emailed the pictures."

Rory turned and watched the clerk open an attachment. He stepped closer. The screen filled with the scene from the lobby earlier that afternoon. Christmas tree, Christmas tree with lights, Water Works girls with Christmas tree behind, close-up of punch and Christmas cookies, garland draped around the sergeant's desk. Ah, finally, the children. There they were. Smiling eyes. Dancing eyes. Bright eyes. Damn, it was worth it!

"They are soooooooooo cute," cooed the clerk.

"Yeah," Rory said.

There was a shot of the chief of police with Hansen and Lloyd from patrol. They blocked out the tree, and each took a somber, Eliot Ness and the Untouchables pose. Not like the movie poster but a no-cheer, no-humor carriage—the look of men who would joyfully deprive you of a beer. The clerk clicked the mouse, and the screen refreshed.

A new picture appeared, this one of Arlo Chuckey with his arm around Thacker, both men grinning ear to ear. Next image—Arlo Chuckey with his arm around the chief, one man smiling, one man not. Chuckey had taken one pain pill too many. Then more pictures of the kids, singing, eating, and finally, collecting their coats to go.

Rory was about to straighten up and move on when a picture filled the screen.

"Shucks. It's not in focus. Sunny must have snapped it as she put the camera down," the clerk moaned with disappointment.

Rory, however, wasn't disappointed. He grabbed the phone from his hip and madly punched icons to open it, the email, and then the pictures. He scrolled through to the last and flicked his thumb and middle finger to enlarge the image. "Gotcha," he said and turned for the squad room and Thacker.

He walked-ran down the hall, studying the image on the screen as he went. He shoved his arm out, extending his phone toward the rookie as he stepped behind the officer's desk. "Thacker, you've got to see this."

Looking up, he saw the monitor filled with the same diagonally framed picture, the wisps of raven-colored hair, the image of a slender neck peeking out from a navy turtleneck. And on the perfect neck—a flowery heart perfectly centered between the loops of a figure eight.

Chapter Twenty-Two

Following the station's party, everyone was distracted and suffering from sugar overload. Rory needed to think, and the office wasn't going to be an encouraging environment. While Thacker went to Bo-Peep KinderCare to question the workers about the girl with the tattoo, he decided to walk the foot path leading from AAA Liquor back to the subsidized apartments. Maybe he'd find something, but his real purpose was peace and quiet.

His attention had gone the way of a watered-down drink—too diluted to do anyone any good. He had a clue, but a tattoo might prove worse than a needle in a haystack. Sidetracked and his efforts spread too thin, he worried. The more time that passed, the less likely he was to solve any one of the crimes. Homer Coot murdered and left in a field; Lydia Mullins, whereabouts unknown; truck hijacking linked to a tattooed girl. If only he could find that one thing that would propel him toward resolution. He was a fish out of water—and a solo investigator without a reliable network to depend on. Seasoned informants and contacts were vital. In Omaha he'd cultivated a community and used those resources.

Unfortunately, his position in the WPD left him with a much narrower field of opportunity—an overly willing rookie, and if he was lucky, a laid-off bookkeeper. He was in trouble, and he knew it.

As he waited to cross the street, Jesse Wallace turned down Front Street, honked, and gave him a wave. He felt a twinge of embarrassment over his early assessment of the doctor. Since Esther only had kind words to say about her sister, he figured Jesse was okay. It was a shame the Mullins sisters couldn't help each other out. He wasn't getting any closer to finding Lydia Mullins, and they would need each other—especially if the outcome ended in tragedy.

The thing that puzzled him most was the unprecedented number of crimes in Winterset, an innocent small town without the usual big city woes. There had to be a connection between the cases, he just needed to find it. Reason told him the hijackings had everything to do with the construction business and Elliott Construction the local contractor. The fire destroyed precious resources belonging to the company. Esther Mullins, daughter of the missing Lydia, had once worked for Elliott Construction. That only left Homer Coot without a tie to the construction industry, and Jonathan Elliott specifically. Or even remotely. He was stretching, forcing the cases to relate to one another. As much as it would help him to consolidate his efforts, clarity would only come with feet-on-the-ground, nose-to-the-grindstone investigation. He shoved his hands into his pockets.

Stepping off the curb, he continued on to the foot path intending to pick it up behind the Golden Leaf Diner. Like all businesses on Main Street, an alley separated the building from the railroad tracks and the path running parallel to them. Next to the open back door of Wallace Realty, he found Jesse's car parked in the alley. He poked his head into the realty office and caught her examining a paper at her husband's desk. "Doctor Wallace?"

"Oh, hello, detective." Mouth open, eyes wide, she dropped the paper, and stepped toward him. "Out for a walk or nosing around?"

"It's a good day for a walk, and there's a lot of commotion at the station. Is your husband available?"

She gave him a wary look, then said, "It doesn't appear so. I thought I'd catch him, but as you can see, he isn't here."

"Do you mind if I ask about his business interests? It seems his finger is in a lot of pies. Diversifying, I presume."

With a feminine snort, she returned to the desk. "His main interest is money."

Rory tipped his fedora back. "Is the realty business his?"

"Yes, and no. It's in both our names, but Neil runs it. I have a key—but no interest, and absolutely no inclination to be involved. He's also on the town council, where he hobnobs with the big boys to make himself feel important. And if you haven't already discovered, he does drafting, construction drawings, and bid estimates on new jobs when Jonathan Elliott needs help." She wrinkled her nose. "Drafting. What he ended up doing when he couldn't manage to make it as a civil engineer. I don't play a part in any of his endeavors."

"It sounds like you disapprove."

"Oh, I don't care, not anymore. He can do whatever he likes with his time." Rory raised his brows.

She continued, "You think I'm cold hearted? It's been one scheme after another, each more hare-brained than the last. I've grown tired of it. It's no secret that we'd have been divorced a long time ago, except neither of us wants to bother."

She opened the middle drawer of the desk, rummaged through the contents, and pulled out an appointment book. Opening it, she said, "No showings today. That leaves Elliott Construction, the bars, and loose women."

Rory came up from behind to peer over her shoulder, wondering about Neil Wallace's working relationship with Jonathan Elliott. He'd love to look at the previous pages and check Neil's appointments on the days matching his cases. Before he could ask, Jesse dropped the book into the drawer, and abruptly shoved it closed.

Fingering the edge of the desk, she sighed. "I don't know why I thought I'd find it here."

"Are you after something in particular?"

She looked at him, as if deciding whether or not to explain, then answered with a small nod. "It's nothing important."

"Sometimes nothing turns out to be something big." He took his hat off, smiled, and gestured for her to take a seat.

She studied his face. "Esther seems to trust you."

"I try to be accommodating."

"You lost some ground when you pulled the plug on the search and rescue."

He felt his face flush. Was he that transparent? His code of ethics dictated his professional conduct, namely upholding a detached distance and an unbiased perspective. A relationship with a victim, even a family member, clouded judgment and led to careless mistakes. Esther had caught his eye, there was no denying it—a rookie screw-up. These cases were enough for him to contend with, and his interest in Esther Mullins didn't have a place in his calculations or assessments. It wasn't the first time his personal life had to take a back seat to his professional. Esther, or any woman for that matter, had no business in his thoughts.

"Moving out of the church basement and closing the center was a matter of economics and resources. The search deserved the efforts of greater channels: county, state, federal law enforcement. Your mother's case is still open, and it will continue to be so, until she's located."

"When she's located. As I recall, you gave us an assurance. We're counting on you."

Rory let her rant for a moment, and when she wound down, she said, "All right, you win. I'll tell you about my problems."

He pulled over a chair while she perched on the edge of the desk. "During Thanksgiving dinner Neil and I had a tiff. It started out as a disagreement about the handy man Mother was using, a vet who lived in the apartments across the street from her home."

"You don't mean Homer Coot?"

"Yes. Esther uses Axel but Mother thought she should help my Homer out. He'd been doing odd jobs around the church and it seemed perfectly natural for her to ask him. Neil didn't like the arrangement. Mother mentioned that Homer had been over to look at her Catawba rhododendron the previous Wednesday. The leaves were spotted, and he had a plan to treat them. But since he was no longer with us, she wasn't sure what to do. Neil went ballistic. It soon became my fault that Mother had offered Homer the job, and naturally, in my husband's frame of mind, there was no reasoning that could persuade him to think otherwise. It pretty much ruined our family gathering."

"Thanksgiving? By that time Homer was already dead."

"Yes, exactly. So, you see, it was ridiculous, his getting upset."

"It does seem an over-reaction." Rory kept his voice calm and tried to keep his expression from giving away his thoughts, a jubilant, *Ah-ha! Homer and Lydia—a link between the victims.* He wanted to pull out his note pad but didn't want to discourage Jesse by making a sudden move that might disrupt her thoughts.

She stared at the front window where the drawn blinds blocked the street from their view. Looking into middle space, she said, "Unless it was the money."

His hand went to the notebook in his chest pocket. Jesse didn't notice.

"That morning Neil and I had a real row. Money. It was always money. The week before, he'd asked Mother to invest in his senior center project, a hideous suggestion for someone of Mother's means. And appallingly, she was thinking about doing it." She turned to Rory, and pleaded her case. "Neil and Mother get along famously. I don't know what they see in each other, but there is no denying it. Maybe he's the son she always wanted? Who knows? She makes his favorite meals, bakes his favorite pies, gives him gifts, and takes his side. He, in turn, plays up to her. And that morning, before we left to join her and Esther for dinner, I found an envelope full of cash. Don't you see? She'd do anything for him—it had to be money he'd conned her out of. I demanded he return it to Mother. He said it wasn't hers. We'd had a doozie of a fight."

"So, you think he directed his anger at your envelope discovery and not the use of Homer as the handy man?"

"Giving up money trumps a man who's been dead for seven days."

"And you're looking for the money now?"

"It's not at the house, and I didn't see him return it to Mother on Thanksgiving. To make things worse, Esther says an envelope with Neil's name on it was at Mother's the day we discovered her missing, and the envelope has since disappeared."

"You don't think Neil had anything to do with your mother's disappearance?"

"The fact that he'd convinced her to invest in one of his schemes grates on my nerves."

"I wouldn't jump to conclusions."

She checked her watch, then fleetingly looked around. "The envelope might be in the file cabinets, but I don't have time to search through every drawer and every folder. There's always the safe." She pulled a card from her wallet, crossed to a small safe closer to the alley door.

Rory went with her. Jesse crouched down and using the information on the card spun the dial to unlock it. It took three tries to line the numbers up correctly, but finally the door swung open. Before she blocked his view, he caught a glimpse of the contents— a velvet pouch, bundle of documents, small wooden box. His heart leapt, as did his interest in the box. She pulled out the documents and rifled through them. "Not here."

"Maybe it's in the box?"

Still sheltering the contents of the safe from his view, she reached in, then jerked her hand back. "No!"

He heard the box lid snap shut. She'd hardly had time to see what was in the box. Whatever it held, she hadn't liked it. "He's a weasel, but I don't want to believe he stole from her. And there's no way he would hurt my mother."

She closed the safe, spun the dial, and stood to face him. "I don't know what I'm doing here. Nothing makes sense anymore."

Rory quietly put his notepad away. "Perhaps your sister…" He wasn't sure what Esther could do and let the suggestion drift away.

Jesse searched his face. "I don't think she… Well, it isn't her problem is it?"

"You're in this together. Family can be a comfort."

Her face drained of color. "I have never felt so alone—I miss my mother."

His chest tightened. What more could he do?

"Find her," Jesse said.

As soon as he could tactfully leave, he did. After traveling less than a hundred feet down the path, he called Esther and suggested she find time to talk with her sister. "I don't want to interfere," he said, "but Jesse could use your friendship. It's not a good time for either of you to be alone."

Chapter Twenty-Three

Esther saw the white lights along the roofline of Jesse's house as she turned onto the street. She pulled into the cleared driveway, turned off the engine, and pushed the button to pop the trunk. Framed by the open doorway, Jesse appeared small and frail. Esther caught her breath. For a second, she thought it was her mother, then her mind returned to her sister and the reason for the visit.

"Merry Christmas, Es," Jesse called, waving a hand.

"Merry Christmas." Esther took her overnight bag out of the trunk and then retrieved the cat carrier from the rear seat. She moved somberly toward the house.

The traditional Christmas wreath was missing from the door, and the oversized picture window was a dark spot where Esther expected to see an eight-foot tree covered with glimmering lights. "Where's the tree?"

Jesse looked confused. Her appearance was haphazard as if she'd picked random items from her closet, a loose-fitting sweatshirt, wrinkled dress slacks, gardening clogs. Her beautiful blonde hair piled on her head, where a barrette struggled to contain it. Loose strands graced her shoulders. She searched Esther's face before she said, "Oh, you mean the Christmas tree?" They stood woodenly in the doorway until she opened her arms and hugged Esther. "Not this year. It doesn't feel right."

"But you have lights on the house and—"

"A service does those. I didn't call to cancel." Jesse took the cat carrier and stepped through the living room and out of sight. "There wasn't any point," she called from the utility room. "The neighborhood association would stick us with a fine. Neil didn't want to risk it."

"Neil's a jerk," Esther said, gingerly stepping into the room before Jesse returned.

"Thanks for bringing Commander. If Neil wasn't allergic…" She swallowed, pulled a tissue from the box on the table beside the sofa, and dabbed at her eyes. "You know, if I could, I'd keep him until Mother gets back."

Esther felt helpless. If only their mother was back, or they knew what kept her from coming back. "It doesn't seem possible that next week is Christmas, and we still don't know where she is."

"I keep hoping," Jesse said.

"I know. Me, too." Esther moved awkwardly to the center of the room. "I'm glad you asked me to spend the night. We haven't done this since… Well, I guess we've never done it."

"No, we don't do sisterly things, do we?"

"Where is Neil?" Esther asked, trying to sound interested. "Working late again?"

"Who knows?" Jesse shrugged. "Did the police come up with anything new?"

Esther shook her head sadly, clutching the handle of her overnight bag with both hands.

"Then what is it? You look like you have something important to say."

Her stomach tightened. Convincing Jesse was going to be harder than she thought. She cleared her throat. "We need to talk."

Jesse stared at her, her face changing from curiosity to defiance. Before she could complain, Esther rushed on. "Without Mother, it's just the two of us. You might have Neil, but I'm pretty much alone on this island. I don't think I can handle it. I need help."

"I can let you have Neil," Jesse said. Her forced smile fell short of humor.

Esther shifted her weight from one foot to the other, waiting for a serious response. Jesse sat on the sofa, picked up a throw pillow, scooted back, and began to pick at the fringe along its edge. In the awkward silence, a plastic toy rolled across the hardwood floor. Commander streaked in from the hallway and batted it under the sofa at Jesse's feet. She picked him up. He protested and then settled down on her lap, purring.

Esther carried her suitcase to the guest room, tossed her coat on the bed, and sighed. Returning to sit next to Jesse, she reached out to pet their mother's cat. She was reluctant to jump-start the conversation and searched for a way to solicit her sister's help without alienating her. "How about a glass of wine?"

"A glass of wine?" Jesse asked incredulously. "You and Neil. Serious talk, serious drink."

Esther frowned.

Jesse stood and abruptly dislodged Commander from her lap. She stomped to the kitchen, uncorked a bottle of Chardonnay, and stomped back. Sloshing the contents into two glasses, she handed one to Esther. "Okay, I'm here. What is it you expect me to do?"

The right question, wrong attitude.

"We've celebrated some great Christmases. Do you remember the one when I cut up your shoes?" Esther said, taking a sip.

Jesse waved the topic away with an impatient hand. "That was years ago. We were young."

"I remember it like it was yesterday. You got my shoes. I mean, I think Mom and Dad got us mixed up. I'd asked for the shoes with the bows and was angry when you ripped away the paper and there they were."

"You were ten. As I remember, you locked yourself in the bedroom, and Mom had to beg you to open the door. After all, it was Christmas morning, and we couldn't start breakfast without you."

"Christmas pancakes smeared with cinnamon baked apples," Esther said, remembering, trying to turn the conversation to pleasant memories. "We should make some tomorrow morning, just for old times' sake."

Jesse nodded. "But it won't be the same without Mother." She brushed imaginary crumbs from her lap and added, "You not only wrecked the shoes, but you also destroyed Mom's pinking shears by using them to cut through the patent leather. You ruined Christmas."

"Yes," Esther agreed, "and for that, grounded."

"No, you were grounded because you yelled that you hated them and wanted to go live with Grandma."

Esther dropped her hands to her sides. The outburst wasn't what she wanted to remember.

"Unforgivable," Jesse mumbled. With fast, impatient movements, she released her hair from the barrette and shook it loose. The action left her with a wild, angry—desperate air. "And in the long run, you got exactly what you were after."

Esther grimaced. "Truly, I didn't want to live with Grandma. I wanted them to be fair. I wanted them to treat me like they treated you."

"Treated me? What are you saying? You're the one that had everything. Class valedictorian. Most likely to succeed. Do you know what it was like living up to those expectations? Not to mention you were Grandma's mini-me."

"And what did I get?" Esther asked. "Dad died. Grandma got old. Mom was in no shape to manage on her own. I succeeded, all right—in becoming a small-time bookkeeper. I was eighteen, and I gave up my dreams."

"What dreams? You never wanted anything more than to stay in Winterset. You made a tight little family, you, Mom, Grandma."

"Of course, we were close. Dedicated to making sure you didn't need anything."

Jesse opened her mouth to protest. Then she closed it as if deciding she better not go there. After a moment, she said, "I don't want to fight."

"Who's fighting!" Esther folded her arms over her chest. Jesse glared at her.

"You were our dream," Esther said sadly. "Don't get me wrong, we were happy to do it. You made us proud."

"But you had them," Jesse declared. "Grandma left you all her possessions, even the house."

"You want the house? You can have the house."

"No. Of course not. I wanted what you had, their devotion."

"And I wanted what you had—opportunity, husband, career. You don't even realize how lucky you've been."

"What about you? You can do what you want. You're not accountable to anyone. You don't carry the world on your shoulders. You don't hold life and death in your hands every day and worry that one little mistake and you'll break a mother's heart or be responsible that a father will never walk his daughter down the aisle. People don't expect you to have all the answers. You've had everything handed to you."

"Be fair, Jes." Esther pinched her lips together and looked around the room, searching for an appropriate response, waiting to get her temper under control. "Grandma was needy. Sure, we had a special relationship, but it cost me. I spent my entire life in this place. You got a degree and a license and traveled the world. My world has always been limited to less than thirty miles in any direction from the courthouse in downtown Winterset."

"I didn't have an opportunity to decide what I'd do with my life. It was expected."

"You want to talk about expectations?" This was unbelievable. Esther rose and started to pace. "I was the eldest, and when Grandma needed help, it was expected I'd be the one to provide it." She turned to her sister and declared, "And what did I get—a small life in a small town."

Jesse watched her through large, glassy eyes, her expression blank except for the sadness, the desperation, and the loneliness Esther saw plainly on her features.

"Maybe this wasn't such a good idea," Esther said, sitting down again.

Jesse's voice was barely audible as she said, "They loved us the same, Esther."

The clock on the mantel chimed, and the lights in the entryway lit suddenly. Esther looked at Jesse. "What just happened?"

"They're on a timer. Neil is out late most nights. I get spooked here by myself, and I don't want it to appear as if I'm home alone or that the house is empty. And I don't want to stumble around in the dark. They come on at ten and go off again at six in the morning."

Jesse went to the entryway and flipped the deadbolt on the door. She selected a CD from a stack on the entertainment center and adjusted the volume so soft jazz filled the room. Esther watched her cross to the kitchen and heard the back door open and then close. Shortly, Jesse returned with an armful of wood, laid a fire in the hearth, lit it, and then rejoined Esther on the couch.

"Do you remember the Christmas you got the saxophone?" Jesse asked.

"I remember the year we got the toboggan and Dad took us sledding all day." Esther smiled, encouraging Jesse to remember more, but Jesse's face grew pale. Esther set her glass down.

"Christmas season always brings back memories," Jesse said.

"Part of the season."

"They're not all good memories. Parties, presents, obligations, it never ends. And always wrapped up with too many traditions and too many demands." She looked intently into Esther's eyes. "I miss my son."

"I imagine you do, and then Dad, and now Mother."

"He would have been twenty-one this year," Jesse whispered.

"You were the most beautiful pregnant woman I'd ever seen. I envied you."

A tear teetered on Jesse's lower lashes. "I think my life would have been very different had he lived."

Esther slid closer and stretched an arm around her, pulling her close. "I'm afraid I wasn't much comfort to you. Grandma was in hospice, and I wanted to be there when—"

"I couldn't give him up. My heart was broken. He'd been a part of me for nine months, and no one was ever going to see how beautiful he was. It happened so fast, I didn't have time to count his little toes. Do you know that I asked the nurse to let me hold him? She wrapped his tiny body in a blanket, and I held him to my heart, refusing to give him back." The tear broke loose. She swiped it with the back of her hand. "We planned to name him after Neil, Neil Alexander Wallace. Everyone encouraged us to give him the name, even though...even though..." She choked on a sob. "But I couldn't. I named him Chance because I'd rolled life's big dice and lost it all in that one throw."

"You weren't alone," Esther argued. "You had family, Jes. You had Neil. You had the strength to go on. You lost your child, but you moved on and made a good life. Look at you, Doctor Jesse Wallace. You are someone. You do important things."

"None of it matters. My family has fallen apart, and I'm a crummy sister. My marriage is a sham. At first, I blamed Neil. Sure, he hasn't been perfect, but what has it been like for him? I loved him, Esther. I loved him, but I was never there for him. And even now, when I know what a lousy husband he is, I can't give him up."

"Maybe you don't need to."

"Oh, yes, I do." Jesse shuddered. "He's seeing Lacey, that girl from the grocery store. No telling how many others there have been. Then today, I found a gun hidden in a box and locked inside his office safe. You can't imagine the crimes I pinned to him because of that sin."

"What do you mean? What kind of gun?"

"What does it matter? It was just an ugly revolver of some kind. And don't suggest he had it for protection"—she narrowed her eyes—"it wouldn't do him any good locked in the safe. He knows how I feel about firearms."

"I'm sorry." Esther picked up her glass but just ran her finger along the rim, half-listening, and curious about Neil's gun.

"No need to be sorry. There seem to be many things I don't know about my husband. I chose to be blind while he tomcatted around. I guess that empowered him to branch out in multiple directions."

"You can't be responsible for Neil's actions."

"Truthfully, I'm more concerned that I wasn't there for you or Mom, the two people in my life that do matter. I just throw myself into work, hoping it will all go away."

"Oh, Jesse. We can't wish it away."

"And the worst of it is, the very worst, is I blame you for losing Mom." She looked through teary lashes at Esther and then dropped her chin to her chest. "I'm ashamed. I know it isn't your fault."

Esther's throat tightened.

Jesse looked up. "Can you forgive me?"

"Sure. You're my sister."

"I haven't acted like one for a long time." Jesse started to sob. "I haven't been thinking straight, but I'll do whatever you think we should do. We have got to find her! I want her back."

"As do I," Esther said, "but Detective Naysmith says we may never find her or even discover what happened to her, just like we'll never know why you lost your precious son. Rory says we need to face the fact that her disappearance may remain a mystery."

"But we can't give up!"

"We won't, even though it's been days. And even if it takes forever."

Jesse struggled to control her tears. "The police will still look?"

Esther brushed a wisp of hair off Jesse's shoulder. "Naturally, Rory will continue to work with the FBI, and the case will remain open, but we need to face the possibility that she may never return."

"I love her, Esther. Even if I seem disconnected, I truly love her."

"Me, too."

"Are you sure we're not giving up? I don't want to give up."

"Jesse, we'll go on looking."

"I'm so sorry. Can you ever forgive me for being so selfish?"

"You don't need to ask. It's already done." Esther patted her sister's hand. "Now, let's get in our pajamas and try for some Christmas cheer."

Jesse asked, "Just exactly who is Rory to us, and since when do we take his advice?"

Esther's heart sank. Then she noticed the sly smile twisting Jesse's lips.

Chapter Twenty-Four

There wasn't a vacant spot in front of Neil's office even though two were clearly marked *Wallace Realty Only*. Irritated, he wheeled into the first empty slot, then slammed the car into park. As usual, he'd have to hike. Regardless of the weather, the designated spots were always claimed by farm vehicles. Not that he used the office often. He preferred to work from the house. Since Jesse had seen fit to keep that dumb cat of her mother's, he couldn't get a moment's peace. When he sat down at his comfortable desk at home, the beast insisted on jumping on his lap, clawing at his crotch, and loudly purring.

Forced to work from the office downtown, he locked the car and marched down the street, clutching the backpack in his arms. It was after ten, and still, the Golden Leaf Diner was full, and his parking spot taken.

Entering, Neil turned on the overhead lights and slung the pack on the desk. He glanced around the room, something felt off. The office was divided into two separate areas. The front used for a one-man office, while the back offered utility, storage, and access to the alley. The office came to life, while the utility area remained in shadow, blocked off from the front behind a row of five-foot-high filing cabinets. Everything in its place. Finding nothing amiss, he shrugged the feeling off.

Even with the snow gone, the winter cold remained. He checked the thermostat and pushed it up from sixty-five. He walked to the windows and turned the blinds to let in the light. The rays did nothing to enhance the drab furnishings of the room. Specks of dust hung in the air and settled on the travel posters tacked to the walls. From next door, he could hear the scraping of chairs and murmur of voices. He booted up the computer and opened the Internet radio icon to mask the hum with a blend of saxophone and piano. After removing the documents from the backpack, he unfolded the list the boss had given him. Smoothing the page, he tucked its edge under a paperweight and reached for the phone, dialing.

"Wallace, here. I'll expect you in an hour."

Neil banged the receiver back into the cradle. Taking a roll from the storage bin, he unfurled an architectural drawing. One last review and it would be ready. Concentrating on the job, he missed the dance between a weather-beaten farm truck and the battered pickup as they did the do-si-do outside his front door.

An hour later, Neil rolled up the drawing and stowed it in the tube. He stood, stretched, and crossed to the back of the office, where he unlocked the door to the alley. From the fire safe tucked between the water cooler and the cabinets, he took a small wooden chest and a velveteen pouch and returned to his desk.

Opening the chest, he lifted out a twenty-two-caliber pistol and wiped it down with a soft cloth. Since the clasp on the box no longer locked, and his wife had the combination to the safe, he decided to move the handgun behind the hanging folders in the bottom drawer of the strongest filing cabinet. The task complete, he verified the drawer was secure.

Back at his desk, he was placing the velveteen pouch in the wooden box, when the bell over the front door tinkled. Without looking up, he calmly placed the box in his middle desk drawer.

"Morning, Neil," sang Marilyn Beauregard.

"Marilyn, what a pleasure. Are you out shopping?" He nudged the drawer closed and placed his hands, fingers laced, on the desktop, smiling tightly at the older woman.

"No, I'm looking for my friend." She took the seat in front of Neil and stared directly into his eyes. "My best friend—your mother-in-law."

"Yes. Jesse is very concerned." He quickly added, "We're both concerned. But after so many days, I think it best to leave the looking to the police."

"I'm not leaving it to anyone. And that is precisely why I've come."

The paperweight sat in the far-right corner of the desk next to a leather-bound day planner, both precariously close to Marilyn. He didn't trust her, and nonchalantly moved the planner in front of him. Taking the list from under the paperweight, he folded it in half, and slipped it into the closed day planner.

Marilyn's eyes followed his movements. With a jeweled hand, she reached for the planner. Before she could touch it, Neil picked it up, placed the book in his desk drawer, and arrogantly snapped it shut. Marilyn's gold bracelets clinked as she withdrew her hand and settled it on the clasp of the purse in her lap. A simple gold and garnet ring adorned her pointer finger, and a vintage filigree diamond graced the middle finger of the hand she laid on top of both. He wondered where this was going.

"I don't think we should play around, Neil. Lydia has been missing for over a week. She's your mother-in-law. You saw her at Thanksgiving because it was a family obligation. I see through your pretense to be the dutiful son-in-law so don't think you've pulled one over on me. You don't really care. If you did, you'd have participated in the search-party effort. According to Esther, you haven't offered to help in any way."

"Now, that's not true."

"Yes, it is. And what's more concerning is that you're absent from Jesse's life as well."

"What do you mean? How dare you accuse me—"

"Just listen." All business, she leaned forward, squaring her body on the chair. "Lydia is one of my oldest and dearest friends. Her girls are like daughters to me. I will not sit quietly and watch them fall apart. You will answer my questions, and you will answer them now." Neil chuckled as he relaxed into his seat, not meeting her challenge. "Mrs. Beauregard, Marilyn, you are overwrought. Lydia's disappearance has affected us all."

"I'm concerned," she responded stubbornly. "I can't see the girls hurt any more than they already are. You know something. I want you to fess up."

"I don't know what you mean."

She opened her purse and removed a business envelope, held it up, and silently examined the front flap. "For one thing, you can explain this."

The plain back faced Neil. *Could it be the envelope containing the bribe money?* Recognition settled around him like a spider web, and he felt the blood drain from his face.

"The day after Lydia vanished, we were at the house, Esther, Jesse, that detective Naysmith, even Axel," Marilyn said. "We were looking for clues, what was missing, what was out of character, or anything that would help explain Lydia's absence. Unfortunately, everything looked normal. Everything except for this."

She raised the envelope defiantly. Her bracelets slipped down toward her elbow and clinked. The sunlight played off her rings, throwing a rainbow of color on the wall. "I took it from a pile of things sitting on Lydia's kitchen table. I think you need to explain."

Neil wasn't new to the game of "demand and deflect." It took little effort to place an innocent expression on his face.

She barked, "I don't know what you were doing with Lydia. I can't imagine how you managed to deceive her. She never had two nickels to rub together, and this is unforgivable."

"Tampering with the U.S. mail is a federal offense."

"There's no stamp. The offense is your single-minded greed."

A field mouse peeked out from behind a stack of for-sale signs leaning against the east wall. It hesitated before scurrying across the linoleum to duck into a small crack on the Golden Leaf side of the room. Neil watched its journey, making a mental note to call pest control.

Marilyn opened the envelope and removed the contents, fanning the crisp bills out like a hand of playing cards. "If you don't tell me, I'll be forced to turn this over to the police."

Neil excelled at Go Fish. *Pick one, any one. Marilyn, do you have any hundreds?*

"They're new. Crisp. The serial numbers are consecutive, Neil. What is this?" Marilyn flapped the currency at him. "And don't give me any lies."

"Lydia owed me money."

"Rubbish."

"I was blackmailing her. There was a wild weekend in Odebolt—"

"Hogwash."

"What makes you think the money is mine? Not that I couldn't use two thousand dollars."

Her eyes widened. "It is two thousand dollars! If you are taking this kind of money from Lydia, what else have you done?"

"Be reasonable, Marilyn. That was just a wild guess. How would I know how much money you've got in there?"

"Exactly!" She ceremoniously slipped the bills back into the envelope. She shoved the packet into her purse and then leaned over the bag to stare unwaveringly into his face. "You better come clean."

He never flinched. "It could be anyone's money."

"Not in an envelope with your name on it. I should have given it to Esther or Detective Naysmith right away."

"Give it to them now. I don't see what this has to do with me." He glanced at his watch before adding, "I'd accompany you to the station, but I have a business meeting. As a matter of fact, I'm late for that meeting."

He checked the clock on the wall behind Marilyn and then his watch again.

Marilyn stood. She did a little body shimmy in front of her chair. Neil had seen his mother-in-law make the same maneuver. If Marilyn were a bird, she would be fluffing her feathers. It made him wonder if she was nudging her slip down over her hips, her girdle was too tight, or if she was making a deliberate effort to rev-up before taking flight.

Her head turned toward the picture window. "No need. Axel will take me."

Neil followed her gaze. There was no mistaking the figure standing there, the tip of his nose spreading a grease mark on the glass, his hands cupped around his eyes, and his forehead leaning on the pane.

"Ah, there he is," she said.

Marilyn held herself stiffly as Neil ushered her to the door. He hesitated before opening it, contemplating a final comment. He decided against it and merely held the portal open for her to pass through. He watched as she joined Axel on the sidewalk, weighing his options.

****

The alley door opened, and the cool air swept around the cabinets to find Neil. He turned toward the irritation and discovered Branch Dubois standing in the opening to the utility section, overcoat unbuttoned, hands buried in his pockets, watching.

"Didn't I say an hour?"

"You did." Branch shifted his weight to his right leg and scraped the heel of his left boot on the linoleum. A briefcase hung at his side. "I didn't think it wise to interrupt."

"Good man. That woman is a pest."

Neil pulled the wooden box from the center drawer and added, "We better get this finished and over to the courthouse." He took the building plan from its tube and spread it on the desk.

Of the two visitor chairs, Branch took the one Marilyn had vacated and set the case on the floor. He leaned back, tipping the chair, and placed a heavy booted foot on his knee. He stretched out an arm to rest on the back of the other. Handsome by most standards, Dubois had dark hair, a dark complexion, and an unshaven jaw that added to his overall look of youthful arrogance. His dress shirt and slacks didn't hide the fact that he was tall, lean, and every bit muscle.

"There are four permits and the plans," stated Neil as he reviewed the drawing for a final time. He reached for the box.

"Still under lock and key?" Dubois sneered.

Neil gave a short, dismissive snort and slipped the unsecured clasp. The hinge on the wooden chest opened with a squeak, revealing the black velveteen pouch. Reverently, he removed a silver handled stamp from the bag and took the guard from the instrument's face. He held the stamp in his hand, turning it toward himself to review the surface. Satisfied, he affixed the signature to the lower-right corner of the drawing by firmly placing the right edge on the paper and rolling it firmly to the left, and then he briskly picked it up again. He leaned forward and blew softly on the ink.

"You have enough time to get the papers filed. They break for lunch at noon, but that is in our favor. The clerks will be in a hurry to take their breather. It's not like they aren't used to seeing you in the queue. Be sure to get the permit for the park excavation."

Neil took a handful of papers from the backpack. To each, he attached the signature. After inspection, he placed them one at a time into separate manila envelopes. With a flurry, he scribbled a project name on the outside of each envelope. He rerolled the drawing and stuck it into the tube, before returning it to the bin. Last, he took the list from the day timer and reviewed the items.

"Better get going."

The chair thumped to the floor. Dubois picked up the briefcase, opened it on his lap, and stuffed the envelopes inside. He closed the case and stood, all in one motion. "That all?"

"For now, but don't get lost."

Dubois nodded and headed for the back, stopping at the water cooler.

Neil joined him at the safe, squatting to spin the dial. He placed the wooden chest inside, picked up a packet, and extended it to Dubois. "You'll need enough money for the permits and the inspectors."

"Enough for now," replied Dubois.

The alley door creaked as it was opened. Neil stood in the doorway with the cold air drifting in around him as he watched Branch Dubois climb into the vehicle. He was still there when the mammoth black truck crunched down the alley, leaving a dissipating haze of diesel exhaust hanging in the frigid air.

Chapter Twenty-Five

Esther stepped into the Golden Leaf Diner, bundled in a pea coat, with a crocheted scarf wrapped around her neck and pulled up over her nose. She paused near the cash register to scan the community bulletin board that hung by the door, searching. When she found the poster of her mother, she heaved a heavy sigh. It had been two full weeks since her mother disappeared, yet it seemed only yesterday she had sat over a cup of tea with her. Time marched on—with or without her mother. Life was unfair.

"Over here," Marilyn called out, waving her jeweled arm in the air and scooting over to make room. Beryl, the waitress, beat Esther to the booth with a mug of streaming coffee.

"The usual?" asked Beryl. Esther nodded absently and unwound the burgundy scarf from her head and handed coat and scarf to Axel before she took the seat beside Marilyn.

Axel picked up the menu sitting between the napkin holder and the advertised specials. It hadn't changed in fifteen years, but he handed it to Esther anyway.

"Coffee. Black," he said as Beryl refilled his mug.

Ignoring her breakfast of rye toast and scrambled eggs, Marilyn frowned at Esther. "I can't believe this weather. It must be thirty degrees out there and, with the wind factor, down in the twenties. Aren't you frozen? That's all we need."

The restaurant was full to capacity. The large, round table was crowded with the usual group—farmers out for the latest news, weather, and gossip. Each sported a ball cap in the "indoor fashion," well back on their head. Esther felt removed from the comfortable din.

"I've been to see Neil," began the older woman.

"Is he doing all right?" Esther asked.

"Of course. He'll always be all right." Marilyn plopped her forearms on the tabletop with a clamor of silver bracelets. "Why not? He has the best of everything."

Esther raised her shoulders and dropped them slowly as she stared at the table, the coffee mug ignored.

"I went to see him about the envelope I found at your mother's," stated Marilyn.

Esther turned the upper half of her body toward Marilyn. "Oh?"

"Yes, I think he should explain why it was there. As soon as we're done here, you are going with me to the police station. We're going to find that Detective Naysmith, and we're going to turn him in."

"Detective Naysmith?"

"No, sweetie." Marilyn patted Esther's hand and nudged the coffee mug in her direction. "Neil."

"But Miss Marilyn," Axel said, "we need to talk to Miss Esther before we do anything rash."

What were they talking about? Esther's first thought was that she'd missed something, either that or Marilyn was talking in riddles.

"This isn't rash." Marilyn frowned. "I just don't get Neil. He can't be this callous."

"What has he done?" Esther was confused. "What's this about an envelope?"

"That's it. He didn't say. I demanded to know, and he sidestepped. Little weasel."

Axel said, "He's not so little, and he has lots of friends. Geez, he knows half the town."

"Well, he probably knows the *entire* town. I don't care. I'm in it for my girls."

"The girls aren't so little, either." Axel looked sheepishly at Esther, then unrolled the utensils and placed the paper napkin in the neck of his shirt. It was too coarse for the purpose and stuck straight out over his red flannel shirt, pointing an accusing finger at Marilyn.

The doors to the kitchen flapped, and Beryl's voice announced, "Tall one in Vermont and a short one with a slither." The diner was peppered with a lively discussion on the weather. Comments like "planted before the full moon..." and "early freeze will kill..." drifted over from the round table.

The Price brothers entered and headed for the booth behind Esther and Marilyn. There was a volley of greetings from the round table. Bob took off his cap and bowed to the crowd. Joe pantomimed the swoon of a Southern belle and flopped onto the seat. Beryl arrived with two tall glasses of water. "On the city," she announced as she set them down.

Joe leaned back, placed his head between Marilyn and Esther, and asked the ceiling, "Any word on Mrs. Mullins?"

"Not yet," Esther whispered in response and straightened her silverware. Unfair. Just when she'd managed to control her emotions—another reminder. Well intended, but it pieced her heart none the less.

In the booth behind Axel, two men held a muffled conversation. When Beryl appeared with a fresh pot of coffee, they stopped talking. She filled their cups and whisked away the empty platters before they resumed. "It's not like we're at fault," one said.

"Maybe not, but I'm not going to risk it," added the other.

Axel straightened, leaned back in the faux leather seat, and moved as close to the pair as the booth allowed.

Marilyn persisted, "With his talents and resources, you'd think Neil would fall all over himself to help us out. But no, he has to be cute. He's on the council, for crying out loud. He could rally the troops." She eyed Axel. "Take off those earmuffs. You're not listening to a word I'm saying."

Axel reached a hand up and pushed the muffs back on his head, leaving his ears exposed. He looked at Marilyn but tilted his head toward the rear, angling his ear toward the booth occupied by the men.

"I was saying, 'Council, rally, troops.' "

"Yep," Axel said, but his body was inclining left, following his ear.

"Cow with a pig alongside the mess," announced Beryl setting the platters down in front of the Price brothers.

"We're going straight to the police," continued Marilyn. She began to consume her breakfast and said around a mouthful, "See what he does." She shook her head in disgust. "Axel. Open your eyes. This is no time to daydream."

As the two men behind Axel rose to leave, the bench rocked, and he was jostled. The muffs fell from the back of his head and landed somewhere under the table. He ducked down to retrieve them. As he rose, he lifted the tabletop with his shoulder. The dishes slid in disarray, and coffee sloshed out of the cups. He peeked guiltily at Marilyn, his eyebrow over steel-gray eyes even with the tabletop, his nose and bushy lip below.

Beryl steadied the table with one hand while balancing a platter in the other. "The usual," she said as she set the biscuits and gravy down in front of Esther.

The two men donned their coats and tossed a bill onto the table. Axel stiffened and turned to watch. "Dang, now I'll never know," he said.

"Know what?" Esther asked.

"Those two guys. They were talking. It sounded sinister."

"Axel?" Esther took a quick glance at Marilyn. "What kind of sinister?"

"Yep, I think they might be the ones."

"The ones?" challenged Marilyn.

"Ah, Ms. Marilyn, you should have heard them talking about guilt and exposure. The guy with the gravelly voice said things like havoc and chaos together." He placed his forearms on the table and balanced the weight of his upper body on them. Leaning in, he added, "They sounded intent."

"Intent, indeed." Marilyn said.

"It's just Red Darcy," Esther offered. "I do his books." She didn't look up as she sliced off a piece of biscuit with sausage gravy and lifted it to her mouth. "I don't know the other guy. He's probably a day laborer."

She looked up to find Axel staring at her. "What?" she said, wide-eyed, her head swinging back and forth between her friends.

Axel was first to respond. "We should go after them." He started to rise.

Marilyn dabbed at the coffee spill with her napkin. "Not until we see Detective Naysmith. Esther, you finish up your breakfast, we'll go on ahead."

After her friends departed, Esther wiped the corner of her mouth where a drop of gravy had settled and pushed the platter away. The door to the diner opened. Red Darcy entered and made his way to her booth.

From the kitchen, Beryl's voice rang out, "Drop 'em and flop 'em."

Chapter Twenty-Six

Rory puzzled through the encounter with Jesse Wallace. What had been in the wooden box that she didn't want him to see? It had more than piqued his interest. She didn't want to share and without her consent he couldn't find out. There was no way he could get a search warrant. And then there was the mystery of the tattooed girl. The party had been long over before he'd begun to ask if anyone could identify the girl in the picture. No one had seemed to know who she was, and Thacker had enthusiastically headed to the daycare, but he'd come back empty-handed. Here it was, a day later, and Rory didn't have the hijackers or the girl. Was it possible that she wasn't known? Rory couldn't believe that in Winterset, a girl could simply vanish. Well, there was Mrs. Mullins. He rubbed his head.

He was studying his picture wall and working on a plan when Sunny called him to the lobby. He was in no hurry as he rounded the doorway to find Marilyn, in billowing skirt and scarves, alongside Axel, in open galoshes and with an armload of coats.

He approached the older woman wearily. "Ms. Beauregard?"

"Oh, there you are. Has there been any activity in the search for Lydia?" Her tone felt accusatory. She rushed on, not waiting for the answer. "We've given this disappearance further thought, and we're certain that Lydia has met with foul play." She motioned to Axel as she spoke. "We have evidence that Lydia was involved in a sinister plot formulated by her son-in-law." Rory saw Axel flinch and wondered if it was Marilyn's comment or him that made the hippy uncomfortable. Rory raised his brows.

"I have it right here in my purse." She opened her bag and pulled out an envelope, waving it at him. "Why he didn't lock it in that little box where he keeps all his secret documents and private papers—the one he thinks no one knows about—is beyond me."

He felt the hackles on the back of his neck begin to twitch. He knew the feeling—it was a break. And he felt certain his network was beginning to grow, first Thacker and now, of all people, Marilyn Beauregard. This would require some investigation. Should he take them to his office? Marilyn Beauregard could be persuasive and long-winded when the need suited her. Mention of the locked box, had his mind ticking.

"Interrogation desk," Sunny said with her back to the drama.

"Let's sit down and go over what you have." Rory turned and led the way to the interrogation desk.

The pair followed, with Marilyn talking as they made their way. "It was right there. I shouldn't have picked it up, maybe. I had to think about the girls. There was the possibility that it was just loose money, something Lydia was handling for someone else. Well, I didn't want just anyone to take it." She'd run out of steam as they arrived, and Rory cleared the chairs for them.

"Make yourself comfortable," he said.

Marilyn made a production of sitting, scooting the chair up as close to the desk as she could, and placing her handbag on its surface, her hands folded on top. She peered over it at the detective as if she expected an arrest.

"This is additional information that you didn't have at the time of the disappearance?" he asked.

"I had it at the time. I just didn't know I had it. You see, I thought, well, I thought Lydia…" She looked at Axel, perhaps expecting clarity of explanation. She gave a little snort and turned back to Rory. "Well, here it is. You judge for yourself." She plucked the envelope from her purse and thrust it at him. Then she sat back tugging her scarf righteously across her chest.

Rory accepted the envelope and turned it over in his hand. The back was pristine white, with no markings. The front contained a scrawled "Neil Wallace," underlined with a flourish of curly cue that he recognized as an old woman's mark of endearment. Opening the flap, he saw the money.

"See! It's right there under our noses. Neil Wallace."

Rory turned it over again but found no additional markings. "Where did this come from?"

"Right there on Lydia's kitchen table."

He pulled the bills out and took a look.

"There were utility bills, greeting cards, and that envelope," said Marilyn.

"This wasn't there when we went through the house," he said.

"No. I didn't want the girls to worry about the money. With everyone traipsing in and out, I picked it up for safekeeping."

Rory eyed her suspiciously.

"Truth is truth," she said and smugly glanced at Axel, who had moved to the window and was silently looking out. He held both his and Ms. Beauregard's coats in his arms, but he still wore the pair of earmuffs on his head. "Axel, sit down," she commanded.

He looked blankly at her but complied. "I'm watching Miss Esther," he said as he took a seat. "Looks like she's talking to the conspirators."

"Not now, Axel," she said and reached out to lay a hand on his arm. "You should dust them for fingerprints or something."

"Ms. Mullins' prints wouldn't prove much. This looks like gift money. Or payment of some sort," Rory said, fanning the bills out before returning them to the envelope.

"Payment? In a pig's eye. Lydia didn't have that kind of money. She barely made ends meet. Cashed her social security check once a month and lived on that."

Rory pulled out his notebook, flipped through it, and settled on a page. "This is from an earlier interview, Ms. Beauregard, and I quote, 'She carries as much as a thousand dollars around.' And this from her daughter, 'She didn't like banks and carried a lot of cash.' "

"This is two thousand dollars. Two thousand dollars with sequential serial numbers. You're not listening to me. Lydia didn't have that kind of money."

"Have you asked the daughters? Perhaps…"

Marilyn waved a bangled arm at him and shook her head frantically, not interested in discussion. "No, they're of no use. Jesse is Jesse. Esther is grieving."

At the mention of Esther's name, Axel perked up. "Say, we need to see what Miss Esther is getting herself

214

into out there." He rose and crossed to the window. "Look! Look, they're leaving together. We can't let her go!" He rushed back to the interrogation desk and all but threw Marilyn's coat at her, donning his own in a hurry. "They'll get away!" Tripping over the chair in his haste, he dragged it into the middle of the room and rushed out the door.

Rory and Marilyn stepped to the window. From its view, they looked down Main Street toward the Golden Leaf Diner. A battered pickup backed out and headed down the street, Esther sitting inside. All seemed quiet until moments later when Axel appeared, his long, skinny legs pumping as he took off down the center of the road in the same direction.

"We better go," Rory said. He handed the envelope to Marilyn and reached for his fedora and coat. "Do you know who's driving the pickup?"

"Esther said it was Red Darcy. She does his books. I don't know the boy. However, the father has a small construction business, or he did before he went batty. It's on Twenty-Second Street."

Rory conducted her from the dispatch office, through the vestibule, and toward the front door.

Once on the street, they faced a dilemma. Marilyn Beauregard's giant old car with the cushy blue interior or Rory's nondescript city-issued vehicle. Rory steered them toward the city-issue. If he couldn't control anything else, he would at least control their speed. However, Marilyn declined, agreeing to follow him in her own vehicle.

Turning down Twenty-Second Street, Red Darcy's business was easy to find, the house a nondescript wooden slat residence sitting in the middle of a muddy yard. Huge ruts crossed the front and ended at a ten-by-ten prefab building attached to the front of a Quonset hut. Rory pulled over and parked on the street. From where he sat, he could see the front bumper of the battered pickup peeking from behind the Quonset.

Marilyn turned into the lot, stopping ten feet from the office door, and hurried back to join him at the curb. "I don't see Axel."

Rory unfastened his seatbelt and exited the car. "We'll just take a look around."

Marilyn was right behind. "That boy will be the death of me. What does he think he's doing? And Esther. Oh, Esther, what would possess her to get into a truck with the likes of Darcy?"

Rory stepped to the door of the house and gave it a rap. Then he looked around the yard and fleetingly at the Quonset. Across the rutted yard, the entrance of Darcy's office opened. Esther Mullins and Axel Barrows stepped out, each struggling with an armload of brown paper grocery bags. They headed around the building.

"Esther!" Marilyn shouted. Rory couldn't tell if her voice carried relief or despair. She left his side to scurry toward the couple. "What are you doing?"

The tall woman stopped, peeked around the parcel, and said, "I'm working. What else would I be doing?"

Axel kept on walking. Marilyn, clearly exasperated, upped her stride to a walk-run. "Axel, stop where you are!"

Finding himself alone, Rory headed for the Quonset and knocked on the door. A middle-aged man with faded red hair opened it. "Mister Darcy?" Rory asked.

"No other," Darcy said. "Come right in, Detective Naysmith." He held the door open and waved him into the room.

Rory knew most people could pick out a cop in a crowd, but it always threw him for a second when someone unknown to him knew who he was. No need to identify himself, Winterset's grapevine had tagged him and voiced opinion on his performance. Not only did he need to do his job, where his actions would speak for him, but he battled from the unpopular position of town outsider.

Behind the tacked-on office, the space under the arch panels of corrugated steel was stacked high with lumber, power tools, and racks containing boxes—most likely fasteners, nails, screws. A desk sat against a windowless wall. The back wall contained barn-style doors that slid open from the middle, where a crack between them allowed outside air into the room. There was no heat in the room, although Rory saw a space heater next to the desk. Whoever had been with Darcy at the diner was not in the building.

"What can I do for you?" Darcy asked, taking a seat in an old office chair. "This must be my day for company, you just missed my bookkeeper."

Rory swiped the hat from his head and took the mismatched chair next to Darcy. He could feel the chill on his head and popped the fedora back in place. "I'm surprised to catch you here on a weekday."

"This time of year, things are slower than usual."

"Slow enough you have time for breakfast out and a moment to catch up with your paperwork?"

"Sure, a man's got to eat. And Esther is a bear about my receipts. What's this about?"

Rory expected denial and was surprised when Darcy readily agreed. "You had company at the diner."

"More of a silent partner."

"I thought your father was your partner?"

"Sure, but he's not much help nowadays."

"So, you took on a partner to help you out?"

"Not that it's any of your business, but Dad left me pretty much flat-footed. We were hoping to expand into commercial projects, and then he goes and gets old on me."

There was no need to point fingers. He'd heard the family history from Sunny, one of the many tales she'd thought he needed to know about Winterset. Dementia was a tragedy. No one was immune to its devastation. "So, you took on a partner in order to expand?"

"Looking to expand," Darcy said. "We've always done a lot of work on domestic buildings. But once someone remodels a kitchen, they're not doing it again right away. No more babies, no more room additions. I gotta go somewhere."

Rory nodded. It made sense to him.

"I started putting out bids last spring, but I didn't win any contracts. It seems businesses are hesitant to let the new guy get the bid even if it's the lowest. And even if he's been around all his life."

An idea struck Rory. "Did you bid on the senior center?"

Darcy gave him a started look, then answered, "Sure. That's the best piece of construction to come along this decade. I woulda been crazy not to. Thought I had a shot at it, too."

"Who's your partner?"

"A fellow outa Omaha, a lawyer named Dubois. Branch Dubois. He'd be happy to stick it to Elliott. I didn't ask any questions. Besides, so far, we haven't been what you'd call successful. He's got money. That's good enough for me. You just curious, or do we have a problem here?"

"No problem. How'd you find Mister Dubois?"

"He found me. But I don't see what any of this—"

"You're right. It's not my business. I guess, once a detective, always a detective." Rory wanted to know more but had no reason to question Darcy further on the matter. He'd check into it once he got back to the station. "I saw you leave the Golden Leaf with Miss Mullins. There was another man, unknown to me. And with Lydia Mullins still missing, I wonder if you've found something."

"Couldn't I use that twenty-thousand-dollar reward," Darcy said. "But no. I don't have any new information."

A telephone rang. Darcy began slapping his hands down on the papers scattered about his desk and didn't stop until he located the ringing device.

From the ringtone Rory thought he was looking for an old-fashioned rotary phone. Darcy surprised him by pulling a cell phone out from under the confusion and checking caller ID.

"I gotta take this," he said.

"Sure." Rory stood. "Mind if I take a look out back?"

Darcy shrugged a suit-yourself gesture and answered the call.

Rory exited through the same door he'd entered. Marilyn's Cadillac was gone. Esther, Axel, and Marilyn were nowhere in sight. He rounded the building and headed toward the nose of the battered pickup. The side yard was empty, but he found plenty of tire ruts where the melting snow had turned the area to mud, none of which told him anything more than there had been activity recently. How recently, he didn't know. The back was a jungle of equipment. If there was a method to the madness, it eluded him. Crusted cement mixers, wheelbarrows, and hand trucks clustered against the building. Cinder blocks and bricks were stacked haphazardly. Portable light towers stood, rusting among ladders of every height and description as if ready for a giant game of pick-up sticks.

Darcy had stacked dozens of wooden pallets, and it looked as if, left to their own devices, they had toppled during a frantic effort to escape. A forklift parked by the barn doors had a load of sheetrock resting on the forks, maybe ready to move into the Quonset or perhaps staged to load onto a truck for delivery to a job site.

As Rory moved closer to the doors, he heard Darcy's voice echo inside, "Yes, ma'am. I will," followed by a hollow chuckle. Rory decided the call was not so much business as pleasure, especially when Darcy added, "It's a date, then."

Behind the light towers, Rory saw blue canvas, and figuring nothing ventured, nothing gained, moved through the scattered debris to inspect what was underneath the tarp. He only got as far as the lights.

Darcy popped out between the barn doors. "Hey, Detective Naysmith. I'm going to have to shut her down for a while. Gotta run out for a minute."

"I guess I'm through here," Rory said. "Lots of stuff."

"It just collects over the years."

"I'm curious how you keep track of your equipment and supplies. Inside, it's pretty organized. Out here, wow!"

"Wow is right," Darcy said with dismay. "Most of this stuff is left over from past jobs or damaged beyond repair. Dad never wanted to get rid of any of it. He said you'd never know when we might find a use for it or strip out a part. Our own Darcy Pick-A-Part operation." Darcy smiled halfheartedly. "You can come back anytime and have a look-see. Only, right now—"

"Sure," Rory said. "I'm just interested in how a construction company operates. Never had the opportunity to see one up close." He hoped he sounded sincere. He wanted to check under the tarp, but this wasn't going to be his chance.

Darcy stepped back inside, sliding the doors closed with a thump. Rory could hear him attaching a chain on the inside.

Rory trudged across the yard to his parked car. Seated behind the wheel, he took out his notebook and jotted down "Branch Dubois," "tarp," and "girlfriend." He added a question mark after "girlfriend" and underlined "Branch Dubois." Moments later, Darcy came out the front door of the Quonset and rounded the building, headed for his truck. Rory heard the pickup start and waited while it, too, pulled around. He contemplated following Darcy but decided he had no reason.

Darcy stopped in the yard. Rory could see him looking through the windshield at the city issue. Damn, it looked like he was going to wait for Rory to pull out.

Curiouser and curiouser.

Chapter Twenty-Seven

Rory parked on the street and walked around to Esther's kitchen door. She opened on his first knock. "Hello, Miss Mullins. I hope this isn't an inopportune time."

"Esther," she said and waved him in. "This is a perfect time. I was about to wrestle with Red Darcy's books. And to be quite frank, I could use an excuse to keep me from the drudgery."

"I saw you at Darcy's earlier." She looked surprised, and he quickly explained. "I followed Mrs. Beauregard over from the station. She'd been to see me about…well, you were at Darcy's when we arrived, and then you left with her."

"Oh, Marilyn. I see."

"You were just leaving, and she joined you and Axel. I had a brief visit with Darcy, and when I finished, the three of you had disappeared. I thought I'd check to see that everyone got home."

"Have you been to Marilyn's?"

"No. I came here straight away."

"Oh, I see." Her lips lifted at the corners. It wasn't a full smile, but he felt encouraged.

Until he remembered his vow to stay detached. "I have a few questions. Perhaps you can help me out?"

"I can try." She headed into the kitchen. "Do you want coffee?"

"Sure, that'd be fine, Miss Mullins."

"Esther," she said.

They sat at the kitchen table with their mugs. "Have you done Darcy's bookkeeping for a while?"

"I started helping him after his wife left. She managed to keep things running until she didn't care enough to bother. And Red doesn't have the sense he was born with." She studied the back of her hands. "I shouldn't have said that."

"It's got to be tough losing your wife and then your father, both key to the business."

"I suppose so."

"He says he has a silent partner." Rory took his notebook out. "I've got the name right here. Perhaps you know him?" He flipped to the right page. "Dubois. Branch Dubois."

"No. I'm fairly certain Red doesn't have a partner."

"How about a girlfriend?"

Esther laughed. "Red? I don't think so. But relationships are more Marilyn's thing. Why do you ask?"

"No real reason. I'm trying to get a complete picture."

"The full picture is sad. Red struggles with the business and the fact his wife left him for parts unknown while his father is on lockdown in an Alzheimer's ward doesn't help. I've known Red since high school and he doesn't have an ambitious bone in his body."

"But he is a client."

"I do his books for next to nothing because he needs help. Yes, he's a client." She looked over her shoulder at the grocery sacks on the desk in the backroom and frowned.

Rory filled in. "And a headache."

"Yes. That, too. It'll take me the rest of the day to sort through his mess."

On the table between them, Rory spotted the sudoku and picked it up.

Esther said, "I didn't have a chance to finish the puzzle this morning. What was that name again?"

"Dubois. French, I guess. Darcy claims he's a lawyer from Omaha. Branch Dubois." He took his pen out and put a nine in the top box of the unfinished sudoku. It helped him fill in a missing three and a six. He studied the puzzle.

"Unusual name, Branch Forrest," she said. "Like Rob Roberts, or Will Williams, or Rich Richards."

Rory didn't get the connection. "I took a couple of French classes. The only use I've found for them is the crossword. If memory serves me right, Dubois means woods or forest."

She took the puzzle from Rory and placed it face down on the table.

"So, it's probably not his real name?" Rory asked.

"I didn't say that. Just that it's unusual, and I've never heard of Branch Dubois."

"I wonder why Darcy told me he had a partner if he doesn't."

She frowned at the sacks again. "I can tell you he hasn't had an influx of cash, and no one is paying his bills."

"Maybe he keeps two sets of books."

Esther gave him a skeptical look. Well, maybe not, he thought.

They sat in comfortable silence like old friends, then Esther asked, "Any progress on your murder case?"

"I'm working it." He wasn't willing to share the details with her and changed the subject. "Second question. I have a key that I'm trying to match to a lock, say a box about the size of a child's lunchbox and most likely smaller than a tool chest. Any ideas?"

She hesitated, as if uneasy, then said, "Last night Jesse mentioned Neil keeps a locking box in his office safe. I have no idea what size, but the safe isn't that big."

"Any idea what's in it?"

After a moment, she said, "No. Important papers, I imagine." There was a sad look in her eyes, and he wondered if she knew but didn't want to say.

The back door opened, startling them both. "Hey," Axel said. "I saw your car, Constable."

"Detective," Rory said.

"Whatever. I got the boxes loaded, Miss Esther. Is there anything you want to throw in?"

"That's the lot of it," Esther said, rising. "Can I offer you something before you go?"

"I hope Miss Jesse is ready." He stepped into the kitchen and stomped his galoshes. Mud clumps the size of walnuts fell onto the rug. "Sorry, ma'am," he said, picking up the larger chunks and shoving them into his pocket.

Esther wrinkled her nose. "Don't be silly. Get out of your coat and have a snack." She set a fresh cup of coffee on the table. As Axel struggled with the rest of his winter gear, she took cookies from the cupboard, then joined them at the table.

"Jesse said come by any time, she'd be ready," she said to Axel. "I'll give her a call when you head that way."

Axel picked up two cookies and started to chew on one while swinging the other in the air. "Haven't had anything to eat since breakfast." He took another bite and said through a mouthful, "If Miss Jesse has a lot of stuff, I'll have to make a second trip, and that'll mean no lunch."

"Oh, detective," said Esther, "I should mention that my sister, and I have joined forces." Rory raised his brows. "We had a long talk last night," she added, taking a cookie and extending the plate to him. "We've decided that just because we're not in a Christmas mood, there's no reason to spoil it for others. We're donating our extra decorations to the hospital and the daycare."

Rory looked around the small kitchen. A single Christmas candle sat on the window ledge over the sink. "Do you have any tattoos?"

She bristled. "Of course not!"

"I was asking Axel," he said, grinning. "But what I wonder is where would you get a tattoo in Winterset. That is, if one had such a desire?"

"Gonna ink WPD on your arm?" Axel asked. "Some guys have 'em. Brotherhood bond and all comrades in—"

"No," Rory said. "I need to find a woman with a particular one. Tattoo artists have their specialties, a signature of sorts, you'd say. I'm interested in a flowery heart. Know anyone who specializes in those?"

Axel and Esther both shook their heads. "The guy on Main Street does serpents," offered Axel.

226

"There's a girl at the market, a checker with a tattoo. Mom always says..." She swallowed hard. "She says they aren't allowed, but Lacey keeps it hidden with her hair."

"I guess that's where I'll start," Rory said, standing.

"You better run along, too, Axel," Esther said. "I'll give Jesse a call."

It took another ten minutes before Rory was willing to leave. He wanted more information on the box in Neil's office, but when Axel wasn't around. It was clear Axel didn't want to leave Esther alone with him. In the end, Rory left without pressing her for further information about Neil's locked box or its contents.

****

Esther cleaned up before going into her office. She booted up the accounting program and logged into the Darcy file. The very idea that someone would be interested in investing in his business was a joke. His accounts would need to be up to date and not stuffed into sacks which she eyed with disgust. Wouldn't any investor insist on seeing the books? Red worked hard, but not wisely. His payments were always behind, and if it weren't for his father's business reputation and extended credit, Darcy would have been out of business long ago.

What was the name Rory said? Dubois. She'd never heard of a lawyer named Dubois. Maybe it was worth a look. She opened the Internet browser and Googled the name. A dozen attorneys came up, none of them with the first name Branch or the initial B. Maybe the police would have better luck, and right now, she needed to get back to business herself. But before she could, her cell rang.

"Hey, Piglet," Jesse said. "I thought Axel was coming by. Everything is ready."

"Sorry. I meant to call you and got sidetracked. He left a little while ago," Esther said. "Thanks for last night. Say, do you know an attorney named Dubois?"

"The only lawyers I know are Winton and Thornburg. And I only know them because I have malpractice insurance. Why?"

"Something Rory mentioned."

"Is it important?"

"Red Darcy has taken on a partner, and the guy is an attorney."

"Who'd go into business with Red? Isn't he a little—?" Esther imagined Jesse twirling a finger around her temple.

"I've always thought so," she said. "Hope springs eternal. Maybe now I can get paid."

"I think Neil works with a Dubois, but he's not a lawyer, more like a jack of all trades. Oh, here's Axel. Got to go, see ya at the Christmas Gala tonight." She disconnected before Esther could reply.

Esther closed the flip phone and set it on the desk. Neil and Dubois? What business would Neil have with someone that Red Darcy knew? Neil was a realtor. Red was a domestic contractor. There was a possibility that Neil had passed on the name of Darcy Construction to those needing home improvements in order to sell, but she didn't think it likely.

Returning to her task, she emptied another sack, smoothing the crumpled papers flat and using the return address as an indication for debit or credit, she created stacks for each. The last envelope had "Elliott Construction" printed in the upper left-hand corner. Confused at that, she stopped. Using a silver letter opener, she slit the business envelope and extracted the contents. A business card fluttered to the desktop.

Unfolding the correspondence, she scanned it, and gasped. Ignoring the butterflies in her stomach, she dialed Rory's number.

Chapter Twenty-Eight

Rory left the Mullins house disappointed. There were too many threads and too few answers. Dubois—what did he have to do with Winterset? Who was the girl with the heart tattoo? Where was the girl with the heart tattoo? Where was Lydia Mullins? Why was someone hijacking trucks and their cargo? Who had murdered Homer Coot? What was in Neil Wallace's safe?

It all seemed unrelated, yet he had the feeling that if he could solve one problem, he'd have the answers to them all. How did that Theory of Separation go? You're one degree away from everyone you know, two degrees away from everyone they know. As the degrees fan out, your acquaintance linked you to their acquaintances, and eventually you were linked to every person on the planet. Many believed six points of separation accomplished the task. But in Winterset it turned out to be closer to one point of separation.

Esther was one degree from her past employer, Jonathan Elliott. Lydia Mullins' church friends included the Elliott family. Homer Coot helped Lydia out and the church she attended. Neil Wallace did contract work for Elliott. The hijackings involved construction equipment. Lydia Mullins had an alleged investment in a construction project. There he lost the connection. How did a tattooed girl, a down on his luck vet, and a lawyer fit into the picture?

After driving around for fifteen minutes, he remembered the blue tarps behind Red Darcy's Quonset. Were the stolen Bobcat front loaders under the tarps? There was one question he could answer pretty quickly. He headed back to Darcy's office to find out.

The yard between the Darcy house and the office was empty when he drove past. He circled the block. Behind the property, he found undeveloped lots. Perhaps it was part of Darcy's holdings, or maybe not. He parked on the back road and walked over through the trees. The ground was still muddy, and under the trees, sheltered from the sun, small mounds of snow were turning to slush. Rory wished he had on boots and frowned at the prints he left with his dress shoes. He could see the blue through the brush and, judging from the area surrounding it, more than one tarp. His cell phone rang.

"Detective Naysmith," he said.

"The chief is looking for you," Sunny chirped. "He says front and center, his office."

"What's this about?"

"Not for me to say, but I can tell you he just came from the mayor's office."

"Crap. I'll be right there. Where's Thacker? I'd like a word with him."

Rory heard the squeak of her office chair. "He's signed out to street patrol."

"See if you can route him back to the office." Her huff came through loud and clear. "Pretty please?" he added.

It took ten minutes to reach the police station. Rory checked the city car into the parking lot and shot a glance at his apartment across the way. Darcy's back lot was muddy, and he'd like to save his dress shoes from further damage. He could run in for his overshoes now or wait until after the meeting with the chief. Either way, he'd need them before he went back. Bryce Mansfield wasn't a man to put off. He decided after would work best.

"He's waiting," Sunny said when he walked in.

Sergeant Powell was balanced on the back legs of his chair, studying his cuticles. Rory waved, glanced at the monitors, and headed back to Mansfield's office.

Chief Mansfield leaned against the front of his mahogany desk, scowling at a forty-two-inch monitor installed on the opposite wall. "Technology!" he exclaimed as Rory entered. "Did you know that I can check on any patrol car? Right from here in my office, a measly flick of a remote." He held a small black object in his hand. "It's revolutionary. Let me show you." He motioned for Rory to enter and pushed a button. "Let's check on your young associate, shall we?"

The monitor lit with the image of Thacker seated behind the steering wheel of his patrol car. He peered left, then right. They watched as he leaned toward the camera, out of focus for a moment, then returned with a walkie-talkie in his hand. His lips moved, but there was no sound at Mansfield's end.

"No audio?" Rory asked.

"Minor irritation," Mansfield said. "I had the techs disable the sound. Every time one of the cars comes into range, the video downloads. Downloads and plays, mind you. I couldn't get any work done for the distraction. I turn the monitor off as well." He gave Rory a devious grin. "Most of the time, that is. I have important business, as you know. Of course, it turns back on automatically when a download starts. In an effort not to get sidetracked, and to get my business completed, I ignore the monitor or click it off again."

Rory said, "What did you want to see me about?"

"Progress report," stated Mansfield. "The mayor will field questions at the holiday festivities tonight, and he wants to be ready with a statement. I told him you had everything under control." He clicked off the live stream and settled behind his desk. "Start with the murder."

Rory filled him in. But to be fair, there was very little progress to report. The key found in the stomach contents was unusual, but so far, he hadn't identified the lock with which it was associated. And whether the key had any direct connection to the murder itself hadn't been established either. Rory felt foolish that with all his experience, he wasn't closer to solving the case. "I plan to revisit the vets. Something there isn't right."

"Well, do it and do it before the end of the year. I want this case closed. Truthfully, Naysmith, I'm starting to agree with popular opinion."

"And what would that be, sir?"

"Winterset needs a younger man. Mind you, it's not my opinion, but…"

The cell phone on Rory's hip vibrated. He glanced at the caller ID—Esther. *Great timing!* Reluctantly, he pushed decline.

The chief stood and started to pace. "There's the morale of the men to consider. I have to answer to the mayor who has to answer to the citizens…"

The phone vibrated again. Sunny. Rory pushed decline. "Your trust isn't misplaced, Chief."

"It better not be," Mansfield said. "What's going on there?" He nodded at Rory's phone.

"I'm not sure, but it seems important."

"Well, get on it, man!"

"Yes, sir." Rory tugged his hat on. Before he cleared the door, the monitor filled with the interior of Officer Garth's unit and Chief Mansfield turned his attention to the screen.

****

On his way to the apartment, Rory checked in with Sunny. Her message was simple. Christmas Gala tonight, eight o'clock sharp, and he better make an appearance if he knew what was good for him. *He didn't need a mother!* Esther's call could wait until after he had his overshoes and was headed out. He met Thacker in the back parking lot.

"I have a request."

"I'm still on patrol," Thacker said. "But I'm free tonight. What you got?"

"I think there's something fishy going on at Darcy Construction. This morning, I spotted tarps behind the Quonset, and I'm wondering what they're hiding."

"I'll swing past and take a look," Thacker said, his voice eager.

"No, I'll check that out for myself. What I need from you is your binder. I'd like another look at what you've put together."

"You know it isn't the official murder book." Thacker rubbed a spot behind his ear and tightened his lips. "It's just stuff I'm collecting to help keep the cases straight."

"It has all your notes? All the cases?" Rory waited for him to confirm it did, and then added, "I might want to keep it overnight."

The young officer hesitated before answering. "Don't show it to the guys, and you can keep it as long as you like. I'll get it from you later."

"Done." Rory glanced at his watch. It was already getting late. "Drop it by the apartment before you head out."

They parted. Thacker to the station and Rory to the apartment where he took the stairs two at a time, arriving out of breath on the third-story platform. Fumbling with the door key, he cursed his body's response to the burst of activity and wondered if he'd ever get used to post-heart-attack physical condition. He knew he'd never be young again, but he felt disgusted that daily workouts weren't letting him do what his mind said he could handle. Maybe Mansfield was right, and policing was a young man's profession.

While he waited, Rory checked the mail and built a sandwich. His two-minute stop stretched into forty-five. He could always get the rookie's binder and tomorrow would work just as well. He scribbled a note to hang on the door, telling Thacker the change of plan. Then worried he was wasting valuable time, snatched up his crusty overshoes and donned his hat.

Before he cleared the apartment, the cell phone vibrated at his hip—Esther.

This time he answered with a smile. "Detective Naysmith."

Chapter Twenty-Nine

Thacker stepped into the station with renewed confidence. If Rory wanted his notes, it meant he was a valuable asset to the investigations and not just an annoying hindrance and Winterset tour guide. Before he could stop her, Sunny talked him into working a second shift. He knew the value of experience, and she had a way of refusing to take no for an answer. Still, he felt manipulated and disgusted with himself for setting aside his own desire—detecting—*real police work.*

He was late retrieving the binder from his parents' home and delivering it to Rory. He knocked and endured a short wait on the exposed platform before the door opened. The detective waved him in with one hand while clutching a cell phone to his ear with the other. Concentrating on the conversation, Rory turned his back and walked away.

He stepped in timidly. Dim sunlight fell through a dingy window, revealing a wooden kitchen table and a bare concrete floor. Newspapers and pill bottles crowded the tabletop. A pair of overstuffed chairs shared the living space with a recliner. Waist-high book towers were stacked on the floor and a tapestry hung on the wall behind the sofa. The fifteen-foot ceiling loomed overhead, and the radiators hissed. Thacker swept litter out of the way, making space for the binder on the table. His hand lingered on it, reluctant to release his thoughts into Rory's care.

Rory crossed to the table, picked up a pill bottle, slipped it into his pocket. "You're right. It is important," he said to the party on the other end of the phone. He gave Thacker a nod and pointed to a chair.

He sat. He had learned many things from Detective Naysmith in their time together. One of them was vigilance, and another, patience. Naysmith was often abrupt with him, but he knew it was just the detective's way of keeping useless ideas at bay. This was the first time Rory had asked for advice. Why else would he want the binder? Thacker knew every page by heart and wondered what the detective was looking for.

Rory disappeared into another room, but his voice filtered back. "I'll want to look into it first." And a moment later, "Don't do it alone. I'll check on the connection, then we'll talk."

Thacker wondered who the detective was speaking to, what the conversation was about, and if he could help.

Rory stepped back into the main room. "You go ahead with your plans. I'll drop in before it's over, and we can discuss your discovery."

His ears perked up. *A discovery?*

"Chief Mansfield insists we put in an appearance," Rory said. "All right, I'll try to squeeze it in. If not, I'll see you there." He disconnected and frowned. "That the binder?"

"Sorry it took me so long. I don't keep it at the station—too many prying eyes."

Rory tapped the top of the binder. "This includes all your notes? Mullins' disappearance? Coot's murder? Truck hijackings?"

"It's just my musings, sir."

"But they're all in there?"

What was Rory after? He straightened his shoulders, ready to defend his actions. "Yes, plus some observations that don't have anything to do with criminal cases."

"Good," Rory said, distracted. "I want to look at all of them together. Build a timeline. See where the times intersect." His gaze drifted to the ceiling as if he were studying something only he could see. Then he asked abruptly, "If I need you later, where will I find you?"

"I volunteered to do duty at the tree lighting. Then there is the Christmas Gala tonight—"

"Keep your phone on," Rory said. "If I need clarity, I'll call. If I need help, I'll have the night sergeant contact you on the radio."

"We'll keep digging. We'll find it." The puzzled look on Rory's face made him feel he'd overstepped an unspoken boundary. "Well, I'm off, then. Keep the binder as long as you need."

"I'll read through it after I get back from Esther Mullins' and the blasted Gala."

****

Night settled on the winter-shortened day. Thacker had an hour to kill before reporting to the town square and traffic control. A slow roll down Front Street proved things were quiet, citizens preparing for the tree lighting and community sing-along. Main Street was no busier. He wondered if the binder would help Rory. Thinking about the detective, he realized Rory's visit with Esther Mullins would postpone the check planned for Red Darcy's tarps. Thacker checked the dashboard clock. He had time, Rory didn't. Turning toward Darcy's part of town, he was confident the detective would appreciate his help.

The street was empty, and the bare bulb above the Quonset door too dim to light the yard. The house was cloaked in darkness. He crept past the construction company. No battered pickup in the front lot or along the side. The coast was clear for a quick look around. He had a niggling thought about obtaining a search warrant. Not that he needed one, this being a reconnaissance mission where anything in plain sight was fair game. All the same, he decided to come in the back way and avoid a possible run-in with Darcy.

There were no streetlamps on the back street, which he considered a plus, but a parked unit was bound to look suspicious. He pulled as far off the road as possible, coming to rest with the passenger-side wheels alongside the drainage ditch. Locking the car, he adjusted the utility belt on his hips and decided the situation called for a heavy-duty flashlight. A search of the trunk yielded a portable spotlight. He grabbed it and tested the batteries. Technically, his second on-duty shift hadn't started. He thumbed off the radio and silenced his phone.

The moonless night hindered his passage. The storage lot was less than a quarter mile walk through the trees. All the same, equipment abandoned between the pines, their dark silhouettes jumping up on the path without warning, slowed him down. The spotlight would help, but he thought the search required stealth and stumbled through the darkness holding it at his side. The soft ground sucked at his shoes. More than once, he stepped completely out of one, realizing its loss only when the cold, wet mud oozed through his wool sock and found a naked foot. An owl hooted. He caught his breath. Winter silence crowded in from all sides.

Breathing hard and disoriented, he emerged at the rear of Darcy's holdings with his night vision engaged. Stacks of discarded lumber, ladders, and pallets leaned against the building. He couldn't see beyond twenty feet in the darkness, but he felt utterly alone. Turning his back to the building, he began to search for the tarps. On the opposite property line from where he'd entered the yard, a mound loomed against the trees. He flicked on the spotlight. Blue, which could be the questionable tarps, was illuminated at the rear of the mammoth pile. Outside the spotlight beam, all else was black. Picking his way through the discarded debris toward the mound, he stumbled and lost his balance. A creature scrambled in the lumber piled to his right. *Rats!* He gave a shudder and swung the spot in that direction. No beady red eyes flashed. He squared his shoulders, marshaled some nerve, and moved on.

At close inspection, the mound turned out to be scrap lumber, dumped in a slipshod manner, and blocking access to the items under the tarps. He couldn't reach the covers from his side while holding the spotlight. He balanced the light on top of an abandoned pallet and swung it around to illuminate the area. In doing so, it caught a silhouette—a man waiting in the shadows. Thacker sucked in his breath and forgot to let it out again.

"Evening, officer." The man stepped forward into the eerie glow. His face was angles and edges, his size menacing. Dressed in black, the large bulge under his coat did nothing to dissipate the policeman's alarm. He stepped closer and tapped Thacker on the chest with an index finger. "You and I need to talk about your future."

Thacker stumbled against the mound.

Another thump to his chest. "Just exactly what are you doing here?"

Thacker didn't feel a need to answer such an obvious question. He tried to right himself, make a show of protest, but the man's presence had thrown him for a loop. He hesitated. The man took advantage, grabbing him by the lapels and shoving him farther into the lumber. "This is private property."

"Just—just a routine check," he stammered. "Part of my job." His voice held no authority.

The man scoffed. "Get up."

He managed to get to his feet. The intruder pulled a gun from his jacket and pointed it at Thacker's chest.

"Drop the utility belt. Slow movements. Nothing funny."

He fumbled with the belt, until it finally fell to the ground.

The brute kicked it out of the way, making sure to keep the gun on his captive. "We're going for a ride."

Thacker flinched. Why had he turned everything off? Eyeing his radio and then his weapon, he felt ill. "Who are you?" he croaked.

A light rain began to fall as he stumbled through the trees ahead of the intruder, headed back toward the parked cruiser. Where was the guy's car? Why Darcy's lot?

God, he wished he'd called the dispatcher and reported the stop. His gut felt like a knot of worms. Some help he was to Rory. Soon he'd be expected at the tree lighting. Very soon, it would become clear that he wasn't going to show.

Chapter Thirty

Old Orchard Restaurant was as close as it got to
fine dining in Winterset. Only open for lunch and
dinner, they catered parties and special events in the
evenings, offering a fare that drew patrons from
Winterset, the newer country club development, and
neighboring bedroom communities.

The proprietors boasted food to savor and an
atmosphere to enjoy the craftsmanship that went into it.
Esther considered the restaurant contemporary in an old
farm setting, made light and airy by way of large plate-
glass windows that looked out over a garden with a
pond. She loved the peacocks that wandered the
grounds during spring and summer. Tonight, the apple
orchard, its bare trees draped with strings of white
lights, could be seen beyond the gardens, and seasonal
decorations decked the landscape. She thought about
the rumors that said Irene Elliott inherited the property
and remained a silent partner without interfering in the
business. The Elliotts denied the rumors, but the
restaurant was the site of the Christmas party they
hosted each year—coincidence?

Esther arrived early. The Christmas Gala didn't
start until nine, but after receiving Rory's call
cancelling their pre-gala meeting, she was anxious to
see him face to face. Had he changed his mind on the
Elliott-Darcy-Dubois connection she'd discovered

while going through Darcy's papers? *Why-oh-why hadn't she told Rory about the gun in Neil's safe?*

Not because she felt any loyalty to her brother-in-law. Rory might have been at the community tree lighting, but he'd sounded busy, saying he'd see her at the gala. Esther wasn't up to standing around in the elements with the holiday-celebrating public. Her mother was still missing, and there was a limit to her cheerfulness despite what she'd said to Jesse. A Christmas party wasn't the place for her discussion with Rory, either, but she'd promised to attend. She couldn't back out at the last moment, no matter the reason. She looked for her sister's car, but it wasn't among the first arrivals. Rory's wasn't there, either. To get out of the wind, she went in alone. They'd be along shortly—she hoped.

Invitations to the Christmas Gala were coveted. As a past employee, Esther was on the yearly invitation list, but she seldom went. Jesse, because of her physician status, and Neil, due to his city council position, made the cut. This year, the main dining room lights were dim. Strings of softly glowing bulbs draped from the ceiling, transforming it from eatery to winter wonderland. The tables lined the edges of the room and opened the center to allow mingling space for the expected guests. The waiters wore red holiday bow ties, complementing their usual sleek black uniforms and crisp white shirts. Evergreen garlands adorned the tables and soft music carried string renditions of holiday favorites. Glasses clinked behind the bar. Murmured conversations accompanied the muted preparations going on beyond the kitchen door.

Esther entered and looked for a friendly face. She met Irene Elliott's eyes from across the room. Standing beside her was Jonathan Elliott looking elegant, festive, and impatient. Not her best friends, yet being civil outweighed standing alone. Maybe she could pick up some information while Jonathan wasn't guarding his every word. *Nothing ventured, nothing gained.* Esther strode toward them with her mind swirling with unanswered questions.

It didn't take long after exchanging holiday greetings for Esther to discover she was out of her element and unable to turn casual conversation to business or lawyers. Irene acted superior and Jonathan preoccupied.

"How is business, Jonathan? Are you still retaining—"

"My goodness, girl—"He looked down his nose at her. "—I'd think you'd be relieved to be away from the nuts and bolts of the construction industry."

"I was hoping you could advise me on business in general."

"My best advice is to leave the heavy lifting to men. We're better suited for it."

Was he joking? He wore a charitable smile, but his eyes were flat. Esther had seen the same face the day he'd cut her loose from Elliott Construction after three decades of service. She often thought Irene was responsible for her lay-off, or at least contributed to the justification for his doing it. Dismissal came at the end of thirty years when Jonathan had relied on Esther to manage all his business details. At that mile marker, Irene became Jonathan's second, and much younger wife, and a lot of things changed. Esther accepted that love was blind; youth, intoxicating; Irene, beautiful.

The threesome fell into an awkward silence. Esther turned expectantly toward the maître d' station each time a new arrival was welcomed. Where was Jesse? And what was keeping Rory?

"May I get you a glass of wine?" Jonathan offered.

"Yes, thank you," Esther said. After he headed for the bar, she turned to Irene. "I've been thinking about engaging an attorney to look over the legal aspects of my CPA business. Can you recommend someone?"

"No," Irene said quickly.

Too quickly, Esther thought. She wanted to shout, "I know Jonathan knows Branch Dubois! He's involved in some shady business with him." Her expression must have given her thoughts away because Irene added, "Jonathan handles all the business details. If you dare, ask him for a recommendation."

Saving her from accepting Irene's spurn, Jesse and Neil appeared at the maître d' station. Jonathan, coming from the bar, stopped to greet them. Esther watched as he handed her wine to Jesse and took Neil by the elbow, leading him toward the far corner of the room. *What were those two up to?* She narrowed her eyes. She didn't trust either one. Or Irene, for that matter.

"Oh, I wouldn't bother Jonathan now," Esther said. "There's Jesse. You'll excuse me?"

Esther walked over to join her sister. "What are those two so hot to discuss?" She nodded at Jonathan Elliott and Neil and took the wine glass from Jesse. "Must be something important."

"I doubt it," Jesse said. "Neil welcomes the distraction. By the way, I asked him about Mr. Dubois on the way over. He says he doesn't know anyone by that name. When I pushed further, he said he didn't even know a lawyer and, if he did, it would naturally be someone from Winterset."

"Didn't you tell me he used a handyman named Dubois?"

"Jack of all trades, but I must have been mistaken." She eyed Neil suspiciously.

Esther sipped her wine. "You'll never believe what I found this afternoon among Red Darcy's receipts."

"Proof he's a twit?"

"No, we knew that."

Jesse, her scrutiny still on Neil, said, "Axel managed to get all the extra Christmas decorations into his truck. I can't believe how many were in the attic."

Esther was going to share her discovery with her sister but decided it would be best to wait for Rory. He might have a different take on the information. Instead, she said, "Speaking of Axel, I understand he's Marilyn's plus-one for tonight's party."

"Lord, help us all." Jesse rolled her eyes. They giggled.

"Imagine Irene's reaction to that pair," Esther said.

The room filled up fast. Drinks were poured, enjoyed, and refreshed. Waiters moved among the crowd, offering flutes of champagne and canapés. The noise level rose above the soft music. Irene played hostess to the crowd and they reciprocated by spreading holiday joy.

When Marilyn arrived fashionably late in a floor length chiffon evening dress, complete with sequins and six inches of bangles on her arm, conversations stopped. Esther thought Marilyn looked stunning in her finery and wondered if Axel could outshine her. He did, making his entrance in a Santa-red velveteen vest, black leather pants, and spit-polished, pointy-toed boots. Jesse went to welcome them with open arms. When Esther looked, Irene stood in the center of the room, her back stiff, lips downturned. Turning away from the couple, she headed for the bar. Esther wasn't surprised Irene would resent losing the limelight. She considered doing a fist pump—but resisted.

Moments later, she discovered Neil and Jonathan had moved from their corner. She couldn't find the pair anywhere in the crowd. *How had she let them slip out of her sight?* They were probably conducting city council business in another dark corner, but she felt uneasy. She felt betrayed by both, Jonathan for playing fast and easy with her career, and Neil for deceiving and lying to her sister. She wouldn't put anything past those two—not even murder.

She felt a chill and her stomach butterflies were back. Rory had said he'd be there before the party got underway. He'd said her find was significant—there were rumblings below the surface, and he'd appreciate her help unearthing them. Now she had a growing feeling that something had gone wrong.

Chapter Thirty-One

Acts of theft, murder, and abduction are far
different crimes. Over the span of his career, Rory had
tackled each—and always brought the perpetrators to
justice. Well, almost always. Winterset wouldn't be any
different. He needed to identify the motive and pinpoint
the opportunity. But the elements behind the current
offenses eluded him. He considered the predictable
motivations: lust, loathing, loot. He couldn't make his
crimes share a motive—and he was sure they did. He
felt it in his bones, deep within his investigator soul.

He lost the evening reading Thacker's binder.
Written in a precise, compact hand the daily details had
been added to a single log much like a diary. Read from
front to back, the rookie strung the separate crimes into
a "what's happening in Winterset" story.

He read it a second time. Made a cup of tea, and
started on a third run through, taking notes.

He thought of his office photo wall clustered in
separate categories: hijacks, Coot, Lydia. It was a
collage very much staged by crime. Rory rearranged the
pictures in his mind, laying them out chronologically—
a fluid sequence of events. All at once, clarity jumped
off the pages. Rory discovered the common motive—
greed.

If controlled by a single mastermind, these crimes, starting with the first hijacking and ending at the third, magically fell in place to form a distinctive picture. As he saw it, the two earlier construction equipment hijackings resulted in material gain. Esther Mullins' removal from Elliott Construction in June was necessary for the gains to go undetected. The week before Thanksgiving, Homer Coot's death, well…he wasn't sure about that one. But the disappearance of Lydia Mullins was surely because she knew something, was too close to someone, or threatened to expose the whole scheme. Maybe Coot knew something, too. Perhaps Coot had thoughts of using his knowledge for blackmail. Maybe he was the first hijacker. Rory rolled right into the second hijacking—loot, quest for power— old fashioned greed. There it was; one of the seven deadly sins, the single motivation for his doer. Then using the timeline and the single point of separation theory he felt compelled to name Jonathan Elliott as the mastermind.

As much as Rory hated to admit it, he wanted to bounce the idea off the young officer to see if it held water.

Thacker had volunteered to work the community tree lighting. A glance at the clock confirmed the outdoor pageant was most likely over. Rain pelted the window. He imagined parents and children scurried homeward when the lighting ceremony ended and the chilly winter rain began. He donned his hat with the hope of catching Thacker at the after-festivity cleanup.

Rory drove through the park but found it empty. He pulled to the curb near a pair of evergreen spruce and slumped low in the seat, mulling over what he knew. Red and green lights splashed onto the windshield. On the deserted street, light flashes danced across the standing water turning to ice. He cracked the window letting in the tinny sound echoing from the abandoned gazebo. Park maintenance must have left the music playing, because he could hear a child's voice singing a melody that drifted in the air. Before he could identify the song, a frosty breeze carried it away. He knew the sentiment—prolonged yearning. Any other time, the song might have calmed him, but as it was, he felt a sense of urgency and the blinking lights brought an eerie feel to the moonless night.

He ran through Thacker's list of lockable items: jewelry box, diary, family bible, toolbox, tackle box, drawers, safety deposit box, medicine cabinet, treasure chest… Good thoughts, but he had a favorite—the locked box in Neil Wallace's safe. Rory patted his breast pocket where he carried the duplicate key Petey had given him after the autopsy. Empty. Then he remembered putting it in the office filing cabinet for safekeeping. What was he thinking? Break into Wallace's office? Crack open the safe? He was out of step. And what was more, he was out of time.

He tried Thacker's phone. No answer. Rory lowered the cell. Was it possible Thacker had gone back to the station? To the apartment? Rory would pass both on his way to Old Orchard Restaurant and his mandatory appearance at the Elliott party. It was worth a look, and he didn't think the young officer would be at the restaurant unless he'd volunteered for yet another duty.

The third floor of the Hillard department store was dark. If Thacker had been to the apartment, they'd missed each other. Rory turned into the station's lot and entered through the back door. Before he had a chance to unlock his office, Powell's voice filled the vestibule.

"Couldn't stand to have a night off?"

Damn cameras! Rory stepped into the dispatch office and found Powell sitting behind his desk and Sunny's usual station unmanned. "Anyone around?" He pushed his fedora back and rubbed his forehead.

"Some of the boys are riding patrol. Hansen and Lloyd just left. I'm hoping for a quiet night."

"It's raining. That should put the damper on any big plans."

"Say, ain't you going to Elliott's fandango? I heard there was an edict demanding your attendance." Powell grinned. "I heard every detective had to show. The chief is enforcing the mayor's orders."

He wondered when Powell would stop resenting him. Damn, the sergeant could have taken the detective's test himself if he'd wanted to become the department's solo investigator.

Powell propped his feet on the desk. "Your lap dog must be spending the night with mommy and daddy."

"Officer Thacker worked a double shift." Powell gave him a glum smile, and Rory sighed. "I thought I might catch up with him here."

"Not here." Powell spread his arms and gestured at the empty room. "Just me, the radio transmitter, and an occasional call from county dispatch. It's always quiet when Sunny's off duty."

"How about trying to contact him?"

"Tsk-tsk. He just got off a double. That wouldn't be nice."

"I want to talk to him, and he's not answering his phone."

"Maybe he's avoiding your call?"

They looked at each other. Rory knew that wasn't true. Powell did, too. "If he calls in, tell him I'm looking for him."

"Yeah, sure. But if Thacker's smart, he'll just lay low."

Rory eyed the monitors. Nothing was happening. "Fine. I'll be in my office for a minute. Then you can report to the powers that be that I'm on my way to the Christmas Gala."

Powell grinned like a Cheshire cat. Rory left him, and entered his office, glanced at the camera, and decided Powell could watch all he wanted. Rory crossed to the filing cabinet and removed the duplicate key from the Coot file. Thacker was right. It wasn't large enough to work its magic on a door, or even a piece of luggage. That still left jewelry box, diary, and treasure chest. Plus, Neil Wallace's secret keepsake box. If only he had reason to obtain a search warrant. Even with Neil's box, he'd need an explanation for Coot to swallow the key rather than be caught with it on him. Rory rubbed the key between his finger and thumb, then dropped it into his pocket.

He could stop by the realty office, the streets were empty, and he was already late. Another few minutes wasn't going to interfere with community schmoozing. His stomach felt hollow. Breaking and entering—not his best idea. And once inside, the box was locked in the safe, adding safecracking to his list of felonies. A swift look—legal or illegal—could end with a lock fitting Coot's key. He had to know if he was on the right path. So, yes, he wasn't just slow and old, he was pathetic.

As Rory locked his office door, a light danced in the window above Chief Mansfield's door. In the otherwise darkened hallway, it glowed like the blue light cast from a TV screen. No one should be in there at this time of night. Rory could have stepped back into dispatch and looked through the CCTV camera into Mansfield's office, but it was just as close to check the office himself. He tried the door, expecting it to be secured. The knob turned. Either Mansfield had been in a hurry to leave or the cleaning people hadn't locked the door when they'd finished. He was in either way.

The room glowed. The hum of electronics greeted him. He stepped in, crossed to Chief Mansfield's desk, and pivoted to face the forty-two-inch monitor on the opposite wall. Shaken by what he saw, he half-fell, half-backed against the desk. Grasping the edge with both hands, he squeezed until his knuckles ached. *Thacker!* Thacker's cruiser—a wild man had commandeered the vehicle!

The scene was surreal without the sound. A dark, muscular man in a black watch cap yelled without uttering a word. His head whipped from facing the windshield to jerking over his right shoulder. There was a gun in his right hand, which he brandished at the rear seat while steering with his left. From the jerky body movements and the degree to which his mouth opened, he was beyond agitated. Thacker's head popped up between the seats. He wasn't shouting, nor was he waving his arms. Blood ran down his face from an ugly gash on his forehead.

Rory jumped up, planted his palms on the polished desk, and looked wildly about the room. *The cruiser was in range and the in-car video was downloading.* He rushed to the window in time to see a pair of taillights disappear, leaving the street outside empty.

He didn't need the sound to understand the situation: Thacker was in big trouble!

Chapter Thirty-Two

Rory roared out of the parking lot. Was Powell watching through the CCTV camera? Should he call in, request backup? He didn't have time for discussion or horseplay. He didn't need the chief or the mayor's blessing. His partner was in trouble. He shook his head, freeing his mind to speed along the path dictated by his training. The hows and whys, even the motivations of other men, were irrelevant when a friend found himself on the wrong end of a gun. What mattered most was what Rory did next. *Thacker!* He was too close to the kid and too far away, all at the same time. His palm slammed the steering wheel, and he stomped the gas pedal.

He sped through town on rain-slick streets, traveling north toward the disappearing taillights. As he raced out of the town limits, he realized, crazy as it seemed, the wild man was leading him toward tonight's most populated site—Old Orchard Restaurant.

Rory slowed before reaching the entrance to the restaurant's drive and came to a complete stop before turning in. The party was in full swing. Merrymakers moved beyond the lit windows and a pair of parking attendants stood under the doorway canopy, out of the rain. The parking lot was full, and no cars moved in or out. He didn't spy the cruiser. He turned off the headlights and crept up the lane, searching. Close to the building, he spotted Esther's car, the mayor's Crown Victoria, and the chief's Buick. Had he guessed wrong? Had the madman taken Thacker farther into the country? Time was of the essence. He wiped clammy hands on his thighs and tried to think. They wouldn't waltz in through the front door, not with Thacker beaten and bloody—not a wild man wielding a gun. He followed a paved route around the side of the restaurant, past a sign that read, *Delivery Entrance*, and found the cruiser behind the building.

Dark and damp, the area looked foreboding. He flicked off the car's overhead light to keep it from coming on when he exited. He silenced the phone and two-way radio and slipped out. Thacker's unit sat in a muddy puddle of rainwater, its engine ticking as it cooled. Signs of a struggle were clear near the rear tires. Thacker might be captive, but he wasn't making it easy. They hadn't gone into the party. He tracked the pair's progress to a rear door. It wasn't the kitchen service entrance, which was off to his left, along with the ruts made by earlier delivery trucks. He jiggled the handle, found it locked, and pulled the gun from his shoulder holster committed to shooting the lock. He hesitated. Thacker was in there somewhere. He thought better of blazing in. There had to be another entry. He spotted a window-well fifteen feet closer to the delivery door and moved along the building's outer wall toward it.

As he reached the well, the rain diminished to a mist. His already rain-saturated coat and hat allowed the cold to penetrate to his body. He felt more icicle than a man. A metal grate covered the well opening, and fallen leaves blanketed the bottom. The windowpanes were opaque, and the putty holding the glass in place broken and brittle. Squatting, he made out movement beyond the glass and heard indistinct, muted conversation. Words eluded him. A climb into the window-well and the gymnastics required to get closer didn't appeal to him. The well was large enough to accommodate, but once in, he'd have limited mobility, making him a duck in a carnival shoot. Someone was in the basement. He had no way of knowing where the window was in relationship to the inhabitants. Or how many they were. If he was lucky—one, plus Thacker, and with their backs turned to him. But the way things had been going, he'd better count on more and assume they would see him before he saw them. He dismissed coming in from another direction. He wasn't likely to find his way to the basement without asking for directions or attracting attention. No, it was from here, and it was now.

He sucked in a big breath, stood, and holstered the gun. He needed to know what was going on, and he needed to find out with stealth. Rain dripping from the trees drew his attention. Off to his right, under one of the larger trees, lay a broken limb. He crept across the lawn to check it out. It had been there a while, with dead leaves withered and locked in place on the branches. He wrestled it to the window-well, trying to limit the noise. The grate opened with minor effort and he lowered the limb along the window side, propping the grill against the building. He had a camouflage and a way to keep the grate from falling back to hinder him.

Every movement echoed in the night. He waited for an alarm to sound from the basement. None came. He lowered himself to sit on the wet ground, then keeping the dead foliage between his body and the window, swung his legs around to hang over the cement well casing. He scooted forward and dropped into the hole. Less than a foot drop, the thud produced on landing sent his adrenalin racing. He froze. Waited. Nothing. When he thought he'd waited long enough, he squatted on his heels, held the stiff leaves out of the way, and peered through an opening where the brittle putty had fallen away.

Luck was on his side. A deep cabinet sat below the window. The room beyond held large wooden racks filled with bottles, crates of plates and glasses, and mismatched cabinets. He watched two men on swivel chairs seated by a table, a muscular, dour man with a dangerous glint in his eye—the madman. And Neil Wallace.

He didn't need a search warrant for Wallace's property after all.

"She knows nothing." Neil's voice sounded stern. "She's so wrapped up in her hospital job and the hunt for her mother that she's blind to our movements."

"That better be true."

"Don't worry, I'm careful. Even the boss is clueless."

"There's always your snoopy sister-in-law."

"I can manipulate Esther."

Rory stiffened. What was going on? Where was Thacker? He eased the pistol out.

The wild man's face demanded a response. "She's asking questions."

"Let her ask all she wants. She will not connect us, or either of us, to the thefts. As far as anyone knows, there is no Branch Dubois. You're a ghost."

Rory's legs trembled from the effort to support his crouched stance. So, this was Branch Dubois, the jack-of-all-trades-lawyer. Neil was on his radar, but he had missed a connection between Neil and Dubois. He was slipping, his old mind dulled with age.

Dubois stood, then moved toward the cabinet and Rory's position. He ducked. Reflex, but unnecessary. The man went out of view. The cabinet and the angle eliminated the danger of discovery.

"Why d'ya bring the kid here?" Neil whined. "And using a cop car? You idiot. The boss will be furious."

"I told you. I found him poking around Darcy's. We need to deal with him."

"Look, Branch, I'm not in favor of killing a cop."

"You didn't have any qualms dealing with the drunken vet."

Homer Coot? Damn! Rory didn't need a locked box to find his way to the murderer. Not when a confession was available. He laid the gun on the soggy floor between his feet, found his phone, pushed "voice memo," and held the recorder against the pane.

"That was different," Neil continued, "Homer's drinking made him stupid, and because he was stupid, he thought he deserved part of the action. You shoulda seen him dancing around in a drunken stupor, waving the key to the stamp box, taunting me. The stupid fool threatened to go to the police unless I cut him in. I tried to grab the damn key out of his hand, and he put it in his mouth and swallowed. He didn't count on my having a gun handy in the desk drawer. You could say his death was the spontaneous result of his stupidity."

Gotcha! Rory clicked off the recorder, shoved the phone back into his pocket, and snatched up the gun.

An agonizing moan rose from below. A yelp followed it as Dubois came back into view, dragging Thacker by the nape of his uniform collar. The young officer squirmed, but he didn't find purchase and collapsed to the floor. Dubois kicked him. "Get up."

Thacker tucked into a fetal position, but not before Rory spotted the tie wraps that rendered the rookie's hands useless. Heart pounding, he made an involuntary lurch, knocking the branch into the window.

Neil looked up. "There's somebody out there!"

Rory clenched his muscles, ready to spring into action.

"Now you're being stupid," Dubois sneered. "It's the wind."

Rory relaxed enough to resume breathing but kept his heightened level of alert. Dubois was still talking. "A hundred people are upstairs celebrating and trading lies with each other. You're imagining things. They don't suspect we're here. And no one is wandering around behind the restaurant in this freezing rain." He jerked Thacker to his feet and shoved him at Neil. "Tend to this one."

Neil returned the belligerent stare and let the helpless policeman fall at his feet.

Thacker was defenseless. Rory wasn't. These men were bigger, younger, and stronger than a middle-aged detective with a heart condition, but there was no way they were meaner.

Here and now!

Rory punched the glass with his free hand, screamed, "Police!" and dove through. As he landed on top of the cabinet, it overbalanced and tumbled forward, sending him flying into the room.

Wood splintered. Glass broke. The gun fired, and a box of utensils clattered to the floor.

Rory landed on Neil, scrambled to his feet, and placed the fallen man between Dubois and himself. Through some quirk of fate, he still had the gun, and held it steady. His gaze darted around the room, taking in his surroundings. Thacker was off to his right, his body in ruin. At his feet, Neil Wallace lay flat on his back, eyes open, with blood spreading across his dress shirt. Branch Dubois, stunned and drenched in wine, stood across the room. An overturned swivel chair pinned his fedora to the floor. Three doors—the locked entrance from outside, the wine cellar access from upstairs, and what looked like a closet door. In the center, a bottle spun in a lazy circle, spewing liquid onto the floor. The winter wind pushed through the broken window and into the room, which smelled of fermentation and cordite and blood. He allowed himself a moment to exhale, then grasped the gun with both hands, leaned forward, and pointed the barrel at Dubois.

"Winterset Police! Keep your frickin' hands where I can see them!" His voice overrode the heartbeat thudding in his ears.

Neil groaned, and in that instant, Dubois shot forward and, with incredible speed and accuracy, kicked the .357 out of Rory's hands. It spun across the floor, under the table, and hit the wall behind with a loud clunk. Rory, taken by surprise, tucked to roll over his shoulder, lost his footing, and fell face first among the broken glass. He closed his eyes and kept them shut. *Brilliant plan. Twenty-five years on the job, disarmed by a thug.* He couldn't save anybody.

"What have we here, the senior detective?"

Rory winced. His face stung. With one hand, he fingered the shard implanted in his cheek. "You and Wallace?" he croaked.

"That's right. And we aren't alone."

Red Darcy and Jonathan Elliott, no doubt. God only knew how many more. Maybe dozens. Upstairs at this very moment, along with every prominent citizen in town.

A gun materialized in Dubois' hand. He locked eyes with Rory, shifted the gun to the other hand and pulled out a cell phone. With astonishing dexterity, he placed a call. "Boss? I have a situation in the storage room." And after a moment, "No need to worry, it's under control."

With Dubois watching, Rory rolled to a sitting position, halfway turned, and looked at Thacker. The rookie, unfolding, struggled, his useless hands bound at his waist. The worst part was his eyes—they weren't frightened, just sad and apologetic when they met his. What had the kid been thinking when he took on Darcy's lot alone? The mystery under the tarps held no comparison to their present plight. It didn't take any imagination to understand Wallace was bleeding, probably dying, and Dubois calling for reinforcements. This wasn't hide-and-seek—this was life and death. And the evil guy had the advantage.

"Pull a car around back," Dubois said, and then clicked off. He waved the pistol from Rory to Thacker and then back to Rory. "Don't try anything funny. You and your curious friend will leave before long."

Wallace made a gurgling sound. It brought Rory's mind back on task. He had no interest in having his suspect die before he got all the sordid details—and not before he solved the entire affair. He needed to control the situation, a plan, a weapon, and the strength to carry through—not necessarily in that order.

While he worked out a practical plan, buying time was an excellent idea.

"You better check on your partner. I can do it for you while you keep the gun on me. He needs an ambulance. Better yet, Officer Thacker is an Eagle Scout, and he knows about first aid, even took the full EMT course. Slip those ties and let him look."

Dubois' face went rigid. "The boss will make that call. You just sit tight."

But Dubois didn't stop Rory when the detective butt-scooted his way to Neil and checked the wound. "He might live if we stop the bleeding."

"He's nothing to me. Let him bleed out."

"Compassion speaks in your favor," Rory said.

"I'll manage fine without the councilman."

"It might be tricky getting away from here with two hostages and a dead body. Riskier to leave one behind." He rose. Dubois didn't stop him. Rory hunched, rounded his shoulders and made his body as non-threatening as possible. He continued, "Impossible with three dead bodies. The Boss won't be pleased."

That gave Dubois pause.

Rory kept his head bowed, watching Thacker, letting Dubois weigh his choices. "Do you need another phone call? I can wait. But I doubt Wallace can."

Dubois didn't answer. When Rory looked up, the sullen man said, "Suit yourself. There's cloth and such in there." He flicked the gun at the mystery door on the opposite wall. "Slow movements. I'm watching." Dubois' gaze snapped to the outside door as if he expected it to fly open at any second. "Anything funny and Boy Scout gets the first bullet."

Rory gritted his teeth. *Not if I can help it.* The first inkling of a plan sparked.

His success depended on keeping Dubois' attention away from Thacker. He started with chatter. "No. No funny business from me. This town can be funny, though. Everywhere prying eyes, everyone related to everyone else. A man stubs his toe on Front Street and three seconds later, Mother Hubbard, living in a bungalow behind the grain silo on 48th, has all the details. Just when you think you can sneak in and meet with Wallace, *voila!* unexpected company. And a bloody wound."

"Get the stuff. I don't need your ramblings."

From the corner of his eye, Rory saw Dubois had the gun fixed on him. He kept his voice even. "Me, I'm used to operating under the radar. But there's no such thing in Winterset. No simple task, you sneaking in and out of town. I admire your ingenuity."

Rory didn't look at the rookie as he shuffled across the concrete floor toward the closet. With his feet, he swept broken glass aside with each measured advance. "It takes cunning to keep your confederates a secret." Dubois made a dismissive grunt. "Neil Wallace." Sweep, step. "Red Darcy." Sweep, step. "Jonathan Elliott." The latter drew a contemptuous snort.

When he reached Thacker, Rory paused, then kicked a broken wine bottle at Dubois. The athletic man performed an awkward two-step and stayed out of the volley. Rory used the moment to send a slender glass fragment in Thacker's direction.

"You're not as clever as you think." Dubois repaid Rory with a backhanded barrel-slap that knocked him to the floor. "Get something to stop the bleeding and shut up."

Straight ahead, Rory's service revolver lay against the wall. Twenty feet of hard surface lay between him and the closet, two more to the gun. It would take a superpower to get the .357. He wasn't sure he had the energy to summon it. Or another distraction.

He made a sluggish rise and stumbled forward. "Agreed, I'm not clever, but many consider me intelligent and witty."

In case he wasn't drawing Dubois' full attention, when Rory reached the closet, he eased the door open a crack and then flung it wide. It struck the cinder block with a loud bang and bounced back with such force it knocked him sideways. He grabbed the doorknob in time to stay upright and cursing himself for not diving for the gun when he'd had the chance.

"Hey! Grab the stuff and quit fooling around."

Rory straightened, arms aching, head spinning. He shrugged it off and stepped in. The closet was a standard six feet wide with shelves down both sides. A bare bulb hung from the ceiling. A pull string dangled above his head. He gave a tug. Napkins, tablecloths, and other linens lay folded and stacked on the upper shelves. Punch bowls, silk flowers, and utensils were piled below. Rory searched the shelves for a weapon, sliding boxes open and peeking at the contents. A meat grinder sat on a waist-high shelf and behind it, their chance at deliverance—a meat cleaver.

Rory sucked in his breath, amazed at his good fortune.

"Grab 'em and get back out here or your friend goes down!"

Back out here? That meant Dubois didn't know what was going on in the closet. Rory snatched some linen, draped them over an arm, and picked up the cleaver. Amazed by its weight and heft, he held it at arm's length against his leg. He sidestepped back into the storage room, buoyed by the thought there was hope.

Dubois had moved to Thacker's feet and stood with the pistol inches from the officer's ear. He turned his head in Rory's direction. Thacker's knees were up, his hands hidden. Rory looked at the kid who'd worked by his side for the last four weeks, the rookie who trusted and believed in him. Their eyes locked. Thacker winked. *Shit, the kid got it!*

Rory hesitated, holding the cleaver at his side, thinking how heavy it was when you only had one hand, chiding himself for not practicing more, remembering how seldom he'd hit the target, picturing the bullseye. His mind was so busy it tripped over itself sorting out the pros and cons. He'd lost his chance to get the gun. That left him with two choices. One, use his ax-throwing skills to toss the cleaver, take that off-balance moment when Dubois ducked to keep out of the way, leap at him, and trust Thacker to do something miraculous to stay out of the line of fire. Or two, cross the room to Neil as if he were cooperating, count on a free-handed Thacker to take Dubois by surprise, and deal with the gun. If Rory was fast, he might use the moment to get off an accurate throw and disable their capturer. His chances with either choice, iffy—fast, he hadn't moved at high speed in a long time.

The outside door rattled. Dubois turned his head. Thacker leaped to his feet, using a maneuver Rory had first seen watching pro-wrestling on TV. Survival instinct kicked in. Rory dropped the linens and bounced the wooden cleaver handle into a firmer grip. *He had a winner!* Rory centered his focus, summoned all his strength, and thrust the weapon at Dubois' chest.

It found its mark.

Dubois' face contorted in disbelief. He released the gun and seized the cleaver's wooden handle. Thacker grabbed the fallen weapon. Rory drop-rolled to his service revolver, and both policemen came up with their gun barrels pointed at the opening door.

Dubois wheezed, then stammered, "B... boss..." before collapsing.

Neil's raspy breathing demanded attention. Rory ignored him, stepped over Dubois' body, and concentrated on the doorway—ready.

It swung open.

Irene Elliott stepped in.

Chapter Thirty-Three

Rory pointed the gun at her chest. He expected to face Mister Big, *the boss*, but he didn't flinch when Irene, face twisted in rage, stepped through the doorway. She drew her lips in a severe slash, narrowed her eyes.

"Step away from the door, ma'am."

She looked past him into the room. "What have you done?" Her voice expanded to fill the space. "Is he dead?"

"Wallace, no. Dubois? I believe so."

She gave a faint shudder, then went rigid. He heard sirens which she didn't seem to notice. In his peripheral vision, he saw Thacker move. Rory kept the gun on Irene. "See if she has a weapon, son."

For a moment, the rookie froze, then stepped in to do the pat-down.

"How. Dare. You?" She curled her lip. Cold, dark eyes bore into Rory's. "Keep your hands to yourself."

Thacker moved into the open doorway as if he couldn't get away from her fast enough. "She's clean."

"You can't treat me this way. You have no right to be here. Old Orchard is private property. I'll have Jonathan sue you for unlawful entry. This is trespassing!"

Siren screams beat the strobe lights through the doorway. Car doors slammed. Heavy feet crunched the gravel outside. Thacker stepped out as Officers Hansen and Lloyd stepped in with their guns drawn.

Irene kept up her tirade. "My husband is the most important man in town. You won't get away with this."

The situation controlled, Hansen huffed, planted his feet shoulder-width apart, and leveled his gun on Irene. "Put your hands on your head, ma'am."

She argued but complied. She wasn't as accommodating when Hansen wrestled her arms behind her back for the cuffs, fighting his efforts. Face a bright red, she shouted obscenities over the vein bulging at her temple. The men took it in stride. Lloyd righted a swivel chair, flipped Rory's fedora to him, and propelled the chair toward his partner.

Hansen shoved Irene into the chair without ceremony. "Ambulance is on the way," he said. Thacker watched, rubbing his wrists.

Rory's mindset shifted as a cog fell into place. If Irene was boss, Wallace became the slick right-hand man, and Dubois, the henchman. Was it possible he'd misjudged Jonathan Elliott? If Irene reigned, was Jonathan a pawn? He shook his head. He wasn't ready to grant the man any leeway.

Irene regained her composure. "You all will be walking a beat before Jonathan is through with you. And you, detective—" Her nostrils flared. "—will be sorry you ever set foot in Winterset."

"Better read Mrs. Elliott her rights, Hansen."

"He is the most powerful man in Winterset—"

Rory cut her off. "You used that power for a smokescreen, knowing that you were the real driving force, hiding behind his affluence to mask your crimes. Did you derive some twisted sense of pleasure, pulling strings—duping a man too trusting to see the truth? A man you hold in contempt." She glared, opened her mouth to deny his allegations, but smirked instead.

"Do you wish to make a statement, Mrs. Elliott?"

"Not without my lawyer present."

"If your lawyer is Branch Dubois, you're out of luck." He turned to Hansen. "Take Mrs. Elliott into custody. Book her with conspiracy to commit murder, racketeering, and kidnapping."

Rory holstered his gun. "Where is that damn ambulance?"

****

Siren screams and pulsing lights brought the partygoers down the cellar stairs. They burst into the basement with Marilyn leading Jonathan Elliott before Esther elbowed them out of the way. Broken glass, upended crates, and the spilled wine hindered their access. Officer Lloyd moved to contain them. The sight of the bodies brought them to an abrupt halt before he crossed the room.

"Crime scene," Lloyd said. "I'll have to ask you to leave."

"Detective Naysmith?" Esther's voice trembled. Her outstretched arms both protected and blocked those behind her from entering. Her gaze locked on Rory, telegraphed a desperate struggle for self-control. The sight of the battle's aftermath, he was sure, stretched the bounds of her comprehension.

Jonathan Elliott burst into a roar. "Irene! Are you..?" He pushed past Esther, rushing into the room. He stopped chest-to-chest with Lloyd. "Release her. Now. You've just lost your badge, hope you haven't lost your freedom, too."

272

Lloyd slowly backed Jonathan toward the others. "I need everyone to remain calm. Don't leave the restaurant. You can wait upstairs until we've taken your statements."

Rory felt unexpected pride when Esther took her old employer by the elbow and led him back up the steps. That he allowed her to do it, that Elliott might be culpable, barely registered.

Exhausted, coming down from his adrenalin rush, the sight of Irene Elliott led to the cruiser gave him no pleasure. Rory couldn't say whether he would have pulled the trigger. He had expected Jonathan Elliott or Red Darcy, although he didn't imagine the local contractor had the makings of a crime boss.

The ambulance arrived. After packing Neil's wound, they whisked him off to the hospital in the custody of Officer Lloyd. Petey Moss, the chief, and the major all made brief appearances. The mayor said he'd recognized the sound of gunfire and thought it prudent to place a nine-one-one call. Rory agreed a volunteer bullet had discharged during his not-so-graceful plunge from the window. The chief said he'd expect Rory's gun in the morning—after all, he'd fired it during the altercation. Petey did the county coroner exam on Dubois, pronounced him dead, and had the body removed.

Thacker's forehead still oozed blood, as did Rory's face. It amazed him how much head wounds bled. An EMT examined their cuts and abrasions. All were declared superficial. Thacker's wrists would be tender for days. The room cleared, taped off, readied for the boys to work the scene, Rory climbed the steps to oversee the statements being collected upstairs.

Christmas music played softly. The strings of lights flashed in random patterns. Rory arrived after the partygoers had gone. He joined Jonathan Elliott, Esther, and Jesse in the empty, dimly lit restaurant. They sat at a table against the wall in the shadows.

"I'm sorry to make you wait," he said. They looked weary, crumpled, faded. He removed his hat. "It's been a long night. I'm afraid it's growing longer—a sorry business."

Esther took Jesse's hand in hers. "I'm sorry about Neil."

Jesse hung her head. "Whatever comes out, he hasn't been right for a long time. Our marriage is over. Has been for a while."

Esther looked askance at Rory before turning her attention to Jesse. "Even so, you should be at the hospital with him. He's your husband. Detective Naysmith can question you another day."

"There is plenty of time," Rory said.

"No. Neil won't care if I'm there or not. Frankly, I don't want to waste energy." After a moment, she said, "The other man is dead."

Jonathan moaned. All eyes turned to him, slumped in the chair, his chin almost touching his chest. His tuxedo bunched around his shoulders, and his hands folded over the bulge of the cummerbund. The knot of his tie had shifted more to the left than the right. He looked defeated. A tear rolled down his cheek.

"Dead?" Esther whispered. "How do you know?"

"There wasn't a second ambulance. The cleaver sunk in up to the shaft, his body almost split from the force of the blow. The trauma alone…" Jesse let the sentence drift away. "Was it Branch Dubois?"

"Branch?" Jonathan lifted his head, looked around, his eyes glassy. "Is Neil here? Esther?" He straightened in his chair as if seeing her for the first time.

Esther patted his hand, her chin quivered.

Jonathan said, "It's a mistake."

"I'm right here."

"What are they doing with Irene?"

"We'll sort it out," she said.

It was after two when Rory finished and dragged himself away.

****

The rain was back the next morning when he made it to the station. He stopped at Sunny's desk to check the roster. Sunny looked up. "You look like somebody dragged you through a swamp. Did you get any sleep, detective?"

"Not yet. Who's in?"

"Peterson took the call about a drunken fool they pulled out of the Missouri this morning. The rest of the boys are here. Hansen and Lloyd came back in about an hour ago. That must have been some party last night. If you want my opinion, and I know you do, they'll be useless today."

"Is the chief in?"

She tilted her head to look at the CCTV monitor, where the image showed Mansfield behind his desk. "Accounted for."

"Tell him I'm here."

She flapped a hand at Rory, shooing him toward the office. "Roger that."

Rory tapped on the door and entered.

The chief laid a report down, cleared his throat, and said, "So, as far as I'm concerned, we wrapped the hijacking cases up last night, along with the Homer Coot murder."

"I agree."

"The mayor will have closure. We've managed to keep the citizens safe."

Rory stepped forward, removing his holstered gun. He ejected the clip, cleared the chamber, and laid it butt first on the desk. Mansfield stared at it and then at the badge Rory extracted from his jacket pocket and put next to it.

"May I sit down, sir?"

"Absolutely."

Rory settled in the chair. He stared out the window at the rain, unable to look Mansfield in the eye. His own image reflected darkly in the glass, reminding him of the horror felt the night before. He pictured Thacker's helpless face.

When he looked back, Mansfield was waiting, his expression unreadable.

"I lost our boy last night," Rory said. "I lost track of time, putting more than myself in jeopardy." He looked down at the fingerprints in the high gloss of the desktop, remembering his shock and the moment he'd made them.

"You did some quick thinking, Detective Naysmith."

"I'd say I engaged in some full-fledged lack of thought. Things aren't like they were when we were at the academy."

"Thankfully, so."

"I wasn't thinking. I've always relied on my strength and my wits to get the job done. Last night..." Rory swallowed, looked Mansfield straight in the eye.

"Last night, it wasn't just me. It was me and that damn blind, trusting rookie you assigned to me. It was the technology that I don't understand and depending on others to accomplish what I've always conquered on my own. I don't want to be responsible. I don't want to think about my body failing me. Or another man dying. I give up. You are right—I'm too old for this job."

In the silence that followed, Mansfield didn't offer an argument. The forty-two-inch monitor came on. Both men watched the image of Sergeant Powell as he adjusted his position behind the steering wheel and turned into the lot. They were still watching when Powell flicked the camera off. Rory sighed.

Mansfield rose. "Welcome to the world of modern police work, Detective." He rounded the desk and picked up Rory's badge. "You have my gratitude. I'll get this polished. I guarantee you'll see things differently tomorrow once you've had some rest. You can pick it up before we meet with the mayor. He'll want a full report."

As he passed Rory, he leaned down and added, "If you want to confess, you'll need a priest—or a wife."

****

Rory entered his office, half expecting to find Thacker there. He wasn't.

Pulling the report together would take hours. Instead of starting, he used the time to run through his conversation with Bryce Mansfield. Would the department be better with a younger detective? How did he fit in an organization with Sunny, Powell, and people like Lloyd? Was it so the department could implement the latest gadgets—and make him look foolish? There was enough to remind him he was slow—outdated. He closed his eyes. Heaved a sigh—it was fatigue talking.

Fifty didn't mean he was archaic. His experience, drive, and determination alone were an asset. He had a lot to offer, he hadn't even tapped his full potential. He recognized a group effort when he saw it. He had to admit he'd been part of that team—like it or not. He could see the department stayed on the cutting edge by melding the old with the new, mixing his experience with fresh perspectives and skills. WPD stayed one step ahead of crime, guaranteed the safety of the people—*because it was the right thing to do*.

He was exhausted. God knew he'd had little sleep. In the early morning hours, he and Thacker had questioned Neil Wallace in Winterset Memorial. Stable but a little loopy, Neil had been happy to toss the blame on Irene Elliott.

Wallace outlined a complicated scheme that included inspection payoffs, altered construction drawings, and forged permits. They'd appropriated materials, juggled funds to keep costs down, and filled their pockets. Irene called the shots, doctoring her husband's books to hide the evidence. A blind eye exchanged for a pocket full of cash, and Darcy's backlot became their waystation. Wallace claimed they hurt no one, at least not in a bodily harm kind of way. He called their graft a Robin Hood venture.

When Rory asked, "What about Homer Coot?" Wallace stopped talking.

"Come on, Wallace. He didn't kill himself. He didn't drag his body behind the senior center."

"I hurt. I'm too tired to remember."

"You can recall the details of an intricate con game? Here's what happened: you shared drinks behind the Triple-A, he was on to you and wanted part of the action, the two of you got into a scuffle, and things got out of hand."

Neil looked beyond Rory, his stare intent as if studying someone in the shadows. Rory turned, there was no one in the room save Thacker, taking notes.

"Where's the nurse?" Neil asked. "I need something for this pain."

Rory waved the rookie toward the door and shucked off his coat.

"We can get you something for the pain, but now, I want to talk about Homer Coot."

Thacker returned with a nurse. They waited while she hung an IV bag, fiddled with the settings, and started the drip. "Morphine," she said. "The pain will subside in a moment. Can I get you anything else, Mister Wallace?" She must have seen the handcuff tethering his right wrist to the bed because she shuddered and left, giving Rory a sideways glance.

"Homer Coot, Neil."

"All right, Coot was greedy."

"So, he was part of your crew?"

Wallace closed his eyes. Rory suspected the drugs had kicked in and feared Neil would drift into a mellower, quieter place, a full confession floating off with him.

Neil surprised him by blurting, "Coot was a drunk. He was a liability." Neil struggled to sit up and then collapsed onto the pillows.

Rory checked on Thacker, who was back in position and taking notes. "Uh-huh. Tell me something new." Rory had recorded Neil's confession from the window-well, but he wanted Thacker to document it. He leaned over the bed, willing Wallace to tell all.

"It was a careless mistake. Coot must'a come up the footpath because he knocked on the alley door. Lacey had just left after—"

"Who's Lacey? The girl with the tattoo?"

"Yeah, like I was saying, Lacey brought the bribe money, and I was putting the envelope in the safe. I let Coot in. Ya see, I let him work around the office some, sweep the floor, take out the trash." Wallace spoke in a monotone, his voice growing weaker. Rory strained to hear the words over the hospital sounds as monitors took the injured man's vital statistics.

"Good. So, what happened?"

"He was drunk. He wanted… I don't know what he wanted. He saw the cash as I shoved it into the box, ready to lock it up. I was foolish, but she'd carped on and on, always the same… give the vet a chance… let him earn some money… self-respect…"

"She? Do you mean your wife? Lacey? Irene Elliott?"

"No, Lydia…my mother-in-law…" Rory stiffened. Wallace continued speaking at half-speed, drifting further and further away. "He grabbed the key… to the box…"

Bingo! "Where is the box, Neil? Where will I find Lydia Mullins?"

But Wallace was through for the night. Rory wasn't through with him—not by a long shot.

Back in his office, everything took shape. Before Irene demanded a lawyer, she claimed she'd never heard of Branch Dubois, much less been in league with him. Convenient since he couldn't challenge her claim. Rory could tie them together. Greed and power created strange bedfellows. They weren't the oddest couple he'd ever seen—not in twenty-five years on the force. The link was there. Only the footwork remained. Irene Elliott was behind it all, and Neil had been willing to do her bidding. Under the radar, Branch had applied pressure and brawn. Rory could tie the tattooed Lacey McKenna in as a willing accomplice, a courier, a diversion, even a carrot to keep the men in line.

Wallace was under guard at the hospital, where he'd stay until they could safely move him. Irene was in lock-up, awaiting transfer to the county jail. WPD had put a warrant out for Lacey's arrest. Branch Dubois lay in the morgue. He didn't see where Lydia Mullins or Jonathan Elliott fit into the picture. That, too, would sort out. Not a bad night's work for a seasoned investigator.

Taking stock of his life was harder. He was tired, but he felt good. He'd sunk a bullseye when it counted. Chief Mansfield hadn't accepted his resignation, at least not yet, so he still had a job, and he'd do it. Take a wife? He pictured Esther Mullins, confident, calm, leading Elliott away from the chaos at Old Orchard and then lending support by remaining at his side until cleared to leave. Level-headed, composed, common-sense Esther. He sighed. *Maybe someday*.

Team player? Perhaps not, but he carried the badge that made him a member of the brotherhood. So what if they didn't accept him? He was too stubborn to let that get under his skin. Winterset's solo detective, Rory Naysmith, *his job*—and now, *his town*.

He buzzed Powell's extension. "Have we been to Wallace's office? Good. Notify me when they bring in the goods."

Rory booted up the computer and started the paperwork.

****

Later in the day, the boys brought the boxes in from Wallace Realty and checked them into the evidence room. Rory immediately checked them out, wheeling a dolly with four large containers into the dispatch office. "This is the stuff from Wallace's filing cabinets." He stopped at Sunny's desk and wiped his forehead. "You want to give me a hand with this, Ms. Gomez?"

She held up ten midnight-blue, enameled fingers and wiggled them. "Look at these and tell me how much of a fool you are for asking such a stupid question."

Rory put a hand to his heart. "I am a fool, a special kind of fool."

"Get lost."

"Only if you'll come with me."

"Oh, for God's sake!" She slammed out of her workspace and stomped away on black platform heels, with earrings and curls bouncing.

He grinned and wheeled the dolly over to the interrogation desk. He lifted his brows at Powell. "I think I'm getting to her."

Epilogue

Joggers were the first to notice the destruction in the city park. During the winter, no one saw the beavers moving along the stream that fed the lake. By early April, they had dammed the water flow on the north end. The flooding covered the softball field and made the four-square courts unusable. Water backed up behind the beaver dam, and the water level of the lake sank, reaching levels much lower than anyone could remember from previous springs. It demanded action.

The *Winterset Gazette* ran an editorial detailing the damage. Not giving it much thought, the mayor suggested eliminating the beavers. Marsha Epperson wrote a letter to the editor, claiming she would go on a hunger strike unless the beavers were rescued and relocated. WPD arrested Harold Eaches when he took his gun out to the stream and began to take pot-shots at the water, claiming to have seen the beavers moving around. Axel rammed PVC piping through the dammed sticks to allow some water through. Two days later, the beavers had dammed up even those holes.

Concern for his image prompted the mayor to call the extension service of the University of Nebraska Wildlife Management in Lincoln. They contacted Wildlife Management Company of Omaha, who contracted with Winterset to remove the animals and take them to a protected wetland in Washington State.

Transporting wildlife across state lines required a State permit. The joke in town was that the governor pardoned the beavers. No one cared where the beavers ended up, only that they were gone.

The first Saturday afternoon in April, Rory stood with the crowd gathered to watch the traps set. The Natural Resources' SUV, Wildlife Management panel truck and the mayor's blue Crown Victoria parked at the edge of the lake. Rory was daydreaming, not paying much attention. Esther Mullins had agreed to accompany him to see *The Nice Guys* at the theater on Main Street. He didn't like cop movies, but she'd insisted that the neo-Nazi, skinhead thriller he'd picked wasn't her style. He expected a pleasant evening in her company. While the wildlife team set up traps along the stream, Rory heard Bob Price shove his brother, Joe, into the lake.

"Hey, a beaver just tried to grab my leg," Joe hollered. Rory ignored the shouts, but when Bob jumped in to wrestle the beast and save his brother, Rory looked beyond the stream and over to the lake.

Bob bobbed up from the water. "Hey, there's something down here. It could be a car!"

The breeze was steady, and the temperature pushing fifty-five, as Rory stood beside the shore, arranging for a tow truck on his cell phone. Bud's Wrecker had one, only Bud, nearly eighty years old, wouldn't agree to dive into the water to do the hook-up. Rory arranged for divers. By the time the tow truck and the divers appeared, so had the reporters and a camera crew. A van from Omaha TV station WBNE was parked behind the Crown Victoria.

It was a slow, noisy, wet retrieval. As the Dodge Charger broke through the lake's surface, Rory's stomach moved to his throat. This day, there would be no time for movies.

****

The next day, the *Omaha World-Herald* ran the following article.

The four-month search for missing 75-year-old Lydia Mullins came to a tragic end at a lake in Winterset City Park. Police say Mullins drove by the small lake on 20th at Lincoln on her way to and from St. Matthews Lutheran Church. Her body was found Saturday afternoon in the water about 20 feet offshore inside the black rental car she was driving. Bud's Auto wrecker driver, David Bolton, said, "The silt had it trapped underwater. You could tell it left the road at a high rate of speed."

Mullins disappeared after the early snow last November. The 75-year-old never showed up for a scheduled bridge game. Nebraska issued a statewide Silver Alert. Police spent hundreds of working hours trying to find her. Volunteers scoured the area, hoping for a clue that would lead to her safe return. The entire time she was in the lake, less than two miles from home.

The Winterset Police Department called in the county sheriff's dive team after discovering a submerged vehicle in the lake. WPD spokesperson, Rory Naysmith, said, "We've been searching for the needle in the haystack for over four months and the Price brothers stepped on it by accident. It was an unfortunate ending that took a toll on the Mullins family." Mullins was discovered with no visible signs of trauma to the body. An autopsy will determine the cause of death. The vehicle has no damage beyond that done by four months underwater.

The Mullins family is at peace for the first time in months. The news was hard to take for her daughters, Dr. Jesse Wallace and Ms. Esther Mullins, both of Winterset. In a statement made by Dr. Wallace, she said, "Four months is a long time to hold on to hope. The Lord was waiting until we were prepared to accept her loss. Maybe it took us this length of time to do it. I can't say it hasn't opened wounds, but at least our worry is over. We pray it happened quickly, and she was gone before she hit the water."

****

The chief notified the family. Rory missed his date with Esther, mumbled a heartfelt apology, and offered his condolences to her over the phone. He wanted to console her. However, guilt for not discovering her mother's whereabouts sooner got in his way.

It was a full week before he worked up enough nerve to call and suggest an outing. Esther insisted he come by instead. He agreed, adding, if she planned to serve dinner, he'd bring a gift.

"That's good," she said. "I have something for you, too."

She stood midway between the garden and the back door with her hands on her hips when he pulled into the alley. Commander circled her feet. She seemed dubious of Rory's intentions, resting one foot behind the other as if intending to run. There was something different about her that he couldn't put his finger on. He hoped it wasn't a new hairdo. He was a failure at noticing such things. Her expression was pleasant enough.

"Okay, are you ready?" he said, snicking the trunk's lock and allowing the lid to pop open.

"And waiting," she answered.

He wore a loose-fitting Hawaiian shirt, beige Bermuda shorts, and neon-green sneakers. The fedora sat at a sporty angle, and he'd tried for everyday casual by leaving his shoulder holster and gun locked in the glove compartment. Rory pushed his hat back, grinned. "I'm bringing it out. No laughing."

"I won't laugh, honest."

"It's not much, just something I built in my off-hours."

"Rory, you know you don't have off-hours." She appeared curious, not coming closer but craning to see what he had hidden in the car.

Commander left Esther and flopped down at his feet. He stepped over the sprawled cat and moved to the car's rear door. "Wait. Let me get the other piece from the back seat."

"How many pieces are there?" Her voice carried a smile. When he looked up, she was beside him.

"Three. Three sizeable pieces." He lifted out a two-by-two-foot wooden box with circular holes cut in the sides. "This is the top. Some assembly required." He realized he was nervous, which was silly—she'd like it. He'd spent a lot of hours—too many hours. He picked up Commander and cradled him in his arms, stepping away to allow Esther space to appreciate his handiwork.

"Is that carving I see along the edge?"

"I did all the woodwork myself."

While Esther admired the carving, he scratched Commander's belly. The tabby soon wiggled free, and Rory retrieved the other two boxes from the trunk. "So, this is the base, and this is the center chamber. You're holding the top."

"These are leaves. You've carved leaves all around the edge. Rory, it's a cat tree."

"Guilty." He beamed at her.

She laughed. " 'The Gift of the Magi.' "

Confused, he stepped back. "I don't get it."

"It's a short story by O. Henry." She shook her head. "There's this young couple and they each give up their most prized possession...well, it's not important." She peeked at him from below freshly cut bangs.

Crap! It was the hairdo. "Did you do something with your hair? It looks swell."

Swell? Couldn't he think of something better than that?

She didn't seem to notice his discomfort. "I've been wrestling with a decision ever since we discovered Mother's fate. It wasn't easy, but after much deliberation, I finally decided this morning. Commander needs to earn his keep, plus your old warehouse of a department store needs a mouser." She paused.

He waited. When Esther didn't go on, he figured it out. She was gifting him the cat.

"You want me to take the cat?"

"Yes," she said. "He'd be much happier living with you. Poor tabby, he's continually shuffled between Jesse's house and mine and he's never quite at home with either of us."

Commander rubbed against Rory's leg. *Sure, he wanted the cat. Why wouldn't he want the cat? They were two old codgers, set in their ways, but not without charm, if he did say so himself.*

"Okay." Rory felt the smile spread across his face. His body let loose a wave of endorphins that made him weak in the knees.

Accepting Commander made it official. Esther—WPD—Winterset.

He was right where he wanted to be.

A word about the author...

Terry Korth Fischer writes mystery and memoir. Her memoir, *Omaha to Ogallala*, was released in 2019. Her short stories have appeared in The Write Place at the Write Time, Spies & Heroes, and numerous anthologies. Transplanted from the Midwest, Terry lives in Houston with her husband and their two guard cats. She enjoys a good mystery, the heat and humidity, and long summer days.

Visit her website at https://terrykorthfischer.com

Thank you for purchasing
this publication of The Wild Rose Press, Inc.

For questions or more information
contact us at
info@thewildrosepress.com.

The Wild Rose Press, Inc.
www.thewildrosepress.com